AN AJ DOCK

DEADLY
EQUATION

GARY GERLACHER

Black Rose Writing | Texas

ISBN: 978-1-68513-528-7 (Paperback); 978-1-68513-556-0 (Hardcover)
PUBLISHED BY BLACK ROSE WRITING
www.blackrosewriting.com

Printed in the United States of America
Suggested Retail Price (SRP) $21.95 (Paperback); $26.95 (Hardcover)

Deadly Equation is printed in Minion Pro

*As a planet-friendly publisher, Black Rose Writing does its best to eliminate unnecessary waste to reduce paper usage and energy costs, while never compromising the reading experience. As a result, the final word count vs. page count may not meet common expectations.

PRAISE FOR
THE AJ DOCKER & BANSHEE THRILLER SERIES

"*Last Patient of the Night* is M*A*S*H* meets Detective Harry Bosch. It's a thriller that won't disappoint."
–Gregory D. Lee, author of *Stinger: An International Thriller*

"*Deadly Equation* is a fast-paced game of cat and mouse (and dog) you don't want to miss."
–Travis Tougaw, author of *Foxholes* and *Captives*

"*Deadly Equation* has all the elements of a great edge-of-your-seat spy thriller, and like the other installments, it stands on its own."
–Dan Burke, author of *Red Screen* and *Vibrations in the Field*

"A cryptic request from a dying patient propels Dr. AJ (Doc) Docker into a maelstrom of political conspiracy in our nation's capital."
–Gail Ward Olmsted, author of *Katherine's Remarkable Road Trip*

"Gerlacher jumps right in, feeding the reader an action-packed mystery sandwich that doesn't let up."
–Paulette Mahurin, author of *Two Necklaces*

"With clues like *National Treasure*, and scenes like *Night at the Museum*, the only thing standing between democracy and autocracy in this Capitol Hill thriller is an emergency room doctor and his superhero canine!"
**–Cam Torrens, award-winning author of
the *Tyler Zahn Thriller* series**

Real heroes out there bring justice to monstrous humans
who prey on children.

This book is dedicated to all the monster hunters.
Thank you for your efforts.

DEADLY
EQUATION

CHAPTER ONE

Three years earlier

Mark Lawton's vacation was interrupted by a pistol pointed at his nose, causing his brown eyes to cross, as he focused on the gun.

"Empty your pockets, Señor. Everything. Hurry."

Mark sighed, looking past the gun into the taxi driver's merciless eyes. The Dominican Republic may be a tropical paradise, but while tourists sought the perfect beach, criminals preyed on them. He had been warned about the dangers of unlicensed taxis, but in his excitement, he hadn't paid attention when he clambered into the car. The taxi driver leaned forward and pressed the gun against his forehead.

"Last chance. Everything out of your pockets, now."

Mark held up his hands in surrender, then slowly emptied his pockets, handing over his wallet, hotel key, and phone.

"Give me that watch."

Mark removed it to be snatched by the greedy thief. The Apple Watch would bring him pretty good money.

The thief reached over the seat and patted down Mark's pockets, stopping on the right front.

"What is this?"

Mark reached into his pocket. "Just a piece of amber I picked up." He held up the golden amber that glowed in the sunlight. The thief squinted at it and scoffed.

"You stupid fucking tourists, paying good money for cheap amber. Keep that crap as a reminder of your time in my country. Get out. Leave the computer on the seat."

Mark opened the door and stood on the sidewalk, as the taxi raced away with over five thousand dollars of his belongings, leaving him with only the amber. He angled it toward the burnt orange evening sun, the rays shining through it in a spectacular prism.

Over ten million years ago, a tropical forest had covered the island. Resin from the now extinct Hymenaea Protera tree trapped insects as they sank into the stickiness and hardened to form the amber, leaving insectile carcasses eternally entombed. Mark marveled at the unusually well-preserved termite encased in his sample. He had searched the Bayaguana area for days before finding this piece. Insects encased in amber were not unusual, and termites were among the most common. He had peered into thousands of samples before discovering this one. If his theory was correct, the vacant eyes staring back at him would change the world.

Mark began the mile-long trek back to his hotel, turning the amber in his pocket. He hadn't told anyone about his hypothesis, as it was too fantastic to believe. His coworkers thought he had taken a much needed vacation to a beach resort, but he had yet to step into the sand. Now that he had found the amber, he might just relax for a day before flying back to work. He kicked a soccer ball back to a group of children playing in the street, as he contemplated the thief who stole his belongings. The one item he had left behind was more valuable than the thief could imagine. Mark clenched the amber tightly, as he planned the next steps of his research.

CHAPTER TWO

Friday, March 13
6:23 p.m.

Mark Lawton never rushed, a trait that would cost him his life. Even as a child, he had been purposeful in movement and action. Spontaneity risked unacceptable error. Mistakes were predictable and avoidable, given the correct information, and Mark had successfully avoided major mistakes throughout his life.

A prodigy in math, his talent had been overlooked at first. His teachers at his Catholic school judged him lazy and disinterested, when his mind wandered in class to imagine complex scenarios unfathomable to them.

His situation changed when he took required algebra in high school. Finally, he found something interesting and vaguely challenging. He devoured the year's lessons within the first few weeks, garnering his teacher's attention. Astonished, she formulated his own curriculum with increasingly difficult problems to solve. By the end of his freshman year, Mark had mastered all the material that the high school math department could offer.

His teachers shared his abilities with professors at nearby Massachusetts Institute of Technology. Ten minutes into his interview, the Dean of Mathematics admitted Mark. Life as a fifteen-year-old college student had its challenges, but Mark's family and mentors maintained a solid safety net around him. By age nineteen, he had earned his first PhD and his second by twenty-one.

His work focused on converting complex data into mathematical formulas that could model and predict data. His expertise impressed private industry, where he generated multiple patents guaranteeing wealth for the rest of his life. It also caught the attention of the government that always has a use for advanced mathematics in its research programs.

Five years ago, at the age of 33, Mark left private industry for a full-time job with the government. With his own lab, access to the most powerful supercomputers, and an almost unlimited budget, Mark focused his attention on maximizing his contribution to humanity, but now, the military wanted to weaponize his technology. Mark couldn't allow that.

Sitting in his lab, Mark systematically erased all traces of his current research. How the military had even discovered his work mystified him. Fewer than ten people knew what he had been working on, all of whom he trusted. He would conceal his discoveries until he found a way to limit its use to benevolent purposes. He had one copy of his work hidden off-site, a precaution he had undertaken since the first day of the project. He had updated it frequently, and he was the only one who knew how to access it.

Now, with his life possibly in danger, he had to leave a way for someone he absolutely trusted to find the data if something should happen to him. He trusted only one person to do the right thing no matter what, his twin. An exhausted smile briefly visited his tired expression, as he prepared the first step for her to find his data. His equally brilliant sister had access to considerable resources. She would figure it out. He dumped the flash drive into his pocket and left his lab for the last time. His backpack, full of meaningless papers and manuals, would hopefully distract anyone interested in stealing his research.

The streets of Washington, D.C. were crowded with workers heading to their overpriced homes, many of them preparing to head back out to be seen next to important people. Mark couldn't care less about the social circuit in D.C. Focused on his surroundings, he scanned for familiar faces and abnormal patterns. Crowd flow followed mathematical predictability, and aberrations were obvious to Mark, which is why he immediately noticed the familiar two men follow him as he exited his building.

To most, they would appear unremarkable and therefore invisible, only another two men in suits heading home after a long day at work, but to Mark, they may as well have had spotlights shining over their too casually indifferent movements, as they awkwardly ignored him. Their poorly cut suits failed to disguise their bulky frames. Most concerning were their empty hands. Everyone else carried phones, purses, or bags, but these two had left their hands free, which would be useful in an assault, Mark thought, as he adjusted the shoulder strap on his backpack.

He weighed his options and stopped in the middle of the sidewalk, turned around, and stared at the men. Pedestrians parted around him with varied looks of puzzlement and annoyance, and the two men abruptly froze and stared back. The deadly game had begun.

·   ·   ·

Dr. John Pastone took another bite from his sandwich, as he looked out over the city, darkening with the setting sun. "Think those snipers could hit us with a clean shot?"

I ate the last of my chips and glanced in the direction he referenced before responding. "Those boys are less than a mile away. They could probably take us both out with one shot."

"True. I wonder if they know we're up here."

"I guarantee they know we're up here. Secret Service knows everything going on in this town, especially on a rooftop near the White House."

Mild spring temperatures in Washington D.C. brought refreshing change from the long, dreary winter. John and I relaxed on the helipad at George Washington University Hospital, taking a break from our jobs in the emergency room below. In his fifties, John was still a good ole boy from east Texas. He'd been working in the ER for over twenty years and showed no evidence of slowing down. He stayed in shape and rode his bike as often as possible. A few inches shorter than my six-foot-two-inch frame, and with hair thinner and grayer than mine, he could outride me with impressive stamina. John had a no-nonsense leadership style that served him well as head of the emergency department.

I had been at GW for only two months, part of a four-month contract to help cover the emergency room. I was finally getting used to life in D.C., a significant change from my last job in Las Vegas. I wasn't much for politics, and everything in this town revolved around politics.

"Where's Banshee?" John asked.

I whistled, and he burst out from around some air-conditioning units. He leapt over a four-foot wall that protected the helicopter landing area and sprinted to a controlled stop in front of us. He sat obediently waiting for his next command, excited by the prospect of a job for him.

"RELAX, Banshee." I poured some water in a bowl, and he lapped it up. Banshee is a Belgian Malinois and former police dog who was injured when he took a bullet meant for me. Unable to continue his police duties, his handler gave him to me. Since then, he has been my constant, loyal companion. He functioned as an emotional support dog to calm patients in the emergency room, as well as a guard dog to enforce good behavior from troublemakers. Outfitted in a custom ceramic vest, he knew hundreds of commands.

"Is there anything that dog can't do?"

"He can't cook or do laundry, but he has a lot of things figured out."

"I need a super dog like that, but in the meantime, we need to get back to work."

"At least while we still have jobs. Are those assholes at the private equity firm still trying to steal your contract?

"Yeah. We have some more meetings scheduled for next week. I can't figure out why the hospital administration would want emergency room staffing determined by private equity guys instead of by a physician-owned company. We know what we need and what the patients need, and they don't."

"What are the new guys offering?"

"The usual bullshit. They can staff more efficiently, and the hospital will make more money, so they can afford to hire more administrators. The truth is, their staffing models are cheaper, but way too cheap. Patients are going to die, if they cut staffing that aggressively, and I'm not sure who will want to work in that environment anyway."

"Hospitals are all the same. They look at what is working and then figure out a way to screw it up. If you randomly fired fifty percent of the administrators at every hospital in the country, the delivery of healthcare would improve across the board."

"Not to mention their bottom line. They pay those guys more than I pay my doctors."

"I'm pretty sure they get bonuses based on how many meetings and memos they produce each year. Maybe they should consider paying them based on how many patients received better care because of their decisions. Of course, that would make sense and would go against the standard operating procedures of the hospital."

"Sadly, you are correct." We gathered our trash and took one more look at the city around us. The Washington Monument and United States Capitol were majestically lit in the distance. Unfortunately, like in any big city, violence erupted after sunset. Somewhere in the distance suffered our next patient.

CHAPTER THREE

Friday, March 13
6:28 p.m.

Mark turned on his heels and continued his march down the street with his two followers only a few steps behind. The crowded streets offered a modicum of safety, but he needed to lose the men and get the information to his sister.

The Ballston metro stop on Fairfax Drive was a convenient three-minute walk away. Mark strolled at a normal pace, resisting the urge to look over his shoulder. He wasn't too concerned about the two men, but did fear others who might be hunting him without his perceiving potential danger. His golden brown eyes scanned the crowds, recognizing patterns and noticing no breaks that would normally be disturbingly obvious to him. He reassured himself that only the two stalkers hounded him at the moment.

He made it to the entry, scanned his card, and took the escalator down to the tracks. He walked to the east-bound platform for the Orange line and waited for the next train. Clean and well lit, like all Washington metro stations, the wall supported his back, as he leaned back to watch his two followers emerge onto the platform. He made eye contact with them, and they split up, one heading to stand east of him, while the other remained to the west.

Mark ignored them to focus on the remaining crowd. Both followers had AirPods and were talking to someone. He wanted to identify those people. The train arrived, and Mark waited until the last possible moment to enter the car. He didn't expect his last second action to fool his followers, but he figured he might as well make them earn whatever they were paid to harass him.

He chose to stand in the middle of the compartment facing the door. His followers entered adjacent cars, watching him closely to see if he would exit suddenly. Mark's smile flickered, as he thought about pretending to exit, but suppressed the urge. He studied each man closely as the train moved along the tracks. Too bulky to be military men and too poorly dressed to be private security, he surmised that they were likely with a foreign government. These guys were muscle pure and simple, meant to intimidate, not to think. They would be trouble in a fight, but Mark didn't plan to fight them. Muscle didn't worry him, but brains did, and he hadn't found the brains yet.

Ten stops until the Smithsonian, and then he would lose them. With his access and the security of the museum, he would get lost in the miles of interconnected tunnels underneath the building. He could hide there for days.

At the Farragut Square stop, eight people entered the train and four exited. All eight appeared to be exhausted workers looking forward to home, but something was wrong with the woman across from him. Jeans and a blazer over a tight t-shirt hugged her athletic figure. Long blond hair spilled out from her Washington Nationals baseball hat, and large glasses magnified her blue eyes. To most people, she would look tired and bored after a long day of sight seeing, but Mark was not most people. He noted that her supposed indifference masked hyper alertness. She studied everyone in the car except Mark. Treating him differently disrupted a pattern, and to Mark, she might as well have worn a flashing light on her hat. Perhaps she was the brains who controlled the muscle men.

He continued his scan of the crowd, not letting on that he had noticed the woman. He made occasional eye contact with the first two watchers, who openly glared at him from the adjacent cars. Everyone else seemed oblivious to the mini drama playing out before them.

The Smithsonian stop approached, and Mark moved to stand before the doors. Four other people positioned themselves behind him preparing to exit, including the woman. The doors opened, and Mark took one step off the train and stopped abruptly, stood still, and obstructed the exit from the train car. The baffled and annoyed throng behind him spilled around him with muttered curses. The woman had no choice but to pass him as well.

Mark stood perfectly still, as the doors closed, and the train moved away. The few people who noticed him dismissed his behavior as commonly eccentric and continued their commute. The woman and one of the muscle men stayed to the north of him and the other to the south. Mark chose to move north, preferring fewer people behind him. The watcher and the woman preceded him on the escalator, as the second man closely followed.

Mark took a deep breath. From the top of the escalator, the Smithsonian beckoned with less than a minute walk to its entrance. Safety was close.

He stepped from the escalator and found his watcher waiting for him at the top, staring straight at him, and functioning only as a distraction. The woman was the real threat. She approached from his left, nonchalantly and casually, easy to overlook, but Mark noticed her subtle angling to the left, freeing up her right hand that rested on her open purse. No one traveled on the metro with an unzipped purse.

As her hand reached into the purse, he swung his backpack at her head with his right hand and at the same time, his left plunged into her purse. The gun lay right where he expected, and her hand fought for it, too. She may have been well-trained, but she had not expected an attack from a research nerd, and Mark closed his hand around the pistol grip. He drew it out and pushed the woman away, tripping her, as she fell backward.

Mark turned to the first watcher, who was clearing his own weapon from his holster. Mark didn't hesitate. The Glock had no safety, and he hoped she had one round in the chamber. Front sights on the target, he pulled the trigger twice, landing two shots into the man's chest. The man fell, as screams erupted from the panicked crowd. Chaos ensued, as tourists and local residents scattered in all directions.

Mark turned to find the second watcher, who had just emerged from the escalator. He lifted his gun, and Mark knelt to one knee to make himself a smaller target, lined up his sights, and put two fatal shots into the second watcher's chest. The gunshots and screams temporarily deafened him, and he lost track of where the woman had fallen to the ground.

Mark stood to scan for other threats, when he felt his stomach burn. His hands clutched his abdomen, as a second shot slammed into him, and he fell backward. Warm blood covered his hands as he looked around for the source of the shot. The woman he had disarmed and tripped grinned from the ground, as she slid her revolver into her belt holster, stood up, and calmly approached him. She reached down and smiled at him, as she collected his backpack. No remorse or empathy inhabited her eyes, only satisfaction at a job well done. She blew him a kiss and turned away to disappear into the chaos.

Mark lay back and contemplated how he had made a huge mistake.

CHAPTER FOUR

Friday, March 13
7:18 p.m.

The GW emergency room supports a Level 1 trauma center, and Washington, D.C. can be a violent city. With every room occupied and more patients checking in at triage, the staff moved to complete protocols in a chaotic choreography. A cacophony of voices competed to be heard above the rest. Occasional shouts of grief, pain, or surprise pierced the baseline noise. I took a deep breath, inhaling the peculiar scent that only the fear and energy of an emergency room produces.

John and I split up to see our next patients. I picked up the chart of a woman with abdominal pain, but a call for an imminent trauma arrival interrupted my review of her chart. I shifted focus to the trauma room to find the team gathering. Nine members, each with defined duties, moved to prepare for a patient with major trauma. Additional members would be added, as needed. Banshee knew his place and curled up in the far corner to watch us work.

"Let me guess. Biker run over by a car?" I asked.

"Nice try, but no. Male in his thirties with two gunshot wounds to the belly. Awake, but pressures dropping," Lisa, the charge nurse reported. A petite ball of energy, Lisa had worked in the emergency room as a nurse for over twenty years. She had seen every type of injury, heard every insult imaginable, and been challenged by innumerable physician consultants, and nothing phased her. Every emergency room had a Lisa acting as a bedrock in the sea of chaos, and challenging her was rarely a good career move.

"Okay, everyone. Let's make sure we have blood ready. I'll take airway, if needed. Make sure the trauma surgeons are awake. As soon as we stabilize him, they'll want him in the OR."

We finished our preparations and enjoyed a moment of peace to gather our thoughts and to prepare ourselves to perform at our best. I took advantage of the proverbial calm before the storm, a last chance to walk myself through what I would need to do. What if it was a difficult airway? What if we couldn't get IV access? What if he coded before we could get him to the operating room? Potential solutions to such scenarios flashed through my head, as we awaited his arrival.

The paramedics disrupted our reverie, as they wheeled the patient in, reporting as they crossed the threshold of the room. "Male, thirties, two small caliber gunshots to his abdomen. One in the right upper quadrant and one in the left flank. No exit wounds. Pressures 90/60 and trending down. Patient is awake."

I watched my team go to work. The patient cried out as the paramedics lifted the backboard and transferred him to the exam table. A medic held pressure on bloody bandages over the two gunshot wounds in his abdomen. One IV was already in place, and a nurse added a pressure bag to speed the infusion. A second nurse searched for an IV on the opposite arm to prepare to infuse blood quickly. Techs transferred the vital sign leads to our monitor, and a quick glance showed a high pulse, low blood pressure, and borderline low oxygen saturations. These were the vital signs of someone in shock, and immediate care was needed to prevent his death.

Medics cut through the remains of his shirt, then sheared through his jeans and boxers, leaving his body exposed on the table. They briefly rotated him to confirm the lack of exit wounds or other injuries on his back. Quiet conversations among staff members coordinated their efforts, as they worked together to save the stranger's life. Our deadly dance would determine the outcome within a few minutes.

In charge of airway and breathing, I leaned over to get his attention. "Sir, can you hear me? Look at me. What's your name?"

The patient focused on me and attempted to speak. I leaned closer to hear him over the other voices in the room. I placed my ear near his mouth and asked him to repeat his words. He responded in a harsh whisper. "My right pocket. Give it to Mac. Don't trust anyone. Only Mac."

This effort to speak drained his last reserves, and he faded to unresponsive and then to unconsciousness. "Preparing to intubate," I announced. I tilted his head back and pushed his chin down, opening his airway, and slid a Mac blade into the back of his mouth. The vocal cords shone in the fiber optic light, and I placed an 8.0 endotracheal tube without difficulty. A respiratory therapist took over ventilating and oxygenating the patient, as I turned my attention back to his overall condition. His oxygen saturations improved, but his blood pressure continued to drop, and his pulse increased despite aggressive fluid resuscitation. The dreaded alarm for asystole filled the room, as his heart, deprived of blood and oxygen, stopped.

A medic started CPR compressions, as a nurse gave epinephrine through his IV. We had a brief window to save him. We pushed saline through one IV and infused blood under pressure through the second IV.

The heart is responsible for pumping blood to the rest of the body and needs fresh oxygen to pump correctly. Blood delivers fresh oxygen. Not enough blood in the body means not enough oxygen going to the heart. When his heart stopped, we knew that no new oxygen had made it to his heart. CPR could manually pump some blood through his body, but if he bled internally, then not enough of the blood could make it to his vital organs. The heart and brain are the most vital and the most sensitive to oxygen deprivation. They would begin to die in minutes without sufficient oxygen.

I ordered a pause in CPR to check for pulses, but he remained pulseless. We gave a second dose of epinephrine and continued compressions, but he remained in asystole. Our efforts at resuscitation continued for thirteen more minutes with forceful compressions of the chest and powerful breaths to fill his lungs, but we tried in vain. We were unable to restore heart function, and at 8:32 p.m., I called the code and pronounced him dead.

All activity stopped, and silence overtook the room, as we stared at the man lying dead before us. Two small holes on his abdomen were filled with dark blood trying to clot. Brighter blood was smeared on the remainder of his abdomen, contrasting with the skin which was becoming whiter as life left his body. His clothes, now bloody rags, lay shredded and scattered on the bed and floor. The team would gather his belongings and clean the heaviest blood stains off him before covering him with a clean sheet, affording him some dignity after his final moments.

What was his story? Why was he shot? Why was this his day to die? Everyone contemplated their own questions running through their minds, as they grieved the loss of our patient. We had spent less than twenty minutes with him and would likely never know the answers. I was always struck by the sudden heaviness of death in the emergency room. In my career, I had probably seen over a thousand people die, often multiple deaths within one shift, and each one was different.

"Thanks, everyone. He was probably hit in the liver or spleen, giving us no chance. Let's finish here, and get back to our other patients," I said to my team. A tough reality of working in the emergency room is the need to get back to work after losing a patient. We never had enough time to process the losses we experienced daily. A life had been violently cut short, and we were expected to see our next patients with comparatively minor complaints, as if nothing had happened. We had no time for prayers or remembrances of the victim. We didn't even know his name or how to honor him through the unknown religion he might have practiced. Was he Jewish, Christian, Muslim, or Hindu? Maybe he worshipped Odin or the Old Gods and the New. Maybe he was an atheist. Whatever his beliefs, we weren't equipped to honor them appropriately. Burnout is high among emergency room staff.

"No one is going anywhere." We turned to one of three large men in dark suits who stood in front of the closed door. The speaker's thick shoulders stretched the seams of his suit. His square jaw offered no hint of a smile, and the scar above his left eyebrow indicated that he was no stranger to violence. Clearly, this man had grown accustomed to being obeyed when he gave orders.

Lisa, unfazed, approached him. "Who the hell are you, and what are you doing invading my ER and barking out orders?"

"Homeland Security, ma'am. This room is now under our control as a matter of national security. We will search each one of you before you can leave this room. Don't try to take anything out of here, or you will be arrested."

Lisa glared at the three men, not backing down one bit. Over her twenty years in the emergency room, she had seen strange things in Washington, D.C., like VIP guests receiving treatment under aliases, politicians conveniently having their stories altered, and even the secret service bringing people in for treatment, but this was the first time Homeland Security had taken over a room and detained the staff, and she didn't like it. She especially did not like them threatening her staff. The agent may have outweighed her by over a hundred pounds, but Lisa got in his face to tell him what she thought of his plan.

Protest arose from the team, as they surged toward the speaker, emboldened by Lisa's actions. The distraction allowed me to reach into the right front pocket of the patient's pants, cut from his body and piled next to his hip. My hand closed around a small object. I palmed a flash drive and weighed whether to give it to these Homeland Security officers or to honor the dying wish of my patient. Since the agent continued to yell and threaten the staff, and our patient used his last painful efforts to admonish me, I decided to honor my patient's dying wish and hand signaled for Banshee. I reached down to pet him, as if he needed to be reassured, and slid the flash drive underneath his vest.

The room settled, as the speaker by the door took control. He appeared to be in his forties and stood rigidly in a manner most often associated with the military. His five-o'clock shadow gave him a sinister appearance. "I'm sorry for any inconvenience, but everyone needs to be cleared before leaving this room. Step up one at a time, empty everything from your pockets, and my colleague will wand you with a metal detector. When you're cleared, you can leave."

A paramedic stepped forward and was quickly scanned and cleared to leave. One by one, team members were processed. Eventually, only Lisa, Banshee, and I remained. Lisa emptied her pockets. The wand alarmed on her chest, and the agent stared at her.

"It's my underwire, Mr. secret agent man."

"You can't leave until we know it's nothing else."

"Seriously? My bra is a matter of national security? Fine." Lisa reached inside her shirt, unclipped her bra, and slid a strap out of one sleeve and then the other. She waved the bra in his face, which flushed redder by the second. The agent scanned and cleared her to leave, relieved to be done with her.

I emptied my pockets and spread my arms out for the scan. "Who did you guys say you are with?"

"Homeland Security."

"Got any ID on you?"

"Not that you're going to see."

"Then how about a name?"

The big man apparently in charge held out his hand. "Agent John Smith."

I ignored his hand. "What's so special about this guy that he has a bunch of feds bullying emergency room staff?"

Agent Smith leaned in closer. "As I said, national security. Now shut the fuck up and leave before I have you arrested."

He jabbed a finger into my chest to emphasize his point. Banshee barked once and stepped between us, emitting a low, deep growl that caused all three men to take a step back instinctively. I reached down to pet him.

"What the fuck is that dog doing in here?" Agent Smith asked.

"He's a former police dog. Now he helps with security and with calming patients. He's really good at detecting assholes who cause trouble in the emergency room. Be careful around him. He senses tension, and if you touch me again, he's likely to use you as a chew toy."

"Whatever." The agent leaned toward Banshee with the metal detector in his hand and Banshee lowered to the ground and growled from even deeper inside. The agent stepped back as the other two reached for their weapons.

"It's okay, boy. Give me a kiss." Banshee calmed down and gave me kisses, knowing he had done a good job guarding me, while he still kept an eye on the agents. "I don't think he is going to let you wand him, but he has only these two pockets. As you can see, they are empty." I opened both pockets, and the agent leaned over to inspect them from a safe distance before waving us out of the room. The two agents by the door allowed Banshee plenty of space as we exited.

Agent Smith followed me. "This room is off limits to all personnel until further notice."

"What the fuck, man? This is one of only two trauma rooms. What do we do if we have multiple trauma victims come in?"

"Not my problem." The two agents positioned themselves outside the door and stared at me until I turned away, shaking my head and hoping that we wouldn't need that room.

As John and Lisa discussed the situation at the nurses' station, I interrupted. "You know I'm new to Washington. Is it normal for Homeland to take over a trauma room?" I asked.

"First damn time for me." Lisa said.

"In my twenty years, I've never seen anything like this, and it looks like the situation is worsening." John pointed to the ambulance entrance, where five more agents strode into the emergency room.

Without a word, they entered the trauma room, while the two agents outside closed and protected the door.

I scratched Banshee's neck and checked the flash drive. Still in place, no one knew about it. I decided to leave it on him until I figured out who Mac was. I moved it to the pocket below his muzzle. Anyone who tried to get to it would have to get past Banshee's teeth first.

CHAPTER FIVE

Friday, March 13
7:37 p.m.

Inside the trauma room, Special Agent Clarence Duff, of recent Agent John Smith fame, issued orders to his team. "I want every square inch of this room searched. We're looking for documents or electronic data storage devices."

"You want us to open all these packages?" an agent asked as he pointed at the trauma packs throughout the room.

"If it's sealed, leave it alone. Search everything that is already open, and every cabinet, drawer, and shelf. I'll take care of the body."

His team spread out as Agent Duff pulled on gloves and began a search of the body. He removed the remains of the clothing, searching each piece for anything in pockets or seams, before placing it in an evidence bag. A brief search of his wallet revealed only the usual cards and cash. He threw it into another evidence bag. Finding nothing else, except a set of keys, he turned his attention to the body itself. Two dark holes surrounded by blood stains in the abdomen of the pale, naked corpse screamed violence. The once muscular frame and brilliant mind no longer looked impressive, as it lay naked and bloody under the sickly bright fluorescent light.

"Find me a body bag and a stretcher. We're taking the body with his belongings. Any word on anything else he had been carrying with him?"

A team member spoke up. "Reports indicate he had a backpack, but it was taken from the scene by the woman who shot him. Multiple witnesses saw her walking toward the Capitol, but no one followed her."

"Do we have control of that scene?"

"Yes, sir. Our agents have taken over for D.C. Homicide. Because the two other gunshot victims appear to be Russian, they're letting us have it without argument."

"Good. I want to know who that woman is and what that backpack contained. I want a media blackout on this entire event. If we have to publicize something, it's just another mugging gone bad. Anyone find anything useful in here?"

A chorus of negative replies left Agent Duff disappointed. He scanned the room. The shelves, drawers, and cabinets were open and empty with their contents piled haphazardly on the floor.

"Let's go. We need the body on our autopsy table as soon as possible, and we can focus on the backpack and any other data we can find. We need to track it down."

A few minutes later, they pushed a stretcher with the body zipped into a bag. Oblivious to angry stares from the hospital staff, Agent Duff's mind groped for possible ways to find that data.

.   .   .

"I'm pretty sure Homeland Security just kidnapped a dead guy," John said.

"Can you kidnap a dead guy?" I asked.

"Good point. Probably more of a theft."

"We should call the cops and report a stolen body. Stir things up."

"I would, if it wouldn't increase the amount of paperwork we already have to do. I can't believe they took his body."

"Did anyone even get a name on the patient?" Lisa asked.

We all looked at each other silently. No one had taken the time to check his pockets for an ID.

"I have no idea, but the incident report on this is gonna be a doozy. At least we got our trauma room back," I pointed out.

"Let's see what they did to it," Lisa responded. I followed her, and we stopped abruptly at the threshold. The room was a disaster with emptied cabinets and drawers open and the trauma room's entire contents scattered all over the floor.

"Looks like they tore through anything that was open, but left all the sealed bandages and towels alone," I observed.

"Whatever, but this is unacceptable. It'll take hours to get this cleaned up and restocked. If I knew they were gonna do this, I would have strangled one of them with my underwire."

I had a pretty good idea what they were looking for and was more determined than ever not to hand it over. Somehow, I would find Mac and get to the bottom of this. "If they come back, I can have Banshee chomp on their legs."

"If they come back they are leaving in body bags," Lisa said, as she stomped away to organize the room's restoration.

I refocused on my next patient with the thumb drive secure in Banshee's vest pocket.

·   ·   ·

Nearing the end of my shift, Lisa tapped me on the shoulder. "We may have a family member of our mystery patient. A woman says she's the sister of the guy who was shot. She's in the family waiting area."

"Thanks. I'll talk to her."

Banshee and I entered the family room to find a woman who had recently been crying, sitting anxiously at the table. She stood and rushed to speak first. "Where is he? How is he?"

I motioned for her to have a seat. "My name is AJ Docker, but everyone calls me Doc. What's your name?"

"Mackenzie Lawton, but everyone calls me Mac. I'm looking for my brother. Police said he was shot and that the ambulance brought him here. How is he?"

Interested that I had apparently met the mysterious Mac referenced by my patient, I asked, "Can you describe your brother for me?"

"He's thirty-six years old and just under six-feet tall with dark hair and brown eyes, like mine. Police said he had been shot in the belly."

"Mac, we had a patient like that come in earlier tonight. He had two gunshot wounds to the abdomen and arrived in critical condition. We did everything we could for him, but unfortunately, he passed away. I'm sorry."

Tears pooled in Mac's eyes, as she processed the loss of her brother. I handed her a tissue from the box and gave her a moment to recover. "Can I see his body and say goodbye?"

"Normally, that would not be a problem, but his death triggered the interest of Homeland Security, and their agents took over the room and claimed his body. I'm sorry, but they left a couple of hours ago, and I have no idea where they took him."

Her transition from grief to anger was instantaneous, as Mac stood and paced. "Those fucking monsters have already been here? They're the reason he's dead. I cannot fucking believe this is happening." She collapsed back into her chair, her body shaking with rage, then with fresh tears.

I gave her a few moments to compose herself. "Mac, when your brother arrived, he was barely conscious, but still able to speak. He asked me to give something only to Mac. Those were his last words."

Her eyes bored into me. "What is it?"

"He had a flash drive on him, and I'm pretty sure the homeland security guys are anxious to get their hands on it. They searched each of us, kicked us out of the room, and then tore the room apart looking for something. I assume they were looking for the drive." I called Banshee over and opened the pocket on his vest. I handed her the flash drive, still covered in some of her brother's blood.

Mac stared at the flash drive in her hand, and an all-business Mac replaced an angrily distraught Mac. "What did you say your name is? Doc? Can I trust you, Doc?"

"How can I help you?"

"Please hold onto this flash drive tonight, and meet me with it tomorrow morning."

"Why don't you take it now?"

"Because those ghouls are probably going to track me down soon to search me, too. If that flash drive contains what I think it does, we can't let it fall into their hands. Can you please just keep it safe tonight and meet me tomorrow morning?"

Her strange request piqued my interest and seemed like only a small favor, and I felt an obligation to help my patient with his dying wish. I tucked the flash drive back into Banshee's vest. "Of course. Where do you want to meet?"

"The Hart Building."

"The one with all the Senators in it?"

"Yes. I'll meet you at the south entrance at eight. Guard that thing, and don't tell anyone you have it."

"The only people who know about it are you and Banshee and I."

She scratched Banshee's ears. "He looks like he can take care of himself. Thank you. I have to go. I have things I need to take care of tonight."

With that, she swept out the door, leaving Banshee and me alone. I leaned back in the chair and considered everything that had happened within the last few hours. It had already been an extraordinarily unusual day before Mac arrived and requested my assistance. Her hints at a shadowy conspiracy would seem crazy, except for the death of her twin and the appearance of Homeland Security so soon afterward.

Mac's instant transformation from grieving sibling to angry problem-solver intrigued me. Her fiery determination led me to believe she was up to the task of discovering what happened to her brother and why, and I was curious to see how this situation would play out. Beaming at Banshee, I looked into his devoted eyes. "Looks like we found a new adventure."

Banshee's tail thumped against the cold, hard tile.

CHAPTER SIX

Friday, March 13
9:43 p.m.

Agent Duff summarized his findings to Lenny Haskins, the Director of Homeland Security, and his senior staff. As usual, Director Haskins sat at the head of the table with his notebook open and pen laid exactly parallel to the spine. He was a precise man in everything he did, from his dress to his note taking. He adjusted his silver wire frame glasses then folded his hands in front of him, centering them precisely in the middle of his notebook. His unblinking eyes focused on the speaker.

The DHS was formed two months after the terror attacks of 9/11 and began operations in March 2003. It has grown to include almost a quarter million employees, making it the third largest of the president's Cabinet behind the Departments of Defense and Veterans Affairs.

The DHS has a broad mission statement, to coordinate the executive branch's efforts to detect, prepare for, prevent, protect against, respond to, and recover from terrorist attacks within the United States. To that end, the DHS incorporated twenty-two government agencies into a single organization. With its nearly unlimited resources and broad charter, the DHS has almost limitless power in the United States.

Over his four years as the director, Haskins had turned the DHS into his own personal kingdom after a meteoric rise through the department. After earning his law degree from Georgetown, he had joined the FBI to become one of the youngest Special Agents in FBI history. His ability to build airtight cases against complex criminal organizations brought him to the attention of Senator Whitehurst, who used her political influence to secure his nomination as head of DHS. His continued success was critical to securing future funding from the Appropriations Committee, which was why Agent Duff's report was unacceptable.

"Do you mean to tell me that Mr. Lawton is deceased, and we can find absolutely no evidence of his work at his home or office?"

"That's correct, sir. We secured them within twenty minutes of his shooting and have searched both extensively. No papers, documents, or notes of significance were found. A desktop and two laptops were recovered, but all three hard drives had been destroyed magnetically. IT is working on recovery, but we can't expect to get anything useful off the drives."

"Nothing on the body?"

"Wallet contains the usual cards and ID, and his keys are for his home and office. Autopsy is unremarkable, except for the two gunshots. One hit his spleen and the other his liver. He bled out."

"What about the shooter?"

"A professional. Pulled her backup weapon and shot him twice before walking away with his backpack. Hat and sunglasses covered her features. We tracked her by camera to a garage four blocks away, but then she disappeared. She could have left out the back of the garage on foot or in a car disguised or hidden. We are tracking every vehicle shown leaving the garage, but we have nothing so far."

"So we have the murder of a top scientist in the heart of DC with theft of secrets vital to national security within spitting distance of this office. I want that shooter; I want that backpack; and I want Mark Lawton's research on my desk. Is that clear?"

"Yes, sir."

"What about the two dead assailants? Are we sure they are Russian?"

""Yes, sir. We have confirmed their identities with the Russian embassy. They are listed as part of a trade delegation, but obviously they were trailing Mark and armed. The Russians are being unusually quiet about the incident. Normally they would be yelling to the media about violence in America and the deaths of their citizens, but they haven't said a word. They want to keep this as quiet as we do."

"It's like the old days, a shadow war battled in plain sight. For now, I'm happy to keep this quiet as well, but I want that shooter, and I want whatever was in that backpack. Dismissed."

Agent Duff left with his team to continue the hunt.

•   •   •

The shooter stood over her desk, methodically reading the contents of the backpack. The random papers and binders appeared to have no connection at all to Mark's research. She set them aside for more detailed review by her team. She searched the rest of the backpack, finding a usual assortment of pens and office supplies in the pockets. After several minutes, she slammed the backpack on her desk in frustration. She had taken a huge risk shooting Mark Lawton in public, but she had been sure that he was running with his research. Maybe it had been on his person rather than in his backpack. She couldn't have searched his body at the time, and she had felt lucky to have grabbed the backpack.

She had made her career by risking bold steps to solve difficult problems and had never made a mistake. Now her audacious effort to get the backpack looked like a colossal failure. She handed the backpack and its contents to her team for further study, but expected nothing. She dreaded her explanation to her boss, but at least she had a plan to retrieve the data.

CHAPTER SEVEN

Saturday, March 14
7:39 a.m.

The idyllic spring foreboded the impending heat and humidity of summer, but Banshee and I happily walked the twenty minutes to the Hart Building accompanied by a gentle breeze under mildly sunny skies. We arrived at the south entrance to greet Mac, who waited on the other side of the security station. Dressed in dark slacks and a blazer over a white blouse with an ID badge clipped to her lapel, her eyes lit up at the sight of Banshee.

"I wasn't sure if he would join us today."

"Hope you don't mind. He hates being left in the house, and it's a beautiful day."

"I don't mind at all." She vigorously scratched behind his ears, and then handed me a bag. "Put your phone in this."

"What is it?"

"It's a Faraday bag. It blocks all signals in and out. No one can trace the device or listen through its microphone while it's in that bag."

"Is that a little paranoid? We're in the Senate building."

Her eyes darkened. "My brother was killed last night. I hope we're being paranoid enough."

"Apologies." I sealed the phone in the bag.

"Follow me, please."

"Do you work here?"

"Yes. I'm Chief of Staff for Senator Whitehurst."

"That's impressive." The third term Senator from California was one of the most powerful politicians in the Capitol. She led the Appropriations Committee, which determined how the government spent its money, and powerful people sought face time with her. She came from a wealthy family and could make a strong run for the Presidency, if she wanted.

Mac directed us to a stairwell to the lower levels. "Is her office in the basement?" I asked.

"We're not heading to her office. Too many eyes watch that door. Most Senators maintain a second, unlisted office for private meetings, where the real work gets done in Washington. The main office is for tourists and photo ops."

We took the stairs down two levels. The polished décor of the upper level surrendered to a utilitarian corridor with bare walls and fluorescent light fixtures. Mac turned down a second hallway to a door marked, "Storage." She unlocked it and led the way inside, turning off an alarm inside the door.

Solid wood floors and walls with recessed lighting, highlighted by a built-in bar and bookcases, gave the room a weighty ambience. Padded leather chairs surrounded a table for eight, and a second, more intimate seating area featured four chairs surrounding a smaller coffee table. Three workstations with large monitors lined the side wall.

"This is the nicest storage area I have ever seen."

"It's one of the perks of being a three-term Senator. There're a few of these hidden in the basement of each building. Would you like a drink?"

"Yes, a Diet Coke, please."

"Have a seat. The Senator should be here in a few minutes."

I sunk into one of the plush chairs, and Banshee laid down at my feet. "While we're waiting, please tell me a little about yourself. We haven't had time to get acquainted," I said.

Mac handed me a can of Diet Coke and sat down across from me. "I went to Georgetown and studied political science, like many others on the political scene. After graduation, I wandered for a bit before interning with a representative for a few years. I moved to Senator Whitehurst's office four years ago. The Senator and I work well together, and last year, I was promoted to her Chief of Staff."

"What exactly does a Senatorial Chief of Staff do?"

"Short answer: whatever the Senator needs done, mostly scheduling and arranging details for her events. I decide who she meets with, and I track down people she wants to talk to. I sit in on most of her meetings, and she usually discusses policy decisions with me before she votes. It's a dream job. I get to meet powerful and interesting people and maybe influence policy. The downside is the hours: 24/7/365. My phone is never turned off."

"What's the Senator like?"

"You're probably familiar with her history. From a wealthy family, her dad was a Senator back in the day. When the previous Senator stepped down, she had the name and funds to grab the seat and hold it. She's very practical and tough as nails. She's more honest than most politicians and genuinely tries to do the right thing. She listens well and asks direct questions. She expects direct answers."

The door opened, and we both stood as Senator Whitehurst entered. In her late fifties, she exuded graceful power, as she crossed the room and held out her hand. Over her firm grip, she introduced herself and said hello to Mac.

"Who is this on the floor?" she asked.

"That's Banshee. Hope you don't mind. He's very well behaved."

"May I pet him?"

"Of course. Banshee, FRIEND, SMILE."

Banshee sat up on two legs and smiled at the Senator. She rubbed his ears, as she praised him. "I may have to have that dog join my staff.

Please, have a seat." We settled around the smaller table, and Banshee curled up at the Senator's feet.

"Thank you for coming in today, and for your help last night. Mac tells me that your quick thinking prevented the drive from falling into the wrong hands."

"I probably would have turned it over to them if they had acted normal, but something about them seemed off."

"You have good instincts. What I'm about to tell you is classified, known only by a few. I did some background checks on you last night, and I'm aware of your past adventures. You seem like a man who knows how to handle himself and remain discreet. Is that a correct assumption?"

"I like to think so."

"Very well. Mac, please share the background."

"Mark Lawton, the man you took care of last night, was my twin brother. He was brilliant. He held PhDs in genetics and mathematics from MIT. After graduation, he worked in private industry for a few years. He holds some patents on his work that made him wealthy, and he decided to focus on research for DARPA. Are you familiar with DARPA?"

"I've heard of it, but don't know anything about it."

The Senator explained. "DARPA stands for Defense Advanced Research Projects Agency, and it is a national treasure. It was formed sixty years ago with the mandate to make pivotal investments in breakthrough technologies for national security. Independent research labs are given grant money for their projects, and DARPA oversees the projects. Some of their more famous inventions include the internet, GPS, stealth technology, and the drones you see on TV. Many more of their inventions remained classified."

"What did Mark do there?"

"DARPA has four main pillars of research, and one of them is to harness biology as a technology. Mark led a team that researched genetic disease. He focused on new systems to deliver more effective therapies. Rumor had it that he was close to a major breakthrough, but no one knew the details."

"Is such secrecy the norm?"

"Many projects are classified at the highest levels, and the scientists can be insanely protective of their work. It is not unusual that few, if anybody, would know the full extent of his work."

"Is that why Mark was killed?"

"We believe so. Mark confided in Mac that he had concerns regarding this technology. He wouldn't give any details, but his last conversations indicated that he wanted to destroy his research. He felt it was too dangerous."

"Can't someone else pick up where he left off and continue the project?"

Mac responded. "Unknown. Mark was a genius. Few people possess the intellect and interest to replicate his work, but until we know exactly what he was working on, we don't know. He never shared his research with anyone on his team, and as far as we know, no copy exists."

"So, who shot him, and why was Homeland in the ER last night?"

The Senator answered. "Homeland is interested in getting the technology for military purposes and will stop at nothing to control it. As for who shot him, Mark returned gunfire last night and killed two of his attackers. A third shot him and escaped with his backpack, according to witnesses. The two deceased men are Russian citizens. The identity of the woman who killed him is unknown."

"I didn't hear anything about a murder of foreign nationals last night."

"Cover-ups are a governmental speciality. The information was sequestered under national security concerns. Apparently, the Russians are just as happy to keep it quiet, probably a good idea since their citizens were the ones with guns."

"The Russians are after this technology?"

"Yes. The Russians pay well for information. We have no idea what they know, but they are interested enough to risk shooting one of our scientists in public."

"This is terrifying. Why am I sitting here learning all of this instead of the FBI or CIA? Seems like a national security problem."

"It is, but the government is part of the problem. Certain segments of the administration, particularly in the military, believe this technology could be weaponized, and they want control. I can't let that happen."

"What am I supposed to do that the government can't?"

"Find his research, and bring it to me before any foreign government, or even Homeland Security, gets to it."

"How am I supposed to do that?"

"You're resourceful. You have Mark's twin to help you, and you have the first clue on that flash drive."

"First clue?"

Mac answered. "Mark was a huge fan of quests. My guess is that he created a multi-step process to find his information. When we were young, we created puzzles for each other. Usually, we had to solve at least five clues to get the answer. I think Mark might have done that to make his work discoverable only by me."

"So, he's not the kind of guy to give you a map with an X on it?"

Mac smiled. "Mark would never condone something so direct. Do you still have the flash drive?"

I signaled to Banshee to sit up, opened the zipper on his vest, and pulled out the flash drive.

"That dog is quite useful," the Senator remarked.

"I figured no one would put their hand near his jaws uninvited." I handed the flash drive to Mac.

She inserted it into a computer. "This computer is air-gapped, so it has no access to the internet and no chance for anyone to hack it. Let's see what we have," she said.

The screen opened with a prompt. "Enter password or request a hint." Mac pressed the button to request a hint and a new prompt appeared.

. . .

I stared impotently at the screen. "I hope there's more or that is the worst clue I have ever seen."

"That's because you probably never studied Mayan mathematics."

"True. The subject never came up in medical school, or maybe it was offered, and no one was interested."

"The Mayans developed their own numbering system based on twenty, instead of on ten that we use. Those symbols are a Mayan number, two, five, and five."

"What does 255 mean?"

"Not 255. That would be written differently. These are the individual numbers two, five, and five. Converted to a date, it's February 5, 2005."

I held up my hands in surrender. "What happened on February 5, 2005?"

"That's the day that Mark's best friend from childhood died in the war in Afghanistan. An IED killed him and three other soldiers instantly. He was nineteen and had only two months left on his deployment when he died."

"I'm sorry. So many lives are lost to war."

"It's unfortunate that so many had to give the ultimate sacrifice for our freedoms, but they lie with honor at Arlington National Cemetery. I think that's where Mark wanted us to go." She removed the flash drive and looked around the room. "This place is supposed to be secure, but I still don't know who might be after this. Can Banshee continue to protect the drive?"

"He would be happy to."

The Senator stood. "I will leave you to your quest. Maclaw will keep me updated. Be careful and protect her. It would be unacceptable for something to happen to her, especially after her brother's murder.

Bring me that research." She stepped out and closed the door behind her.

"Maclaw?" I asked.

"The Senator made that up. She said Mackenzie Lawton was too long, so she shortened it. She's the only one who calls me that."

"Seems a little odd."

"Odd, but endearing."

"I've certainly been called worse things than that."

Mac scratched behind Banshee's ears, as she tucked the flash drive back into the pocket on his vest. "Thank you, good boy. How about a trip to Arlington Cemetery?"

Banshee swished his tail.

"C'mon. We can get an Uber. It's only about a ten-minute drive across the river. Have you been there before?"

"No. With so many sights to see in Washington, I haven't made it over there yet."

"I'm glad you get to see it. It's a special place. Over 400,000 men and women are buried there on 600 acres of land. They all fought and died for this country. It contains a poignant and fascinating history. The estate was established by George Washington's adopted grandson, and the US army seized it at the start of the Civil War to defend Washington. Three forts were built on the site, but after the war, it became a cemetery. It officially became a national cemetery in 1864 and has grown ever since."

"You sound like a tour guide."

"Part of my job with the Senator is to escort VIPs to popular sites sometimes. After doing it a few times, I've learned a few things."

.   .   .

Shortly after they left for the cemetery, Senator Whitehurst called from a burner phone in her main office. "You were right. Mark gave that doctor a flash drive."

"How the hell did they get it out of the trauma room?"

"He hid it in the dog's vest."

"What's on the drive?"

"Not sure yet. She needs a password and thinks it might be at Arlington Cemetery."

"Keep me informed."

The Senator ended the call without another word and turned her attention to her next meeting.

CHAPTER EIGHT

Saturday, March 14
8:53 a.m.

Our Uber dropped us off at the main entrance, and after a brief security check, we entered the cemetery. The transformation from the hustle and bustle of Washington to the serenity of the cemetery struck me, as we strolled the grounds. Tombstones stretched into the distance in perfect white lines, each telling a unique story. Families gathered at some grave sites to remember their lost loved ones. Respectful laughter emanated from one group sharing stories, while other groups shared quiet tears.

We stood aside as a funeral procession passed us. "The cemetery performs about twenty-five funerals a day on average, and each one is special for the families. They do an amazing job. Let's head this way," Mac said.

We walked slowly among the towering trees and rolling hills. "Before we visit our friend's grave, you need to see the Tomb of the Unknown Soldier. It's over here, and they change the guard on the hour. The tomb was established in 1921, and the first soldier was a World War I veteran who died in France. His body was shipped to Washington with full military honors before laying in state at the

Capitol. On November 11, 1921, the first soldier was interred. Later ceremonies interred bodies of soldiers from World War II and the Korean War. An unknown soldier from Vietnam was interred for fourteen years, then later identified and exhumed. The crypt for the Vietnam War Unknown remains empty today and is dedicated to all of those still missing in action. Today, the Tomb is guarded twenty-four hours a day by members of the 3rd U.S. Infantry Regiment, known as 'The Old Guard.' That's who we're going to see."

Mac led the way up a hill toward a white marble neoclassical building standing on a hilltop overlooking Washington. The white sarcophagus stood behind the building, facing the city. A soldier walked slowly back and forth in front of the Tomb, twenty-one measured steps each way before a crisp turn, always keeping his weapon between the crowd and the soldiers he guarded. The sharp click of his heels on the well worn pathway was the only sound to disturb the respectful silence. I had never experienced such bittersweet solemnity.

Another soldier broke the silence to announce the changing of the guard. A new soldier emerged to exchange places with the current guard. In a well-rehearsed ceremony, weapons were inspected, the old guard was relieved of his duty, and the new guard began, heels clicking out twenty-one times, as he passed in front of the Tomb.

A small gathering observed the ceremony in silence, and time seemed to cease, as I focused on the soldiers. Their precise movements, expertly choreographed, repeated around the clock year after year, proclaimed the respect these soldiers held for their fallen brethren.

Mac pulled me away, and after we were a respectful distance from the Tomb, I expressed my gratitude.

"Thank you for showing me that. It's one of the most powerful emotional experiences I have ever had."

"It is special. Everyone should see it at least once to sense the sacrifice these soldiers made and the sense of duty the military invokes. It's one of the best places in this town. Come on, let's go visit Jojo. Section 60 holds remains from Iran and Afghanistan."

"How do you find one grave among all of these?"

She held up her phone. "Every grave is documented on their app. It can help you find anyone buried here, but I already knew where Jojo rests." She confidently stepped down a row and stopped before a white marble headstone identical to the thousands around it.

Andrew Joseph Walker

Sgt. USAF

Afghanistan

Feb 14, 1986

Feb 5, 2005

Friend to all

Never forgotten

Mac knelt down and placed her hand on the stone, tears pooling in her eyes. "He was a great kid, energetic, funny, fearless. I can't believe they're both gone. Mark and he were inseparable in high school with their whole lives ahead of them." She dried her eyes. "Time to see what Mark left for us."

The perfectly manicured grass around the stone revealed no evidence of disturbance, and the plain white marble showed no obvious alteration. Mac felt around the stone, as her hands examined the base. A slight tearing sound preceded her removal of white tape from the base. She quickly examined it.

"What did you find?"

"A password." She turned the tape around and showed me a long series of numbers and letters drawn on a piece of plastic.

"That's the longest password I've ever seen," I said.

"Mark was not a 'password123' type of guy. Let's get back to the office and see what we have."

"That may be a problem. Looks like we are about to have some company."

Two men in suits rushed toward us. Nothing about their appearance overtly threatened, except for the menace burning in their eyes. Their intense gaze alternated between focusing on us and scanning our surroundings. Banshee sensed the tension and uttered a low growl.

·   ·   ·

Across the cemetery, two men observed the confrontation through binoculars.

"Do we intervene?" the first man asked.

"Not unless it turns violent. Get a video."

The first man lifted his camera and focused on the group. Although normal in appearance, the camera contained the latest technology which allowed it to zoom 1,000 times without distortion. He ran video continuously as they watched.

·   ·   ·

Mac whispered to me. "Stay calm. This is not unexpected."

I gave the command for Banshee to relax. He laid back down, but remained wary.

The men stopped a few feet in front of us. "I believe you found something that belongs to us. We would like it back." He held out his hand, allowing his suit coat to fall open to reveal a gun on his hip. His partner's hand rested inside his own suit jacket.

Unfazed by the power play, Mac took a moment to look at the code. She held it up in front of her, facing the man, as she stood up. "You must mean this. Is this what you want?" She slowly held it out to him. "It's yours. Go."

The man snatched the paper from her hand, and the two men hastily retreated. Mac sat down next to me.

"What the fuck was that all about?" I asked.

Mac laughed. "Those idiots have been following me for the last day or so. I figured they would make an appearance here. It's easier to give them the code and let them run away."

"But now we don't have the code."

Mac tapped her head. "Yes, we do."

"That's an awfully long code to remember."

"It's only twenty-eight digits. Give them a few minutes to clear out of here."

"Who are they?"

"I'm pretty sure they're Russian. They work hard to fit in, but there is always something just a little too formal and stiff about them. You can also tell by the clothes. Russians never seem to have a suit that fits correctly. Homeland has been following me, too. They're out there somewhere."

I looked around but saw nothing suspicious.

"You won't see them. They're high-tech fanatics. They're far away with a couple of billion pixels aimed at us. Smile for them." She waved like a beauty pageant queen in all directions.

"You wanted them to have the code as well?"

"Sure. They know we found something. If we try to hide it from them, they'll just break in to try to find it. Now they know the Russians have it and will waste time following them. Doesn't matter, because the code is meaningless without the drive, and we're the only ones with the drive. Plus, they won't be able to decipher the code, anyway."

I thought through everything I had learned, as she lay back on the soft grass. I laid down as well, and Banshee rested his head on my chest. "What exactly did you do after college and before joining the Senator's staff?"

"I was an officer in the Defense Intelligence Agency, working for the office of the Secretary of Defense. We focused on national-level, long-term, and strategic intelligence needs and coordinated with the military and the department of defense intelligence units to provide accurate information for the Secretary."

"That's fancy Washington talk. What did you actually do for them?"

"I was part of the Directorate for Science and Technology focused on gathering and evaluating nuclear, chemical, and biological intelligence about our enemies. Mostly, we developed human assets who provided accurate data for us."

"So you recruited spies overseas?"

"That's one way to describe it, although it's not all that glamorous. I don't get to drive an Aston Martin to a casino in Monaco to meet a source. Mostly it's trudging through the bad parts of bad countries to meet with bad people."

"Sounds dangerous."

"It can be. Americans are not loved in much of the world. A lot of the training involves survival skills, which it seems you have some familiarity with."

"Did some checking on me last night?"

"I am trained in intelligence gathering. You have quite the history, organized crime in Houston, dirty money in Montana, and bombings in Las Vegas. Trouble seems to find you."

"I don't look for it, but I hate it when I see innocent people hurt. When I set my mind to it, I'm in it for the duration."

"Are you in this for the duration?"

"Absolutely. I hadn't met your brother before he was shot, but an innocent man reached out to me for help as he died, and I'll see it through to the end. How did you end up with the Senator?"

"My job involved frequent interaction with senior members of Congress, and I hit it off with Senator Whitehurst. She offered me a job as her Chief of Staff."

"Do you know what is actually going on here?"

She stood up. "Not yet, but I will soon. Someone, probably the Russians, killed my brother because of something he was working on. I'm gonna find his work and hunt down the motherfuckers who killed him and give them a lesson on American justice. C'mon. Everyone should have cleared the area by now. Let's get back and see what Mark left us."

CHAPTER NINE

Saturday, March 14
9:39 a.m.

Viktor and Nikolai, ordered to follow the woman and take whatever she found, hurried from the cemetery with their treasure. Their boss would be grateful, especially after the disaster on Friday that resulted in the deaths of two of their men.

After a cab ride to the Russian Embassy without bothering with evasive maneuvers, they entered through a security gate, relieved to be back on Russian territory. They bypassed the Ambassador's residence, where diplomatic parties were held, and entered the main administrative building. Built with all the charm of a Russian tenement building, the eight stories of square concrete office space felt even more depressing inside than outside. Worn linoleum floors, beige walls, and fluorescent lighting highlighted the dated furniture. They passed through a security checkpoint and stepped into an elevator. Their badges accessed three of the five floors below ground. They pressed the button for subbasement three. They had no idea what the two lower floors contained and knew not to harbor curiosity. Willful ignorance was a learned survival skill in modern Russia.

Viktor and Nikolai arrived outside the office door and quietly waited in the uncomfortable chairs before it. The assistant noted their arrival and turned his attention back to papers on his desk. Well trained to maintain respectful patience, they accepted the wait.

After twenty minutes of anxious silence, the office door opened, and a woman departed. The assistant waved them into the office with a dismissive gesture. They stood at attention in front of a massive desk, as the Deputy Director finished some notations.

Deputy Director Dmitry Petrov had been in charge of Directorate S for the last six years. One of eight directorates of the SVR, Directorate S was the foreign intelligence service of the Russian Federation tasked with illegal intelligence operations outside Russia. The SVR had been formed in 1991 from the ashes of its predecessor, the KGB. Petrov was one of the few remaining officers who had started his career under the KGB. Scars on his arms and forehead reminded him of battles won and lost in Afghanistan. He was a hard-liner who believed in the old ways and longed for the days when the KGB ruled through fear and intimidation.

Petrov set aside his work to focus on the two young agents standing before him. Capable, but ordinary, they were destined for a career of mediocrity, he surmised.

"Sir, we followed the subject to her office, and then to Arlington Cemetery, where we observed her removing a piece of tape from one of the headstones. We approached her and acquired it without resistance."

Viktor laid the tape on the massive desk, and Petrov examined it closely. The code or password was useless without more information, a puzzle piece that may or may not have future value. "And she didn't fight to try and keep it?"

"No, sir."

"Was she alone?"

"No, sir. She was with that doctor and his dog."

"Interesting. One of you file a full report and the other get back on the subject. I want to know everywhere she goes, everyone she meets, and gather any additional intelligence that you can. Dismissed."

Viktor and Nikolai left the office, as Petrov reread the code and then asked his assistant to call Agent Morozova into his office. Three minutes later, she stood before him.

Alina Morozova, only twenty-seven, had begun training for the SVR thirteen years earlier. Her fluency in English with multiple regional accents along with her dark hair, brown eyes, and athletic figure allowed her to blend into American society. With changes to her hair color, tinted contact lenses, different heel heights, and padded clothing, she could change her appearance at will. Listed as a secretary for the embassy, she did not have diplomatic immunity. As an undercover spy for Russia, she was one of his best agents, responsible for shooting Mark Lawton and for recovering his backpack. Unfortunately, it contained nothing of value. Petrov appreciated her bold risk, decisiveness, and willingness to use violence. Alina would have done well in the KGB.

He tossed the tape across the desk. "Viktor and Nikolai got this from the sister."

Alina glanced at it. "A password, meaningless without knowing where to use it."

"Agreed, but it means she is on a trail. We need to find that research before the Americans do. It is a matter of utmost importance to the President himself. Success in this matter will assure that you sit in this chair someday." Left unsaid were the consequences of failure.

"I understand, sir."

"Find it for me. Whatever you need, whatever needs to be done, find it. Dismissed."

Alina confidently exited the office. A master at tracking people, she would never fail. The first step had been electronic surveillance on the homes, cars, computers, and phones on Lawton's sister and the doctor, constantly monitored. Whatever information they uncovered she would take by stealth or by force.

CHAPTER TEN

Saturday, March 14
11:03 a.m.

Back in the basement office, Mac fired up the air gapped computer and inserted the flash drive. On a pad of paper, she wrote the twenty-eight digits from memory in precise handwriting. Twenty letters, eight capital and twelve lower case, as well as eight numbers seemed randomly mixed into the code.

"Why not just enter the code?" I wondered aloud.

"Mark wouldn't make it that simple. The key will be in the numbers." She rewrote only the eight digits, 72828977, and willed them to reveal themselves. "Do you know what's special about this number?"

"Nothing that I can imagine."

"Correct. It's an unremarkable number, and Mark would never use an ordinary number."

"Are you sure?"

"Positive. Every number he chooses will have meaning, and this one is meaningless. We need to figure out the nearest number with special properties."

"I hope you know something about special numbers, because I still use my birthday as my PIN number."

"Do you know what a prime number is?"

"Yeah, a number that can be divided only by one and itself."

"Pretty good for a doctor."

"Even doctors have to take some math classes."

"Prime numbers are important in the creation and breaking of codes. The number here bears a striking resemblance to a very unique number, 73939133. Want to guess at why it's special?"

"Because it's prime?"

"I'll give you partial credit. It is prime, but it's also the largest prime number that remains prime no matter how many digits are removed from the end. That unique quality would appeal to Mark."

"So 7393913, 739391, and all the others are prime? Who figures this stuff out?"

"Usually grad students with an intense desire to be famous in the world of mathematics while avoiding work on their dissertations."

"I had no idea being famous in math was a thing."

"The audience is small, but passionate." She patiently entered the new numbers into the code, and then carefully typed it into the password prompt. Smiley faces flashed on screen before a message appeared. "Don't get cocky, the first clues are the easy ones. Next one: mirror image of 37. Love you, sis."

Mac wiped away a tear as she stared at the message. "Mark was always a smart ass. I can't believe he's gone, and it feels like he's still here with me."

"I'm so sorry for your loss."

"Thank you." Mac dried her eyes as she spoke.

"Any idea what this clue means?"

"Not the slightest idea. I'm gonna need to think on this one."

"Anything I can do to help?"

"No. These clues were meant for me. Give me some time. I'll call you when I figure something out."

"Okay. Banshee and I are happy to help if and when you need us."

"Be careful out there. People are likely watching you, too. They probably won't bother you, but if they do, tell them the truth. You don't know anything. Assume your phone and computers are being monitored. If you need to talk to me or to anyone else without someone listening in, use this."

She handed me a cheap phone from the desk. "A burner?" I asked.

"It should be completely secure. Never been used. The programmed number in there is for another burner I have. Remember, don't be a hero, and you don't know anything if anyone asks."

"Shouldn't be too hard. I am thoroughly confused. What do you want to do with the flash drive?"

"I'll keep it. It's worthless to everyone else, but it's one of the last messages from my brother." Her eyes teared up again.

"Must be tough to lose a twin."

"I imagine it's tough to lose anyone we care about, but no one is like a twin. From my earliest memories, we were in sync with each other. We finished each other's sentences; shared complex thoughts through a glance; and mimicked each other's mannerisms. Sometimes I swear we could communicate telepathically. I wish I could speak to him now. I feel like part of me has been torn away."

"I'm sorry. I never had a sibling, so I can't imagine what you're going through, but I know it's tough. Again, Banshee and I are willing to assist in any way to help you find closure."

"Thanks. That means a lot. I'll be in touch."

We left her seated at the desk, gazing at the flash drive, as if willing it to speak to her. "We need to help her out. Okay, buddy?"

Banshee wagged his tail.

.   .   .

Appreciating the gorgeous day, we stopped at a park on the way home, and Banshee ran around aimlessly, as I enjoyed an ice cream cone. We meandered back to my townhome, a two-story that cost a small fortune to rent, but we had a convenient location and a small yard for Banshee. I unlocked the door and pushed it open. Banshee immediately sat and growled. Trained to detect new odors whenever we return home, he was letting me know that someone had been in the house. Given that I had the only key, the unwelcome guest could still be inside.

I motioned for Banshee to stay alert and silent and entered the house with him at my side. I stepped into the study, the first room on my right, and opened the top desk drawer to retrieve a handgun I kept for security. I confirmed the mag was full with one round in the chamber. The Glock did not have a safety to worry about.

I whispered for Banshee to SEARCH, and he began his methodical trip through the house, sniffing everywhere. We cleared the first floor without incident and headed upstairs with Banshee in the lead. A quick search of every closet and under each bed confirmed that we were alone. I hugged Banshee. Clearing a house with him in front of me was much less stressful than doing it alone.

I returned downstairs and checked all the doors and windows to find them locked. Next, I quickly surveyed likely places a thief might search and found nothing missing. I sat on the sofa and looked around me. Everything seemed in place, but on closer inspection, the room felt a little too neat. Everything squared perfectly with the furniture. The mantle revealed books and a candle misaligned with the light dust patterns.

Someone had searched my home in my absence. I had nothing of value to steal, and Mac had the flash drive. Whoever had been here had left empty handed. The question was whether they had left anything behind.

CHAPTER ELEVEN

Saturday, March 14
5:23 p.m.

A banging assault on my front door interrupted my lunch of reheated pizza and elicited a deep growl from Banshee. "Calm down, boy. I have a pretty good idea who's here," I told him, as I stood to answer the door. I opened it to find my favorite Homeland Security officer.

"Agent Smith, how nice of you to visit."

He pushed some papers into my chest and muscled past me. "Search warrant, asshole. Sit down and be quiet. And keep that dog under control."

Banshee growled, but I calmed him with a touch on his neck. "You're welcome to search all day, but I doubt you'll find anything."

"Why's that?"

"First, because I don't have anything to hide. Second, if I did have something to hide, whoever searched my place this morning would have found it already."

"What the hell are you talking about? Who was here this morning?"

"No idea. I actually thought that it might be you with an illegal search. You don't seem like a strict rule follower."

"Start at the beginning and make some sense."

"When I came home this morning, Banshee alerted for someone's presence in my house. I searched the place and didn't find anyone, but clearly someone had been through my stuff. I noticed nothing missing, but something may have been left behind."

Smith motioned to one of his crew. "Jenkins, I want a blackout on this place and an electromagnetic scan of this entire house."

Jenkins set his case on the kitchen table, opened a laptop, plugged a small antenna into the USB port, and clicked some keys. After a few seconds, he gave a thumbs up. "Area is secure. Safe to talk."

Smith motioned his team to begin their search and directed me to the kitchen table. Banshee sat at my feet, watching everyone move through his home. I stared at Smith and waited for him to break the silence. Finally, he spoke.

"I checked up on you. You've got quite an interesting history with extortion, fraud, even a bit of the cartel in your past."

"I also take care of patients in the emergency room."

"That appears to be where all your problems begin."

"Trouble does seem to find me."

"It certainly does, and it found you again last night. We know you met with the victim's sister and went with her to Arlington National Cemetery this morning. We know you found something, and we want it."

"You already have it. I believe she held it up for you to see before the Russians took it away."

"What do you know about the Russians?"

"That they're bitter about the failure of Marxism and embarrassed to admit that capitalism works."

"Okay, smart ass, maybe some time in jail will make you reconsider your situation."

"It would, but you're not gonna put me in jail, because I will talk about how you guys trashed our emergency trauma room, stole a dead body, and kept the deaths of two Russians a secret to hide something."

Smith glared at me. "So now you're a beacon of transparency?"

"Apparently, I'm more honest than you are, Agent Smith. Show me a real ID, and we can talk. Otherwise, you can complete your search and fuck off."

Smith reached into his back pocket. I expected him to have cuffs in his hand, but he tossed me his wallet instead. "Open it."

I found his Homeland Security ID in the name of Supervisory Special Agent Clarence Duff. I tossed the wallet back to him. "You don't look like a Clarence."

"What does a Clarence look like?"

"A six-foot-five black man who plays the saxophone for Bruce."

"There's some serious shit going down involving some bad people. Three are already dead, and you are on their radar. The next shot may be in your direction. Tell me what you know."

"I don't know anything. Mac asked me to meet her this morning to tell her again about her brother's final moments. I did so, and she asked Banshee and me to accompany her to Arlington. She went to that grave and found that tape with numbers on it, and those guys took it from us. Then I walked her back to her office. I have no idea what is happening, and Mac isn't telling me anything. If you want answers, ask her."

"That's a little complicated given her job with the Senator. You know, politics."

"I don't know anything about politics. I tried to save a guy's life last night, and he died. I tried to help his sister this morning, and now I have strange people searching my house, and you guys showing up with a warrant. I hope you find what you're looking for, but I don't know shit."

Agent Jenkins interrupted us to set seven small devices on the table. "That's everything."

Special Agent Duff lifted one for closer inspection. "Not one of ours?"

"Definitely not. It's Eastern European, military grade, and either state sponsored or from someone with a lot of money," Jenkins replied.

Special Agent Duff focused on me. "I want to put you in protective custody."

"No fucking way."

"I can't guarantee your safety."

"I'm not asking you to guarantee anything. Just leave me alone, and go look for whatever it is you're looking for."

Duff stood up from his chair. "Your choice, but a bad one. My free advice is to stay out of this. You know we're going to be following you."

"I would expect no less from civil servants."

"You know what that makes you?"

"I know exactly what it makes me. Bait."

CHAPTER TWELVE

Sunday, March 15
7:53 a.m.

I arrived to a serene emergency room after the results of bad decisions people made on Saturday night had been discharged or admitted. The pious folks attended church; families breakfasted; and the heathens awoke with hangovers. Sunday morning shifts were reliably calm.

"How's the esteemed Dr. Pastone this fine Sunday morning?" I asked.

"A little sunburnt. I went fishing yesterday and forgot my sunscreen. Don't tell dermatology. I don't need another lecture from them."

"That's funny. When's the last time you saw a dermatologist in the emergency room on a Sunday?"

"Rumor has it that one showed up on a weekend about fifteen years ago, but it may be an urban legend. How was your Saturday? Anything exciting?"

I figured that visits with a Senator, Russian mobsters, and two groups searching my house would count as exciting, but I held back. "Not really. Casual day around the house with a brief visit to the park with Banshee. Are we still on to discuss the new contract with the hospital next week?"

"Yeah, they have our proposal and received a counter offer from Prime Medical Partners."

"The PIMPS are making a run at your business?" Prime Medical Partners, or PMP as they called themselves, were referred to as the PIMPS by everyone in the medical field due to their practice of buying medical practices and then "streamlining" their operations. What they did in actuality was cut salaries by about 20% and staffing by about 30%, resulting in unhappy staff and unsafe working conditions. A private equity firm based in Manhattan, they represented an unspoken danger to medical care.

"Yep. They'll offer a lower price and promise the same level of service, but everyone knows that's bullshit. In six months, you won't recognize this place, if they take over."

"Any way to offer a competitive bid against them?"

"Not really. We focus on maintaining the best staff we can. They don't care about any of that, because they don't worry about the long term benefits of higher quality patient care."

"So how do you plan to beat them?"

"No way they are operating legally. We need to find out how they convince hospitals to take the inevitable public relations hit for lower quality of care."

That peaked my interest. I had a resource for digging up information. "Who would be the targets?"

"Three guys are leading the negotiation. Matt Hyde is their COO. He seems like a yes man and not really useful. Jim Billings, the CEO, is an anesthesiologist, but went over to the dark side years ago. Hasn't seen a patient in over a decade. He's cocky, but insecure. He likes to play the tough guy but really just wants to be liked, which is sad, because no one actually likes him."

"Whose the third person?"

"Don Prost, general counsel for the PIMPS. Biggest asshole I have ever met, and I've been in the emergency room for over twenty-five years. He's usually coked up at meetings, hyper aggressive, narcissistic, and never met a fact that he didn't want to argue."

"Sounds charming. Let me look into these three."

"You got some special talent I don't know about?"

"I have resources you don't want to know anything about. I've met some people over the years who specialize in digging up information. Let me see what I can find."

"Okay, but don't get in trouble for me."

"No worries. I'll find the trouble all on my own."

.   .   .

The number of patients grew steadily throughout the day, but acuity remained low. Typical minor injuries, chest pain, and abdominal pain cases made up the bulk of the work. Called to a trauma room, I was told to leave Banshee at the nurses' station. I found a six-year-old boy crying on a stretcher with his head wrapped in a bandage. Dad, looking like he was about to pass out, leaned over his bedside with his shirt covered in blood.

I walked to the stretcher and introduced myself. "I'm Doc, what's your name?"

Through tears, he responded, "Billy."

"Nice to meet you, Billy. Give me five."

He slapped my outstretched hand.

"How old are you, Billy?"

"I'm six."

"You got a job?"

A smile flashed across his face. "No, silly. I go to school."

"Going to school sounds like a job to me. What are you gonna be when you grow up?"

His eyes brightened. "I'm gonna be an astronaut!"

"An astronaut? Are you gonna go to the moon?"

"Nope. I'm going to Mars. I'm gonna be a Mars astronaut."

"Do you get good grades?"

"Yes, sir."

"That's great! You need good grades to go to astronaut school. I'm gonna talk to your dad for a minute, but tell Nurse Linda about Mars. She loves to hear all about Mars."

He had momentarily forgotten about his head wound and chattered about space and rocket ships with Linda. I turned my attention to his dad and held out my hand. "I'm Doctor Docker, but I go by Doc for obvious reasons. Your name is?"

"Tom."

"You're his dad?"

"Yes, sir."

"Okay, what happened?"

"We were playing in the park, and this Rottweiler was off leash and attacked my boy. Grabbed his head like a toy ball and wouldn't let go. I had to kick him a couple times before he finally let go and ran away. There was so much blood. I called 911."

"Your boy is going to be okay. Dog attacks are scary, and head wounds bleed a lot, but look at him over there. He's doing great."

Dad teared up, as he watched his son tell space stories. "How did you calm him that quickly? He was a mess on the way over here and wouldn't stop crying."

"That's a normal reaction to trauma. I'm sure he was scared and hurt, but distraction works wonders. Let me take a quick look, and see what we have."

Billy finished a story about space suits. "Billy, I want to get you a clean bandage. That one on your head is a mess." His chin quivered, but I held up my hand and reassured him. "Don't worry. I'm not gonna touch anything, I'm just going to change the bandage. Okay?"

I removed it to reveal his bloody scalp. Fortunately, the bleeding was slow. Two long gouges in the hairline oozed, but more concerning were the puncture wounds. Dog bites can be strong enough to puncture bone. I rewrapped the wounds in fresh gauze and addressed them both.

"Billy, I think we need to get a picture of your head and get you some medicine to make sure it won't get infected. Some of my friends will come by to get that done. They have special medicines that let you take a nap while we fix everything. Deal?"

He slapped my outstretched hand and agreed. "Deal, as long as no more dogs get me."

"Billy, I know that other dog hurt you, but not all dogs are bad. I work with a dog here in the emergency room, and he is the nicest dog in the world. Do you want to meet him?"

Billy shook his head. "I don't think so."

"He knows some really cool tricks. Can I show you his tricks?"

Billy agreed, but nervously.

I called Banshee into the room and introduced him from a distance. Billy watched cautiously, as I had him do basic tricks, sit, lay, and beg. "Watch what else he can do." I patted my chest and said, HUG. Banshee leaped into my arms and snuggled into me. I set him back on the floor and said, FLIP. Banshee performed a perfect back flip. Then I commanded him to CRAWL, and Banshee bent low to sneak around the room, leaving Billy laughing at the sight. Finally, I had him stand at the bedside and kiss Billy's hand.

"Billy, now you get to command Banshee. Just tell him what you want him to do."

Laughing, Billy gave commands for FLIP, CRAWL, and JUMP.

I pulled dad into the hallway. "We're gonna get a CT scan, as it looks like the teeth may have punctured his skull. We'll start some IV antibiotics and pain meds, and they'll take him up to the OR to clean everything and close the wounds. Luckily, they're all inside the hairline, so no one will see his scars for several decades. He's gonna be fine."

"Thanks for making him smile, Doc. I was afraid he would contend with a fear of dogs for life."

"You're welcome. Banshee is good for everyone's morale."

Twenty minutes later, the CT results showed two punctures through the skull with one tooth broken off in the wound. The brain showed no bleeding. After a few calls to neurosurgery to take him to the operating room, to an infectious disease consult to work out his antibiotic regimen, and to the hospitalist team to admit him, I had done all that I could. Billy waved to me and Banshee, as he was wheeled to the operating room.

There are few things more satisfying than calming a scared child in the emergency room. "Good job, Banshee. That's why I keep you around."

Banshee curled up under an empty desk at the nurses' station and sighed.

CHAPTER THIRTEEN

Sunday, March 15
8:21 p.m.

I stepped out of the shower, when the phone rang with the Caller ID indicating a call from the US Government. Although unlikely that the IRS or Agent Duff had good news for me, I answered.

"Hello."

"Doc, it's Mac. You have a few minutes to talk?"

"Sure. What's up?"

"Assume our acquaintances are listening."

"Understood." I hadn't really thought through the implications, but I resolved to think about my online presence.

"I hate to ask, but are you available tomorrow? Mark's coworkers are having a luncheon to celebrate his life, and I don't want to go alone."

"I'm happy to join you. I'm off tomorrow. What time and where?"

"I can stop by your place around 11:00, and we can go together."

"I'll be ready. Can Banshee join us?"

"Of course. Be careful, Doc."

"Will do. Goodnight."

I ended the call and turned my attention to my next problem, Prime Medical Partners. I had promised to find information, and I had just the source. The BT is a hacker I had used previously to discover information that had led to criminal charges. The amazing kid could hack into anything. A bit paranoid and fueled by Adderall and caffeine, he was a genius with a keyboard.

I called him from my burner phone, prepared for the rapid answers that The BT would require, but surprisingly, the phone rang four times before a woman smacking on gum answered, "Yeah."

"I'm sorry. I am looking for The BT."

"This is his phone. He's busy." In the background, I heard what sounded like twenty hands on ten keyboards pounding away. The BT was in the midst of a hacking rage.

"Who are you?"

"Fuck you, mister. Who the fuck are you?"

"I'm Doc. I've worked with The BT previously."

"Hold on." I heard her call out, "Yo, Big B, do you know a Doc?" A pause of a millisecond on the keyboards before the clatter returned answered her. "Okay, he says you're legit and have a cool dog. What do you need?"

"Who are you, exactly?"

"He's my boyfriend. You can call me Spike."

"Okay, Spike. I need some information on some people."

"What kind of information?"

"The kind they don't want anyone to know about."

"Got it. The fun stuff."

"As much as you can find."

"Is this personal or business?"

"Business. They're messing with our contract and not playing by the rules."

"No problem. How many names?"

"Three names and one company."

"Send them to me to this email address and wire $2500 in Bitcoin to this address. Have a good day."

She ended the call before I could say goodbye. I shook my head, as I transferred the information and bitcoin to a hacker named Spike. I decided to go to bed with a good book and hope for sleep. Banshee agreed and curled up on the floor beside me.

CHAPTER FOURTEEN

Monday, March 16
10:58 a.m.

Mac arrived promptly at eleven dressed in another black suit with a white blouse. Great minds must think alike, as I was wearing the exact same thing. She looked me up and down, as I opened the door and a brief laugh escaped.

"Well, this is awkward," she said.

"It is a bit much. How about I change my shirt? Will only take a second."

"Thanks. I'll hang out with Banshee."

I changed into a light blue shirt and returned to find Mac sitting on the floor vigorously scratching both his ears. "Careful, he gets clingy."

"It's okay. He's a good boy, and good boys need ear scratches. He's so quiet."

"He can make some noise when he needs to."

"He barks on command?"

"Stand here next to me." I had Banshee sit at attention, then tapped three fingers from my right hand on my left forearm. Banshee viciously howled, and the echo reverberated through the townhouse until I motioned him to calm down.

"That's a bit terrifying. Will he do that for anybody?"

"He has to trust the person giving commands. Want to try? Banshee, OBEY," I said, as I gestured toward Mac.

She tapped three fingers on her forearm, and Banshee howled as loud as he could until I motioned for him to calm down.

"He is the most amazing dog I have ever met."

Banshee wagged his tail, as she rose to leave. "Thanks, again, for going with me."

"My pleasure. Thank you for thinking of me." She led the way to her car, a brand new Mercedes SL roadster in a hypnotic green. I whistled in appreciation.

"That is a beautiful car," I circled it.

"Thanks. It's my one splurge. My dad liked to race and made sure I had an appreciation for fine automobiles. Nothing compares to the performance and luxury of an AMG model on the open road."

We settled into the car, and the tires squealed, as she pulled into traffic. "Made any progress on the latest hint?" I asked.

"Not really. The mirror image of 37 is 73, of course, but I don't know its significance, other than it's typical of Mark, basic, yet frustrating."

"I'll keep my eyes open for a sign pointing to 73. Where is his luncheon?"

"It's at his DARPA lab, probably to minimize the time his coworkers aren't working."

"Do you know any of them?"

"Not really. They're pretty reclusive. Hopefully, we can figure out what Mark was working on at least."

"Maybe someone will have a big sign with the number 73 on it."

She downshifted and punched the gas to take advantage of an opening in the middle lane. She flashed a smile, as she looked over at me, "Not scaring you, am I?"

"You seem pretty comfortable with the car. I feel bad for the folks trying to follow you."

She laughed, as she sped by a car on the shoulder and accelerated into open space.

We arrived in one piece and found a parking garage nearby. The unremarkable glass and metal building stood seven stories.

Mac noted my scrutiny of the building. "Don't let the exterior fool you. This specialized building hosts some of the smartest people in the country working on revolutionary technologies protected by an unrivaled security system."

We entered through glass double doors and approached the front desk, manned by a single guard. "Can I help you folks?"

"I'm Mackenzie Lawton, and this is my friend, AJ Docker. We're here to meet with some of my brother Mark's coworkers."

"I'm sorry for your loss. Background checks cleared for both of you. These badges allow you access only to the first floor. Any attempt to access other floors is a violation of federal statutes and will result in your arrest and prosecution. Please leave all electronic devices with me. Any attempt to take pictures or record any images of the building is also a violation of federal law. Do you understand these rules?"

"Yes, sir," we replied, as we handed him our phones.

"What's with the dog?"

"He's a service animal, trained to calm people during times of stress," I said.

The guard raised an eyebrow, as he looked over Banshee. "He's trained?"

I snapped my fingers, and Banshee leaped into my arms. "SMILE," I said, and Banshee showed off for the guard. "HIGH FIVE," I said, and Banshee held out a paw, which the guard nervously tapped, as he took a step back.

"Seems like he is well trained. You're responsible for him."

We walked through a metal detector and were buzzed through a solid door into a short hallway. The first door clanged shut before the second opened into a lobby area.

"They take security seriously here," I said.

Mac pointed at the vents in the ceiling. "They can probably flood this place with gas in seconds."

The second door opened into a hallway with a large glassed-in conference room filled with a few dozen people. A picture of Mark with an award rested on an easel outside the door. Mac took a deep breath and squared her shoulders.

"You okay?" I asked.

"Let's do this." Mac strode confidently into the room, and conversation dwindled, as about thirty sets of eyes turned their attention to her. The diverse group had dressed casually, many of them wearing white lab coats. Nothing revealed their incredible intellects.

A middle aged man stepped forward and held out his hand. "I'm Mike Snowburn, head of DARPA, thank you for coming today. We're all saddened by the loss of Mark."

"Thank you for organizing this memorial for him. This is my friend AJ, and his service dog, Banshee."

He shook my hand and warily glanced at Banshee. Obviously not a dog person, he led Mac away to meet some people, leaving me and Banshee. I reached down to scratch his ears. "Lets go get a snack and see if anyone likes dogs." Banshee waved his tail, as we moved through the gathering.

As I reached for a cookie, a quiet voice behind me refocused my attention.

"Excuse me, what's your dog's name?" A petite Asian woman in her early thirties, dressed in a fitted black dress, let Banshee sniff her hand.

"This is Banshee, and I'm AJ, but everyone calls me Doc." I offered my hand, and she gently took it in a delicate grip. She withdrew her hand after a brief shake.

"I'm Elise. May I pet him?"

"Of course, Banshee loves attention. FRIEND."

Banshee leaned into her hand, as she scratched his ears, and her soft smile grew. I stood awkwardly with a cookie in my hand.

"What do you do here?"

She looked up. "I work with lasers. It's classified."

"I wouldn't understand much about lasers, anyway. Did you know Mark well?"

Her eyes watered, and she trembled, as she tried to contain her grief. "We never worked on the same projects, but we saw each other around the building. He was a good man. How did you know him?"

"Sadly, I never got to know Mark. I'm a doctor in the emergency room, and I was working when they brought him in on Friday. I wish we could have saved him."

She looked down at Banshee, but couldn't hide the tears dripping into his fur. I handed her a napkin to dry her eyes and gave her some time to compose herself.

"Forgive me."

"Nothing to forgive. He obviously meant a lot to you."

"He was a very good friend. He didn't deserve to die like that."

"No one deserves to die like that. Do you know what he was working on?"

"No one knew exactly what he was working on. Everyone here keeps secrets, and Mark was especially private. He said it had the potential to change the world, for better or for worse."

"That's a bold description."

"It's what we are about here at DARPA. We change the world. Now we'll never know what Mark could have contributed. I hear his work is lost."

"That's what Mac tells me. None of his coworkers has a copy?"

"Rumor has it no one knew his research, except Mark, and he hid it. They emptied his office and took everything away from his lab, but they're still asking questions, so they haven't found what they're looking for."

"Who are they?"

"Creepy government people in suits with no IDs working for nameless agencies."

"Yeah, I've had the pleasure of meeting some of those people."

"Would you please introduce me to Mac? I would like to pay my respects to his sister."

"Of course. Follow me."

We sidestepped through small groups to reach Mac, and I introduced her.

"This is Elise. She does something with lasers and knew your brother."

"Very nice to meet you," Mac said, as she held out her hand.

"Likewise," Elise responded and grabbed Mac's hand more forcefully than she had mine. She shook it, then rotated her wrist to reveal an elaborate tattoo on the underside of her forearm. The number 1001001 was intricately drawn surrounded by a mesmerizing swirling pattern of greens, blues and yellows.

Mac stared at the tattoo for a moment and then locked eyes with Elise, still holding her hand. "That's a beautiful tattoo. How well did you know Mark?"

Elise released her grip and looked around the room. "A conversation for another time. I usually eat dinner at The Golden Chop at eight o'clock on Tuesdays. You are welcome to join me tomorrow, if you are available." She patted Banshee's head and quietly left the room.

"What the fuck just happened?" I whispered to Mac.

"Later. Let's get through this."

We spent an hour in the room with coworkers sharing stories and offering condolences. Mr. Snowburn gave a brief speech praising Mark's contributions to science, and Mac thanked the crowd for their support. Finally, we could gracefully leave.

We buckled into the car, and I couldn't hold back any longer. "What happened with Elise?"

"You saw the tattoo?"

"Of course."

"Did you recognize the number?"

"Sure, 1001001. What's it mean?"

"In base 10, it means one million, one thousand and one."

"I figured that part out."

"Do you know what that number represents in base 2?"

"No idea."

"In base 2, that number translates to 73."

"Seriously?"

"Yes. The mirror image of 37 is 73, and that woman has an elaborate 73 on her arm. I'm pretty sure she was Mark's girlfriend."

"She didn't mention that."

"She's smart and knows that she's being watched. That's why she wants to meet tomorrow for dinner somewhere she feels safe. I hope you like Chinese food."

CHAPTER FIFTEEN

Monday, March 16
1:43 p.m.

Mac hurried into work to catch up on missed calls. The obligations of Senator Whitehurst's office relentlessly accumulated with messages and demands. Mac started going through the messages, filtering those to contact immediately and setting the rest aside for an aide to call back. She was so absorbed that she didn't notice the Senator's entrance and polite wait for acknowledgement.

"How was the memorial service?" she asked.

Startled, Mac met her eyes. "Senator. I'm sorry I didn't hear you approach. The memorial was nice. Mark's friends had a lot of kind things to say about him."

"I'm glad to hear it. Were you able to uncover any information about what he was working on?"

"Not really. Everyone was guarded about what happens in that building."

"Making any progress at all on your overall investigation?"

Mac rarely held back information from the Senator, but her questions seemed a little too pointed. "No, ma'am. I'm stuck on his last clue."

The Senator closely examined Mac's expression. Two decades in Washington had taught her how to read people. Few could hold her intense gaze, but Mac was up to the task. The Senator broke eye contact.

"Very well. Keep me informed of any updates."

"Yes, ma'am."

Mac went back to work, and the Senator secluded herself in her inner office behind her closed door. She sat and retrieved a burner phone from her desk. Government phones were secure, but every call was logged and subject to subpoena. Not all contact was meant to be shared.

She typed a text on the Signal app. "No progress."

The answer came quickly. "Unacceptable. Turn up the pressure."

The Senator erased the messages, threw the phone back in the drawer, and dragged her attention to other matters.

· · ·

I decided on an afternoon run to clear my head. Banshee and I left the house for the short walk toward the Capitol, and I noted a car waiting to follow me. DHS seemed to have chosen intimidation over subtlety. The car disgorged an unfriendly agent to stalk me on foot and continued to follow us.

"What do you say, Banshee? Feel like fucking with the DHS today?"

Banshee swished his tail in anticipation of an adventure, as we walked toward the Capitol along a wide, semi-crowded sidewalk. We arrived at the National Mall to join the usual crowd of tourists and set off at a warm-up pace. The agent following on foot jumped back into the car to follow us. The Mall is wide open enough for them to track me from the street.

My antics began when I came to an empty bench, sat down, and not so subtlety reached underneath the bench before suddenly standing to continue my jog. A few minutes later, I found a Coke can on the ground. I picked it up and looked inside before heading over to a trash can and setting it on the ground beside it, making sure to rotate the can until the logo was visible. I suddenly changed direction, causing the agents to cut across traffic to keep up. I sat on three more benches, bumped into a few strangers, and stopped to make twirling motions with my fingers. I squeezed in a solid four miles of exercise in spite of my admittedly childish, yet amusing, at least to me, endeavors.

Banshee and I cooled down, as we walked more slowly toward home. Car doors slammed, when we turned onto my street, and Agent Duff stood with his hands on his hips backed by two more agents. Banshee's hackles rose with a low growl, and I reassured him.

"That beast gonna be a problem?" Duff asked.

"Depends on what you and your two beasts do next."

The two agents bristled, but Duff cracked a smile and motioned for them to get back in the car. I memorized their faces, as they didn't seem too happy with me.

"Wanna tell me what the fuck you were doing on the Mall?"

"Just out for some exercise to enjoy the beautiful afternoon."

"My men tell me you were acting suspiciously, checking out benches, brushing up against strangers, leaving signals."

"I was just resting my legs, picking up trash, saying hello to tourists, and enjoying my freedom here in the Capitol."

"You're either the dumbest spy in history, the smartest one, or you're fucking with us. Since you seem like neither an idiot nor a master spy, I'm thinking you're fucking with us."

I held up my hands in surrender. "You caught me. Can't fool the DHS."

"Why are you wasting our time?"

"Why are you following me?"

"Because you took something from Mark Lawton and gave it to his sister, and now you're helping her look for Mark's work."

"I think all you have is a hunch, or we would be having this conversation in a room at DHS instead of on my sidewalk."

"I can arrange a more formal interview if you prefer."

"You could, but I don't think you want any publicity."

Agent Duff sighed. "Mark Lawton's work was a matter of national security. I have orders from the highest level of government to find it before certain comrades discover it. Tell me what you know."

"Honestly, I have no idea what he was working on or where that information might be. What I do know is that DHS is hassling me for no reason. Mark's last words were a personal message to his sister. I delivered that message to her, and she asked me to accompany her to a memorial for her brother. That's it."

"Is it normal for a doctor to spend time with a dead patient's family member like that?"

"It is if you have empathy. So, normal for me, but maybe not so much for you."

"All I want is the research, and I will do whatever it takes to get it. If I find you are withholding information from me, or worse, aiding the aforementioned comrades, you'll be locked up for a long time."

"Thank you for the warning. Are your goons gonna keep following me?"

"Yes."

"Tell them to stop the bullshit intimidation tactics, and I'll stop wasting their time with fake dead drops and brush passes. Deal?"

"Deal. All that activity on your run was bullshit?"

"It was one hundred percent bullshit."

"Good to know, but we still have to make sure. We have to waste time checking the tourists you bumped into and watching the fucking park benches. Be careful, Doc. These people don't mess around. Three bodies are cooling in the morgue. My advice to you again is to walk away from this, preferably in protective custody."

Agent Duff turned and left in the car with his scowling assistants, leaving me alone on the sidewalk with Banshee.

"What do you say, boy? Should we quit or keep looking for the research?"

Banshee turned his head to the side and rattled his tail.

"I agree. Let's see this through as long as Mac needs us."

CHAPTER SIXTEEN

Tuesday, March 17
10:23 a.m.

As I sipped my third Diet Coke of the morning, Lisa alerted me to incoming trauma.

"Heads up, Doc. One of your least favorite injuries is heading our way."

"Please don't tell me it's an airbag injury."

"Yep."

"One or two legs?"

"Both."

"Damn. Let's get set up in room one. I'll call Ortho."

Tim, the medical student working with me for the day, asked, "What's the problem with airbags? I thought they prevented injuries."

"They do save lives overall, but they can cause harm. They deploy only twelve to eighteen inches depending on the vehicle, but they do it in less than 0.05 seconds, which means they expand at speeds up to 200 MPH. When passengers rest their feet on the dash and the airbag deploys, their legs are forced back hard at least twelve inches at 200 MPH, even in a minor crash, causing catastrophic damage to the hips and legs."

"Is that why it's your least favorite thing to handle in the ER?"

"It's also because you have to be limber enough to fold your legs onto the dash, so it usually affects young, athletic people. Let's see what we have."

The ambulance arrived moments later and had to maneuver carefully through the door due to one leg sticking out from the stretcher, supported by a paramedic. The patient was in obvious distress.

"Seventeen-year-old female passenger in low speed wreck. Both feet on the dash and airbag deployed. Obvious deformities to both hips, but pulses intact. No other medical history. Name is Julie."

We carefully transferred her to another stretcher. "Julie, I'm Doc. We're gonna get you something for the pain and then get your legs fixed up, okay?"

Julie nodded through tears.

The nurse pushed the first dose of fentanyl, and Julie's breathing slowed, as the medicine kicked in, allowing us to examine her. Her left leg displayed an obvious deformity of the femur, but her right leg concerned me more. Rotated externally at the hip, it was not moving back into position, which indicated a hip dislocation and a likely fracture. Amazingly, she still had good pulses in her foot, so circulation was intact.

The orthopedist arrived, as radiology completed her X-rays, and shared his plan. "Left femur has a clean break mid shaft. Repair should be a simple plate and screws. The right side is a mess. The head of the femur ripped off and blew out the hip joint. She's going to need a total hip replacement on that side, as I doubt we can salvage the bone. We need her up ASAP before she loses pulses in that leg. Is her family here?"

The orthopedist left to speak with the family, as we arranged for her to go to the operating room. Within fifteen minutes, she was on her way.

"What's her prognosis?" Tim asked after she was gone.

"The femur should heal fine on the left. The right side is never going to be normal, even if the hip replacement is perfect, and she will need to have that hip replaced again in 15-20 years. She faces a long road to recovery. Did you learn anything from the case?"

"Never put my feet on the dashboard."

"Congrats. You get an A for the day. Tell all your friends, too. I hate these cases."

• • •

Dr. Pastone found me a few minutes before noon. "You ready?"

"I'm not sure if I'll ever be ready for this. Whose gonna be there today?"

"Senior leadership for the hospital and a couple board members, as well as our friends from the PIMPS."

"We'll probably get some decent food out of it since the big dogs are there."

"What's the matter? Day-old chicken sandwiches not good enough for you?"

"Day-old is fine. It's the three-day old ones that can make you a patient in the emergency room."

We found the Board Room and settled into the overpriced reclining chairs favored by hospital executives everywhere. I bounced on the springs when John leaned over to whisper, "We need to steal a couple of these for the emergency room."

"I'm gonna get one for my house, too."

I turned my attention to the group filing in. A small herd of suited executives from the hospital entered and nodded politely at us before fawning over the two board members who were already seated.

John leaned over to speak to me. "I hope the lunch box contains some ChapStick. Gonna be some dry lips from all the ass kissing going on over there."

Boisterous laughter tumbled in from the hallway, followed by three men strolling into the conference room. The tall, bald man spoke to his friends. "There's no fucking way I'm paying for that. Sue me if you want. I'll drag it out for years." His colleagues apparently found this hilarious as another round of laughter ensued.

I raised my eyebrows at John, and he leaned over. "Don Prost, the attorney."

"The asshole?"

"One hundred percent."

Everyone settled into their seats, as Tina Cantrell, the hospital CEO, called the meeting to order. "Let's get started. Quick introductions and then both sides can present their proposals, followed by questions." Tina had held the position for three years and was known for her no-nonsense approach to management. Smart, confident, and well respected, she tended to ask pointed questions that clarified information for everyone.

After quick and casual introductions, Jim Billings, CEO of Prime Medical Partners, took the floor. He waited a moment until all eyes were on him, then stood from his reclined position. He exuded an instantly unlikable, cocky demeanor, but seemed not to notice or care. Dressed in jeans, a button down shirt with one too many buttons undone, and a blazer, he epitomized a conceited executive.

"Thank you for having us here today. Before we proceed with our proposal, I would like to share with you a little bit about how Prime Medical Partners grew to be a leader in emergency room staffing. The idea started back when I was in college."

He droned on for several minutes in a nasally voice about how brilliant his ideas were and how he had grown the company. Based on the half-closed lids of the audience, his speech impressed no one. Finally, he finished.

"Now, I would like to turn the floor over to Matt Hyde, the COO of Prime Medical Partners, to present our data."

Matt stood and nervously adjusted the notes in front of him. An average sized man in his forties, he dressed identically to his boss, with a blue shirt instead of the white, and with the appropriate buttons done on his shirt. He began in a monotone.

"Prime Medical Partners is the leader in emergency room staffing nationally, with over 110 institutions currently using our services."

I already knew this fact, because it was emblazoned on the slide in front of us, and he had read it word for word. The only thing worse than a power point presentation is a power point presentation read to you word for word in a monotone. Matt confirmed my worst fears when the next slide popped up on screen, and he dutifully resumed his monotonous reading of mundane facts about the industry.

Forty-one slides and twenty minutes later, the test of endurance that should be outlawed was over. Two pages of doodles in front of me had kept me busy, while John had quietly torn a page into a thousand tiny pieces of confetti. Around the table, faces ranged from disinterested to comatose, with the notable exception of the PMP team, who apparently had found the presentation captivating.

Don Prost, the attorney, closed the presentation. "As you can see, Prime Medical Partners is the national leader in providing affordable staffing solutions for hospital systems. Our innovative, data driven approach allows us to staff at the most efficient levels while still maintaining a high quality of care. We can reduce your emergency room staffing costs by 22% with no decrease in efficiency or in customer satisfaction. Stop overpaying for services, and enjoy the increased profitability that can be provided only by Prime Medical Partners. Thank you."

The group offered muted applause. "Thank you. Dr. Pastone, please present your information, and then we will have time for questions," Tina said.

John stood and walked to the front of the room where he could make eye contact with everyone. "Thank you, Ms. Cantrell. As you know, our group has been here for over twenty years, and I have been in charge for the last ten. During that time, we have seen tremendous growth and maintained high quality care and service for all customers. We have been able to recruit and retain staff in a tight market, and we are the leader in our industry. With all due respect to the gentlemen from New York, there is just no way that staffing costs can be trimmed 22% while maintaining quality and throughput."

I was as startled as everyone else when Don Prost leapt to his feet. "Hold on there, son. I will not have you calling us liars. Our system is proven, and our data is clear. We can do this."

Tina slammed her hand on the table. "Mr. Prost, this is unacceptable. I don't know how they do things in New York, but here we are civil at meetings. You had your turn. Please sit down and remain quiet while the other group presents."

Don looked like he was about to explode, but a hand on his arm from the CEO convinced him to sit down. He continued to glare at John throughout the presentation.

John spoke for ten minutes without a single slide to read to us. He spoke passionately about what their group had accomplished, what the community meant to them, and the path forward for the hospital. At the end, he sat down beside me amid applause.

"How did I do?"

"They may be in the lead. Their guy proved that he can read, although you were much more likable."

"Thanks." He coughed a little laugh, although much was at stake.

After about a half hour of questions and answers, Tina called the meeting. "Thank you to everyone for your time. Please have your final proposals to me by Thursday. The Board will have a decision early next week."

We said our goodbyes, and Don Prost grabbed John's arm, as we turned in the hallway toward the emergency room. "I think you owe me an apology for calling me a liar in there."

John looked at the hand on his arm until it dropped away, and then took a step forward. "In east Texas, we are taught from a young age never to call another man son and never to lay hands on another man, unless you are ready to finish the job. Clearly, you were raised by a different set of rules, so I am willing to let this go, but now that you're educated, I suggest you choose your actions more wisely in the future."

Don took a step forward, encroaching on John's space. "I don't give a shit about your east Texas rules. I'm warning you, stay away from me."

John held his stare silently until the CEO pulled Don away.

"I get the feeling that he doesn't like you," I said.

"Feeling's mutual. Let me know what your hacker friend has to say. I ain't losing to that guy."

"I'm on it."

.   .   .

Don still raged as the PMP team ducked into their car. Matt drove, as Jim and Don sat in the back seat. Matt had no idea that he was no more than a glorified chauffeur to them.

"I promise you this. If that country boy calls me a liar again, bad things are gonna happen to him," Don said.

"You need to relax. The vote is being taken care of, and we don't need the extra attention. Besides, that country boy would probably kick your ass back to New York, if you touch him again," Jim said.

"I hate these country doctors and their bullshit sense of duty. Gonna be a pleasure to rip that contract away and fire his sorry ass. First thing I'm gonna do is fire him, and then do my best to make sure he doesn't get any decent recommendations for his next job."

"Relax. This is not the time for personal vendettas. Keep your eye on the prize. That contract will be worth five to six million annually for us, and may open up other contracts for us in this market. We need to close this with as little fuss as possible."

"Who do we have on board?"

"We own the COO and that should be enough to sway the votes. He was vulnerable with his kids going to college and still paying alimony to his first wife."

"What about the CEO?" Don asked.

"No chance. Records clean and finances are in order. No vulnerabilities."

"That's a shame. Easier when we own the ultimate decision makers."

"We'll be fine. It has worked every other time, and it'll work this time. Just try to chill out and don't instigate any problems."

"Fine, but I'm gonna enjoy firing that smug son of a bitch."

"I have no doubt."

Up front, Matt continued to drive them toward home. He had some thoughts on the subject, but knew not to speak unless he was asked a specific question.

CHAPTER SEVENTEEN

Tuesday, March 17
3:15 p.m.

Back in the ER, I checked my email to discover that Spike had sent four attachments. I didn't have time to read it yet, and Mac interrupted any cursory preview with a phone call to my regular phone.

"How is my favorite Senatorial Chief of Staff today?"

"Fine, I have only a minute, and remember, this is probably a party line."

"Duly noted. What's the plan?"

"Meet me at the entrance to the Hart Building at seven thirty."

"Will do. Have a good day."

"You, too."

I ended the call and went to see another patient in what turned out to be a busy afternoon. "Let's go boy. We have ourselves a golfing injury to fix."

The chart revealed only that it was a hand injury sustained while golfing. My guess was that he probably punched a tree after a bad shot. We see a lot of injuries in the emergency room, but not many related to golfing.

I entered the room to find a forty-four-year-old man in obvious distress, holding his left hand under a bag of ice. His golf shirt and hat proudly displayed the logo of his club, and he still wore his golf shoes.

"Good afternoon, Mr. Shaffer, I'm Dr. Docker, but please call me Doc. What happened to your hand today?"

He carefully removed the ice pack and held up his left hand, which showed obvious deformities as his fingers spread in all directions. "I think I broke four of my fingers."

"I think you're right. Does your thumb still work?"

He cautiously flexed and extended his thumb with only a slight grimace. "It feels okay."

"That's a positive. An opposable thumb is what separates us from other animals. It says in the chart this happened while golfing, and I am dying to learn how you managed to do that much damage on a golf course."

"It's easier than you think. I was driving the cart and tried to pick up an extra ball in the grass. I've done it a thousand times, but this time, the cart hit a bump as I was reaching down to grab the ball. All four fingers jammed into the ground and bent backward. The bone cracking was almost as loud as my scream."

"Ouch. Sorry that happened. What hole were you on?"

"Fifteen, and I was three over for the day. Would have been a good round."

"Unfortunately, it'll probably be a few months until you can play again. I'll get you something for the pain, and then we'll get an X-ray, and I will have a hand specialist come see you. We'll know more after the X-rays, but I can guarantee you're gonna need surgery on at least a couple of those fingers. Hopefully, you're right-handed."

"I am. Must be my lucky day."

"Sit tight and I'll get everything moving." I finished my exam, entered the orders, and notified the hand surgeons. John overheard me discussing the case with the hand surgeon.

"What do you think of that?" I asked.

He held up his phone. "I already added 'don't pick up golf balls while driving full speed in a golf cart' to my list of things never to do."

"How many things you got on your list?"

John checked his phone. "That was number two hundred ten."

I shook my head. The emergency room was a great place to learn which activities to avoid to live a long and healthy life.

. . .

Agent Duff received an update a few minutes after Mac called Doc. "They're meeting tonight, but we have no clue what they're up to," an agent reported.

"Don't lose them."

"May be tricky. They're meeting in the Hart Building. It's pretty quiet there at night."

"Flood as many agents into the building as you need to keep it covered."

Agent Duff stared at the ceiling as he pondered what a pain in the ass Doc and Mac had become. He hoped the mess would end soon.

. . .

Alina received the news only a few minutes later than Agent Duff did. The Russian surveillance machine was almost as extensive as Homeland resources in Washington D.C. She did not have the luxury of being able to put agents into the Hart Building and was hesitant to enter herself. Anonymity was her greatest asset.

She decided to monitor the phones and be prepared to intervene if an opportunity presented itself. She rechecked her weapons. If Mac and Doc found the data, she would obtain it no matter the cost.

. . .

Banshee sulked, after I told him that he wouldn't be joining me for the evening. "Sorry, buddy. I need you to stay here and guard the house. Bite any Russians or homeland agents who break in."

I had no worries that Banshee would ensure that anyone who tried to enter the house while I was gone would regret it, but Banshee wasn't happy with my leaving without him. He thumped his tail and barked a sharp rebuke, as I locked the door behind me.

My Uber gently stopped in front of the Hart Building, and Mac waited for me to clear security. She hugged me and whispered, "Play along. We have guests lurking."

I looked around to see only bored workers finishing a long day. Mac led me to the Senator's main office. Behind closed doors, she shared her plan after placing both phones into a Faraday bag.

"This place is crawling with agents, and I don't want to lead them to Elise."

"Please go ahead. I'll follow you."

Mac headed downstairs, passing a cleaning crew on the second subbasement level. She winked at me as we passed and opened the door marked storage to step into the Senator's private office.

"They probably know about this office, but I doubt they know about the emergency escape tunnel."

She approached the back bookshelf, reached under the top molding, and pressed a button. The bookcase clicked and slid forward an inch. She pulled it open to reveal a dark tunnel stretching into the distance.

"I hope you're not claustrophobic. The Capitol is full of these escape tunnels. Since January 6th, everyone wants to make sure they have a safe way out."

"Wouldn't that also let people into the Capitol?"

"Nope. The door here and at the other end are one-way only. There is no way to open them from the other side."

She handed me a flashlight, and we entered the dark, dusty tunnel, a little over six feet tall and only about three feet wide. The fairly smooth sides showed evidence of hand carving into the bedrock. Mac pulled the door closed with a clank. The absolute darkness, except for our flashlights, indeed threatened claustrophobia.

Her voice in the eerie silence startled me. "You okay?"

"Yeah, just give me a minute. Last time I was in a dark, confined space like this, I was hiding in a pizza oven from some violent Ukrainians trying to kill me."

"Sounds like a hell of a story."

"It is. I'll tell you all about it when we get out of here."

Our flashlight beams adequately lit the small tunnel that ran straight into the blackened distance.

"We're headed east under second street. It ends in a storage room in the basement of Thompson-Markward Hall, which provides affordable temporary housing for young women coming to DC for school or work, like a dormitory for young professionals. The storage room remains unused, because no one in the building has a key to it."

We encountered a steel door with a common new door knob. Mac turned it and pushed into a small square empty room with bare, built-in shelves. We left our flashlights in the tunnel, and Mac solidly closed the door that had matching shelves attached to its face, effectively camouflaging its actual purpose.

"By the way, that tunnel is a national secret. If you tell anyone about it, we'll have to throw you in Guantanamo."

"Your secret is safe with me. What next?"

"We head upstairs and catch a cab."

"Not too complicated."

"Sometimes simplicity is best." Upstairs, we passed a couple of residents, and no one gave us a second glance. We quickly caught a cab.

Mac gave the cab driver an address three blocks from the restaurant. "When they realize we're gone, they'll check the local cabs, Lyfts, and Ubers," Mac explained.

"They can do that?"

"They can do that and a whole lot more, sometimes illegal, but potential illegality will not slow Homeland down."

We arrived at The Golden Chop a few minutes before eight. Nothing distinguished it from any other Chinese restaurant. The unremarkable interior housed a cash register at the front and about twenty tables scattered around a single room with a door to the kitchen in the back and a hallway to restrooms in the back corner. Nine other patrons, all older Chinese, enjoyed dinner in small groups. No one seemed to notice us.

Elise waved to us from her seat in the back of the room near the kitchen door. She wore a Georgetown sweatshirt with her hair pulled back into a pony tail, which made her appear even more youthful. She certainly didn't look like a world class laser researcher.

"Thank you for coming today. I trust that you have kept our meeting private," she said.

"Thanks for having us. We took precautions, and our phones are shielded. Is it safe to talk in here?" Mac asked.

"This place belongs to my uncle, and all of the customers are old friends. It's safe to speak openly here. I hope you don't mind, but I took the liberty of ordering for us. My uncle is talented, and the food is delicious."

A waiter came with the first of many dishes, as she spoke. With drink orders placed, Mac got down to business.

"I'm trying to figure out what happened to my brother, and Doc is helping me. As you probably know, he loved to leave clues for people to follow, and the last clue we have obtained led to the number 73."

Elise's eyes filled with tears as she rolled up her sweatshirt and ran her fingers lightly over the tattoo. "I got this years ago. Many believe the number represents growth and progress, and the symmetry in binary is too beautiful to ignore. No matter if I look at it forward, backward or upside down, I am reminded of my own journey. Mark was one of the few who understood its message."

"What exactly was your relationship with my brother? Did you work on projects together?"

"No, my specialty is lasers, and our work never overlapped, but we saw each other often at the office. Our research demands long hours, and security considerations make it difficult to speak with people outside of DARPA. Mark was kind and funny. Our lunches turned into time spent together outside work, and we have been together for the last six months. I can't believe he is gone."

Elise teared up again, and Mac reached to hold her hand as she spoke. "I can't believe it, either. Mark was larger than life, and I never imagined he wouldn't be here. That's why I'm gonna hunt down the people who took his life. Do you have any idea what he was working on?"

Elise dried her eyes, as she answered. "Not really. I know he was working on multiple projects, and one that stressed him out, but he never spoke specifically about it. Mark was a stickler for security. DARPA insists on it from the start, so we all respect each other's privacy about work and never ask about it."

"Mark's clues led us to you. Do you have any idea where we need to look next?" I asked.

Elise looked hard at me, and then turned to Mac. "Can he be trusted?"

"Yes. He took care of Mark in the emergency room, and he's been helping me."

"Mark was worried about his work and concerned about people following him at the end. He was always prepared, and a few weeks before he died, he told me that if anything happened to him, then to share a message with whoever asked about my tattoo. I guess you're the one."

Mac leaned forward. "What was his message?"

"He said to tell you that it's time for you to know about his storage unit."

"That's it? He wants us to know about his storage unit?"

"He was very clear to quote him exactly. 'It's time they knew about my storage unit.' He made me repeat the precise words back to him."

Mac looked confused by the clue, and I asked, "Did he say anything else about where this storage unit might be?"

Elise allowed a soft smile. "Mark would never be so direct, but he suggested that I tell you this at my uncle's restaurant."

Mac's confusion intensified. I sat back and let my eyes wander over the tables. A couple walking by outside drew my attention, and I tapped Mac on the shoulder and nodded toward the front window.

A smile lit up her face, when she saw a public storage facility across the street.

Elise followed our gaze. "That didn't take long to figure out. Unfortunately, I have no idea which unit is his or how to access it."

"No worries. I'll figure it out. Now, tell me about Mark."

Mac and Elise shared stories about him as dinner progressed. Clearly, Mark and Elise had considered marriage. Elise and Mac, now close friends, made arrangements to stay in touch.

"Thank you for your help, Elise," Mac said.

"I'm not sure how much help I was, but thank you for looking for his research. I know he didn't trust anyone else with it, and I feel a little better knowing that you'll make sure his killer is brought to justice and won't be able to hurt anyone else."

"I can promise you that for sure."

After goodbyes, we left Elise to greet other friends finishing dinner and stood before the storage facility.

"I assume that we are gonna follow up on his clue right now," I said.

"We're here, and DHS hasn't tracked us down yet. It's our best chance to do it undetected."

"Then let's do it."

CHAPTER EIGHTEEN

Tuesday, March 17
9:15 p.m.

Agent Duff's anxiety increased by the second. No one had entered or exited the basement office in over an hour, according to video surveillance as well as agents stationed at both ends of the hallway. He spoke into his microphone. "We're sure no one has been in or out of that room?"

"Yes, sir."

Agent Duff knew something was wrong. "Have the maintenance man knock on the door and say he is checking for a gas leak. If no answer, have him enter for a quick peek."

"Please confirm. You want us to enter if no answer."

Agent Duff knew he had no legal grounds to enter the office, but felt he had no choice. "Confirmed. I need to know who is in that room."

The agent, dressed as a maintenance worker for the Capitol, knocked loudly on the door. Receiving no answer, he unlocked it and called out. "Maintenance. We have a possible gas leak, and I need to check this room." He opened the door and scanned the vacant room. He continued to call out and sweep his gas meter, as he searched the entire area. He spoke into his microphone.

"All clear. Room is empty."

Agent Duff pounded his desk in frustration. "Lock up and clear out. All agents, they slipped past us somehow. Start tracking every camera and transportation option in the area. I want to know where they went and who they met."

DHS had access to every camera connected to the internet, and their computers analyzed images from each of them. Thousands of cameras produced millions of images, but he would find them.

.   .   .

Mac and I stepped into the lobby, staffed by a lonely worker engrossed in his phone.

"Help you?"

"No. I just need to get something from my unit."

"Help yourself." He pointed to the security door and returned to his phone.

A computer screen on the door asked for a unit number and passcode. Mac entered unit 73 and passcode 1001001 without hesitation. The lock buzzed us into the storage area.

"What if that didn't work?" I asked.

"I had no doubt. Let's see what Mark left for us."

We marched through tight passages and followed signage to find unit 73, eight feet wide and indistinguishable from the adjoining units. A stout combination lock protected the door.

"Okay, Dr. Smart, let's see if you can figure this one out," she said, pointing to the lock. "I'll give you sixty seconds."

The sturdy, seven-digit lock offered ten million possible combinations. I considered 1001001, but it seemed unlikely Mark would use the same number twice.

"Tick, tock." Mac taunted.

I pulled out my phone and googled the first seven digit prime number, and the answer came back quickly at 1,000, 003. I started to enter it, and then decided to try it backwards. I rolled the last number into place, and the lock clicked open.

"Congrats! You had twelve seconds left."

"Thanks. I'm learning the rules of the game. Let's see what we have inside."

I rolled up the door to expose a cluttered room completely full of furniture and haphazard boxes, all of it significantly worn. Mac looked perplexed.

"This makes no sense. Mark was fastidious. He would never throw a bunch of junk in here like this. He would stack it neatly and efficiently. This stuff looks like leftovers from college dorm rooms. Mark would never buy this stuff, and he certainly wouldn't pay to keep it."

"Maybe a clue is buried behind all this crap," I suggested.

"Let me think for a minute."

I scanned the stack of furniture with no motivation to move everything. It would take all night, which got me thinking.

"It's time they knew about my storage unit," I repeated.

"What?"

"Elise said that Mark was very particular about the message. She repeated it twice. 'It's time they knew about my storage unit.' That must mean something."

Gleeful, Mac hugged me. "Of course it does. You're getting better at this game. The clue is time. He wanted us to think about time."

We zeroed in on a prominent old clock resting on a dresser. Mac picked it up and turned it over in her hands, looking for messages or compartments. Finding none, she set it back down.

"What brand is it? Is it a Rolex or something special?" I asked.

"No. It's just an ordinary clock by Smith & Sons. I think the clue is literally the time. It's set to 12:35. The next clue is 1235," she said confidently.

"Are you sure?"

"I'm positive. This is classic misdirection from Mark. All this stuff is camouflage. It probably drove him nuts even to look at this jumbled mess. He specifically told us that time is the clue."

"What's it mean?"

"No idea, but let's get out of here. DHS will find us soon, and the Russians won't be far behind."

"Should we lock it up?"

"No. Leave it unlocked. They can waste time sifting through this pile for the rest of the night." She moved the hands on the clock to a different time, set it back on the dresser, placed the lock next to it, and closed the door.

Back on the street, Mac opened her bag and handed me my phone, powering hers on as well.

"I'll think about the clue and get back to you. I have a full day with the Senator tomorrow. Thanks for your help on this. I think we're getting closer."

"I'm happy to help. It's kind of exciting." I held up my phone. "How long before Agent Duff is here?"

"If it's more than ten minutes, I'll be disappointed. Let's grab a cab and get out of here."

We hailed one at the next intersection. We dropped Mac off at her home before I headed to my place, greeted by a defiant Banshee. He thumped his tail against the floor and leaned into me as I entered.

"How about a treat and a walk?"

All was forgiven.

.   .   .

The first DHS units arrived eight minutes after Doc and Mac turned their phones on. By the time Agent Duff arrived twelve minutes later, his team had interviewed the storage unit clerk and watched the security video. Another agent led him to unit seventy-three.

"They spent only about three minutes in here. We reviewed the tapes and couldn't see anything they may have taken with them, so they removed nothing larger than her purse," one of the agents reported.

Duff pulled on some gloves. "They left it unlocked?"

"Yes, sir."

Duff scanned the jumbled mess inside. A robust lock rested on a shelf unit, and he rotated it from hand to hand as he examined the contents. "Why the hell would they lead us here and leave it open? And why after only three minutes did they leave apparently empty handed?" he said to no one in particular. His fellow agents had the good sense to remain quiet.

"We need to photograph everything and take it to the lab, as usual."

Enthusiastic "yes, sirs" contrasted with some eye rolling by a few agents. It would be a long night processing the unit's contents.

"Any paperwork on this unit?"

A young agent handed it to him, fresh from the printer. It listed the owner of the unit as Leonardo Bigollo.

"Who the fuck is Leonardo Bigollo?" Agent Duff asked.

"We're looking into it, sir. We don't have anyone by that name in our database."

Duff pulled out his phone and googled his answer. "You can stop wasting time looking for Mr. Bigollo. He's dead."

"Dead, sir?"

"For about eight hundred years. Leonardo Bigollo is better known as Fibonacci, a famous Italian mathematician from the thirteenth century. Mr. Lawton had a sense of humor. Let's start looking through this. Maybe he left something significant in here."

Among the 257 items removed was an antique clock by Smith & Sons, not working, with the time stopped at 2:43.

·   ·   ·

Alina Morozova, frustrated, watched them remove everything from the storage unit. She had arrived shortly before the first agents, but did not have time to look at the unit before they entered. Dreading the conversation, but with no other choice, she called Director Petrov.

As usual, he dispensed with pleasantries. "What have you learned?"

"Director, the scientist had a storage unit that apparently no one knew about before now. DHS is removing everything."

"Did you see inside?"

"No, sir. I arrived before the first agents, but they arrived shortly thereafter and quickly secured the building. Most of what they are pulling out is old furniture."

"No lab equipment or journals?"

"None yet, sir."

"We are falling behind. It is time to get more aggressive. I want to know whatever his sister knows."

He disconnected before she could respond. She looked at the silent phone in her hand and plotted how to increase the pressure on Mac. She would not fail.

CHAPTER NINETEEN

Wednesday, March 18
6:54 a.m.

Mac arrived at her office a few minutes before Senator Whitehurst.

"Good morning, Mac. What's on the schedule today?"

"Good morning, Senator. You will be in session for most of the day, which means I will have a chance to catch up on messages."

"Anyone important on the schedule?"

Mac perused the list in front of her. "Biggest name is Will Tompkins, who wants to talk about pending pharmaceutical legislation with me, and he will be joining you for dinner tonight. Anything I should know?"

"Keep him happy. ARC Pharmaceuticals is making a big push into gene therapy, and he is very interested in some legislation currently pending in the Senate."

"How interested?"

"Interested enough to consider a high seven-figure donation to my reelection campaign."

"I'll make sure he is taken care of. Can you please sign these documents before you head over to Senate?"

She sat down to review them, while Mac turned her attention back to her busy day.

.   .   .

Agent Duff foresaw another bad day in an uninterrupted string of them. No relevant evidence had been gained from the storage unit. Why would a rich, world-class researcher maintain a storage unit filled with useless junk, and why would his sister make such an effort to avoid their following her, but lead them to the unit as soon as she left?

Duff had been with Homeland for ten years after a stint in the Army. His impressive resume listed a series of successful, complicated cases he had managed. The next stop in his career would be as part of the senior administrative team. He would have to give up the fieldwork he loved, but he would gain access to all of the data at Homeland. He would be at the table to make decisions on strategic matters that would affect global policies. This dream was in reach, but not if he lost to the Russians on this case.

It was time to increase the pressure on Mac and Doc.

.   .   .

With nothing vital on my schedule, I slept in past eight. Banshee didn't appear to have anything on his schedule either, as he slept soundly curled up at the foot of the bed. We both stretched before climbing out of bed in search of breakfast, pancakes and bacon for me, while Banshee chose bacon only.

I settled at the table with the documents from Spike about Prime Medical Partners. The thorough documentation included over sixty pages of graphs, text, and spreadsheets. I opened a fresh Diet Coke and dug in.

The first section focused on the corporate finances. On the surface, the PIMPS were a very successful company. The previous year showed almost four billion in revenue with over six hundred million in profit.

They operated at an impressive 16.7% profit margin. Their biggest expenses were salaries, followed by malpractice insurance and billing costs.

Spike highlighted payments of $31.3 million to a company called SGITR, LLC over the last year. They were listed as a consultant's fees on the financial reports, and SGITR was registered in the Cayman Islands, with its ownership hidden from public view. Obscure companies in money laundering countries were like a neon light attracting Spike's attention.

She had hacked into the account and provided a list of transactions over the last three years. Every three months, a series of large payments were dispersed to other accounts set up at the same bank. These payments ranged from $60,000 to $500,000 each, paid on the first day of each quarter. Over eighty million dollars had been dispersed over the last three years.

Spike tracked down the owners of the accounts and listed them on the next page. A quick google search confirmed that all of the individuals were senior healthcare executives at large hospital systems. A few more minutes confirmed that all of these hospitals used the PIMPS as their staffing solution in the emergency room. Most concerning was an account established within the last two months for Francis Littman, the COO of our hospital.

Clearly, the PIMPS were bribing senior healthcare officials to get their contracts, which violated the law. Unfortunately, I had broken a few laws myself to obtain the information. I set the corporate documents aside and turned my attention to the data on the three individuals.

Jim Billings, the CEO, had an unregistered personal account and a second home in the Caymans. Records suggested he had multiple mistresses that he funded there, and none of the information had been reported on his taxes. Matt Hyde, the COO, also had an unregistered account in the Caymans, but without much activity. Both accounts evidenced clear cases of tax fraud.

Don Prost, the attorney, was the most interesting with an account in the Caymans that showed much more activity, including deposits from accounts other than those belonging to the PIMPS. Spike had tracked these accounts, but the trails disappeared before she could find the origins of the money. However, Spike was fairly sure that the extra funds in his accounts were related to laundering money for a drug cartel.

Hunger drew my attention from the documents, and I realized I had been immersed in them for over three hours. Time flies when you're tracking down scumbags who bribe hospital officials to enrich themselves at the expense of quality of healthcare. I made a sandwich of cold cuts and pondered what to do next. I wanted to shut these guys down, but the more immediate priority was making sure they didn't get our hospital contract the next week.

I used the burner phone from Mac to share my information with John Pastone and to finalize our strategy. I made one more call that night to an old friend.

CHAPTER TWENTY

Thursday, March 19
9:23 a.m.

During a calm morning in the ER, we discussed what fields we would have chosen if emergency medicine had not been an option.

"I would be a surgeon," Dr. Pastone asserted.

"Please tell me you wouldn't go into orthopedics," I said.

"Nah, too simple. Bone broke. Fix bone. I'd probably go for trauma surgery. What about you?"

"Knowing what I know now? Dermatology. Triple my pay working seventeen hours a week with twelve weeks vacation every year."

"That would make you one of the hard working ones."

"What do you guys think of general pediatrics?" asked Casey, a fourth-year medical student rotating with us for the month.

John answered with two thumbs down. "I would die of boredom by Thursday of my first week. Pediatric emergency medicine is fine, but general pediatrics requires too much talking. I can't spend thirty minutes on a history and physical for a well child. I barely spend thirty minutes on a major trauma."

"I have to agree with John on this one. Best of luck to you, but you'll never see me in general pediatrics."

Lisa, the charge nurse, interrupted us. "I swear to God I have chairs that do more work than you two. Can I bother one of you to make your way to room one? A neonate with respiratory distress is coming by ambulance."

I jumped up. "Lead the way. Casey, you're with me on this one."

We entered the room to find the team assembling and organizing their supplies. The pediatric crash cart was open and ready.

"Do we know anything else?" I asked.

One of the nurses responded. "A four-week-old is struggling badly. They wanted to tube him in the field, but didn't feel comfortable, so they're coming code three."

"Set up a 4.0 endotracheal tube and a two Miller blade. Start drawing up meds. Assume a five-kilogram weight."

The team rushed to prepare for arrival, as I turned to Casey. "Neonates can go downhill fast. They don't have a lot of reserve and can go into respiratory failure quickly. Paramedics do not like to intubate them in the field because the tubes are so small they tend to fall out during the ambulance ride. Pay attention. This is gonna move fast."

EMS burst into the room, starting their report before the stretcher was locked in place. I listened, but focused on the baby's breathing. His respiratory rate was about eighty times a minute, but the breaths were ineffective, and he struggled for each bit of air. His nose flared, and his rib muscles retracted with each labored breath, and he grunted with each inhalation. All of these were last ditch efforts by his body to move more air into his lungs and signaled impending respiratory failure.

Most concerning was his mottled gray color, the shade people turn before they die. As they hooked him to the monitor, I listened to his chest. Instead of breathing sounds, I heard a cacophony of wheezes and rhonchi, consistent with bronchiolitis. A glance at the monitor showed his oxygen saturation at 78%, despite being on 100% oxygen.

"What's our IV status?"

One of two nurses attempting IV access, one in the arm and one in the ankle, called out, "I've got a 24 gauge in the saphenous. Do we need blood?"

"Not now. Draw up atropine, versed, fentanyl and succinylcholine for me, please."

"Give me thirty seconds, and I'll have this taped down."

I turned my attention to Casey. "What do each of those meds do?" Getting students to think during stressful times was part of the training process for all doctors. The emergency room didn't always allow time to look up information.

"The versed is an amnestic, so he won't remember anything, and the fentanyl is to help with any pain the intubation might cause. Succinylcholine is a rapid onset paralytic so we can more easily intubate and ventilate him, but I don't know why we need atropine."

"Not bad, three out of four. Infants have an exaggerated vagal response, and when you put a tube in the back of their throats, they sometimes drop their heart rates rapidly. This is more common with succinylcholine. The atropine blocks that reaction. Intubating infants is exciting enough without having to deal with a heart rate of forty."

Everyone was ready, and I positioned the infant with the neck fully extended. With the IV secure, the nurse pushed the meds, and the infant became flaccid, as the paralytic medicines took effect. The respiratory distress stopped, but so did the respiratory effort. Now, we raced to get the tube in place, as the oxygen saturations fell even further.

With my right hand on the chin to hold the mouth open, I inserted the laryngoscope blade straight back into the throat. The fiber optic light lit the back of the mouth, showing copious secretions coming from the lungs. I visualized the vocal cords, and held my right hand out for the breathing tube. The respiratory therapist handed me the tube, and I slid it easily between the cords and into the trachea.

I held the tube in place as the respiratory therapist hooked up a bag and began giving breaths. The oxygen saturations were down to 52%, but started to improve, as the chest rose with each breath from the bag. A nurse listened to confirm that breath sounds were equal on both sides, as the oxygen saturations passed 74%. I handed the tube to the respiratory therapist to secure and began a secondary survey of the patient.

Oxygen saturations were up to 94%, and some pink had replaced the horribly alarming gray skin color, but his hands and feet were cold and blue. I turned to a wide eyed Casey. "What do you think?"

"His breathing is better, and his color is better with the tube in place."

"What about his vital signs?" She looked to the monitor and saw a pulse of 184 and a blood pressure of 56/38.

"The pulse is too high."

"Correct. He is in shock. What is the treatment?"

"IV fluids?"

"Yes, but how do you want to give them? Through that tiny IV in his ankle? We need to give it rapidly."

"Should we put in a central line?"

"It's an option, but he's dry and his veins are running on empty. No guarantee we can get one. Other options?"

"Intraosseus line?"

"Yes!" I held out my hand, and the nurse handed me a needle of solid metal designed to be inserted into bone. Fluid could flow rapidly into the bone marrow and then enter the venous system. It hurts like hell, but our patient was already sedated and receiving pain control.

We went over landmarks, then wiped the shin area down with betadine. I had Casey locate the flat area of the tibia just below the knee, and push the needle in with a firm screwing motion. It pushed through the bone cortex and into the softer marrow without pushing out the other side of the bone.

"Great job. Let's push 100 cc of normal saline as quickly as possible." The fluid was pushed in by syringe within three minutes, and the pulse improved to 164. "Better, but let's push another 100 cc over ten minutes, then put him on one and a half times maintenance. Any more, and the PICU doctors will yell at me for flooding his lungs."

The team continued to do their jobs of collecting blood and urine samples for the lab, confirming tube placement with a chest X-ray, getting a viral respiratory panel, and starting multiple medications. Fifteen minutes later, he was on his way to the PICU. There are few things more satisfying than saving the life of a newborn.

"What do you think, Casey? Do you want to quit pediatrics and join emergency medicine?"

"That was a bit more excitement than I could stand on a daily basis. What do you think caused that?"

"We need to wait on the labs, but I would bet my last dollar that he has RSV. It causes only cold symptoms in older children, but can be devastating for infants."

"What's his prognosis?"

"He's sick, but he should make it. The ventilator will breathe for him and allow time for his lungs to rest and heal. He'll be intubated for a week or two, but he should be home in three to four weeks. His lungs will be fragile for a while, but kids heal better than adults, and he will grow new, healthy lung tissue as he gets bigger. By the time he is in school, he may have some asthma symptoms, but should be on his way to a normal life."

"Thanks for letting me help."

"You did great. In fact, even though you are going into pediatrics, I am pronouncing you an honorary BAFERD."

"What the hell is that?"

"A bad ass fucking ER doctor. You earned it. Now finish your note. We have more patients to see."

CHAPTER TWENTY-ONE

Thursday, March 19
11:52 a.m.

John and I entered the meeting room a few minutes before noon. John elbowed me and gestured across the room, where Francis Littman, the COO of the hospital, laughed with the three PMP leaders.

"Probably planning their next trip to the Caymans," he said.

"Hopefully, we can put a significant dent in those plans."

We took our seats, as Ms. Cantrell called the meeting to order. "Thank you for coming today. This is our last opportunity to ask questions of both sides before the Board discusses the contract. We hope to have a final decision early next week."

Board members spent the next hour asking questions of both sides. John answered them professionally, while the PIMPS seemed supremely confident in their position, too confident. Finally, Ms. Cantrell called for a ten minute break. John zeroed in on the hospital COO, while I turned my attention to the PIMPS.

"You gentlemen seem awfully confident today."

Jim, the CEO, responded. "It's easy to be confident when you're the best in the business. We are national leaders, and our track record is unmatched. Our system is proven, and hospitals are ready to upgrade to our program. Sorry, but this contract is ours."

"It also helps that we have the smartest guys in the room on our side," Don, the attorney, said.

"You really think you're the smartest guys in the room? Pretty bold statement. Some pretty bright people are here."

"Sure, but smartest guys in the room is our brand. We have the best and brightest at Prime Medical Partners."

Suddenly, it hit me. Smartest Guys In The Room equated to SGITR, as in SGITR, LLC, the company making the illegal payments in the Caymans.

"Don, maybe you guys are the smartest in the room. You should make that a logo or something for your company, although SGITR sounds more like a vague company name hiding in a Caribbean bank. People would look at the name and shrug, because they would have no idea what it meant. Meanwhile, y'all would be up in New York laughing that you're the smartest guys in the room. You should look into that."

Don's stare had gone cold, while Jim and Matt looked nervously at each other. I should plan a poker game against these guys. I would make a fortune. Don stepped into my personal space.

"You trying to suggest something, Doc?"

"No, just making friendly conversation with the smartest guys in the room."

"I suggest you keep it friendly. I would hate for this to become adversarial. Bad things can happen when business becomes personal."

"It's already personal. These doctors have devoted their careers to this hospital and to providing the highest possible quality of care to this community, and you're trying to muscle in and destroy the trust they've built for years. I don't think it's gonna happen. I think we're gonna win the contract and celebrate with a nice vacation. I'm thinking about a nice beach, maybe in the Caymans. Have the smartest guys in the room been to the Caymans?"

I turned away from them, waiting for a bullet to shatter my spine, but all they had to shoot were icy stares. Mission objective one completed. I joined John and the nervous COO, who were finishing their conversation.

"Hey, Doc, Francis was just telling me that he's canceling his vacation to the Caymans."

The anxious COO could barely hold my gaze. "That sounds like a good idea. John, could I speak with you for a moment?" We left the squirming COO alone with his thoughts and found a quiet corner.

"I assume your conversation with Francis was productive?"

John laughed. "He couldn't have changed his mind any more quickly. He assures me he had no idea they were setting up an account for him."

"Sounds like we got his vote."

"He should be a passionate advocate for us. How did your talk go?"

"I figured out SGITR stands for smartest guys in the room."

"Seriously? How stupid do you have to be to name your illegal company smartest guys in the room? When you get caught, it disproves the entire premise of the name."

"Like all narcissists, they believe their own press. Look at them over there."

We turned to find the three of them huddled in a heated conversation. It ceased when they noticed our watching them. John and I smiled and waved, but the gesture was not reciprocated.

"That lawyer looks pissed. His whole head is turning bright red. Dude is gonna stroke out if he doesn't settle down," John observed.

"Well aware of the quality of care, he probably would feel relieved to receive care at a non-Pimp hospital."

"I would be happy to fill out the paperwork for a transfer to one of his. What about the last part of the plan? Is she on board?"

"Hell, yes. She smells another Pulitzer. She's verifying some things."

"Okay. I hope this works. Thanks for your help on this. We need to keep this contract."

· · ·

Don Prost trembled with rage. "How in the hell did they find out about SGITR and the Caymans? It's buried so deep I have trouble accessing it sometimes."

"I don't know, but this is bad, Don. You promised that no one could ever penetrate the security and learn about the company," Jim said.

"It shouldn't be possible. I've done this before, and no one has ever gotten past the security."

"What if they can access the actual account and see where the money is going?" Matt asked.

"Impossible. No way they can get into that account."

"You also assured us that they would never even find the account. We have to assume it's compromised. We need to get control of this situation," Jim said.

Don flushed even more at the thought of losing this contract and buying the silence of the doctors. "Okay. We offer them some money and get them to sign a nondisclosure agreement, and we walk away from this contract, but after I figure out how they learned about SGITR, I am going to destroy them," Don said.

"Let's buy our way out of this mess first. Then we'll have to shut down SGITR and reorganize our finances to hide future payments. Revenge is a lower priority."

"It's low on your list, but not on mine. I'm going after those guys."

.   .   .

We returned for a final round of questions. John maintained his professional demeanor, but the PIMPS were noticeably subdued. The meeting finally concluded, and Don stopped us, waited for the room to empty, and closed the door before he spoke to us.

"Prime Medical Partners has reevaluated our position, and we are not sure this is a good market for us. We're considering withdrawing our bid for this contract."

"Kind of late in the process to be pulling out, isn't it?" John taunted.

"We have recently come upon new information that has affected our decision. We realize you have spent a lot of time and resources preparing your bid, and we are prepared to reimburse you fully for those efforts. We would like to handle this in a friendly manner, and quietly. A simple nondisclosure agreement is all we require, and we can all move onward with our own business practices."

"Don, we don't want your dirty money, and we're not signing a nondisclosure. I don't care if you pull your bid or not. We have this vote, and we got it honestly. You and the rest of your company can fuck off."

"You're making a big mistake. We're a multibillion dollar company with infinite resources. You don't want us coming after you."

I stepped between the two before things escalated. "You are a billion dollar company for the moment, but I have a feeling that might change. I imagine that you will want to sell your Prime Medical Partners stock, but that would be insider trading added to your other problems. My advice is to find a good lawyer, someone even smarter than you."

"What the hell is that supposed to mean?"

"I promise it'll be obvious in the very near future."

We left Don standing alone, finally the smartest guy in the room.

. . .

I had just returned from an evening run with Banshee, when Mac called.

"Hey, Doc, how was your day? Anything interesting?"

"I saved an infant in respiratory distress and destroyed a shady billion dollar company. How about you?"

"Not quite as exciting, although I'm never quite sure when you're exaggerating."

"It's all true. I'll fill you in later. What can I help you with?"

"I wanted to ask another favor. Tomorrow is one week since Mark's death, and I want to see where it happened. I know it's strange, but I've been avoiding it, and I just want to put some flowers there. Will you come with me?"

"I'm happy to."

"Okay. I'll text you when I'm done with work. Make sure to bring Banshee. He's good for morale."

"Will do. Get some rest."

"In a bit. The Senator is meeting some folks for dinner, and I need to make sure everyone is settled before calling it a night."

"You should have chosen something easy like medicine. Politicians' hours are brutal."

"Maybe I can get you to write me a letter of recommendation for medical school. Good night, Doc. See you tomorrow."

"Good night, Mac."

Banshee twitched his tail, as I ended the call. "Don't worry. You're invited. She likes you."

CHAPTER TWENTY-TWO

Friday, March 20
2:16 p.m.

Mac texted to meet her at three in front of her office building before the short walk down the Mall to the metro stop, where Mark had been killed. Banshee and I caught an Uber and waited for Mac. She approached with infinite sadness in her eyes and reached down to scratch Banshee's ears. She carried a small bouquet of yellow roses to lay at the site.

"Thanks for coming, Doc. I've been dreading this, but I need to experience it."

"Yes, but it's going to be crowded with both of our DHS shadows joining us."

"We could just rent a party bus and all go together."

"That would definitely be more efficient, but it's too nice of a day not to walk."

We set out at a leisurely pace, mingling with tourists that frequented the Mall. At the first cross street, we came upon a line of savory smelling food trucks selling to hungry and dehydrated tourists.

"How about an ice cream?" I suggested.

"That would be nice."

Mac chose a strawberry cone, while I went with a vanilla and chocolate twist. I also had a cone filled with whipped cream for Banshee, and he drooled as he followed us. We found a bench and sat to enjoy the cones. I held Banshee's cone for him, but he still devoured it in one bite. He laid down at our feet licking excess cream that had fallen on his paws.

"Any epiphany on Mark's clue about time?"

"Not yet, but I'm not too worried. His clues have always been increasingly difficult. Something will click eventually. He wouldn't give me a clue I can't solve."

"Anything interesting happening at work?"

"The usual. People lining up to kiss the Senator's ass…"

Mac was pushed violently into me, knocking us both off the bench. I looked up to see a man running away from us.

"My purse! He stole my purse!"

Mac started to get up, but I held her back. "Banshee, STOP HIM!"

Already alert from the push, Banshee focused on the athletic man with a thirty-yard head start. Running fast, the man still didn't stand a chance. After an enthusiastic leap, Banshee hit full speed and quickly gained on him. The man glanced over his shoulder, and his eyes widened at the sight of the beast running him down. He pushed through a burst of speed, but it didn't help him.

Banshee closed the last few yards and launched. The force of the collision knocked the man down, and Banshee's powerful jaw clamped onto the back of his thigh, tearing skin and sinking into the hamstring. The man landed flat on his stomach with Banshee still latched onto the back of his leg. His screams began before he hit the ground.

After making sure Mac was okay, I jogged over and ordered Banshee to let go and guard the man. He attempted to rise, but Banshee's growl convinced him to stay still. I picked up Mac's purse and waited for the circus.

The National Mall is heavily policed, and three officers rushed to the disturbance. Mac approached from behind, and our trusty DHS agents ran to join the party.

"Sorry about that, man. You picked the wrong purse to steal," I said.

He looked up at me and smiled. "Diplomatic immunity."

"What the fuck did you say?"

"Diplomatic immunity."

The first officer arrived with his hand on his weapon and asked me to step back slowly. I complied and called Banshee, who sat calmly beside me. Mac took charge.

"Officers, I am the chief of staff for Senator Whitehurst. This man assaulted me and ran away with my purse, and my friend's dog stopped him. I want to press charges."

"He's claiming diplomatic immunity," I said.

The DHS agents began a subdued but heated conversation with the police, ignoring Mac and me for the moment.

"You okay?" I asked.

"I'm fine. I only scraped my knee. I'm more pissed off about dropping my ice cream, although Banshee's tackling that guy was amazing to watch." Banshee beamed, sure he was the best good boy, as she rubbed his ears.

"He doesn't get to do it often."

"Poor guy is gonna have a limp."

"He'll be fine, as long as it doesn't get infected. He has only puncture wounds. If he had kept fighting, Banshee would have shaken his head and tore the muscle fibers."

"That sounds awful."

"It is. That's why people shouldn't piss off my dog."

The man on the ground sat up and handed a document to a DHS agent. One of the officers was wrapping a rudimentary bandage around the thigh. The DHS agent scowled, as he read the paper and passed it to Mac.

"Ms. Lawton, are you okay?"

"I'm fine. Who is that man?"

"Unfortunately, he appears to be a member of the Russian delegation. I will verify this, but if it's legitimate, we can't charge him."

"You're telling me that a Russian diplomat can attack the chief of staff of a United States Senator, and steal her purse in front of the US Capitol, and there's nothing you can do?"

"I said we can't charge him, but I am sure he will be kicked out of the country with other repercussions that are way above my pay grade. We have the whole thing on video, so you're free to go. We'll call you if we need more information."

Mac, with fury in her eyes, approached the man on the ground. "Why is the Russian government targeting me?"

The man laughed softly. "Bitch."

Diplomatic immunity or not, I commanded Banshee, "SCARE."

Snarling, Banshee lunged at the man's face. Saliva flew from his mouth to rain on the terrified man who tried to scramble away. With a staccato bark, Banshee calmly turned to sit next to me.

The stunned officers hadn't had time to react before Banshee was seated again. The terrified man still tried to distance himself from Banshee. Mac looped her arm in mine, and the three of us walked away to retrieve the flowers that had fallen to the ground.

·   ·   ·

Watching the scene unfold from his car, Nikolai swore in three different languages. Viktor was supposed to grab the purse and jump into the car with him. Useful information might have been found in her phone or journal. The simple plan should have worked, but that evil beast had run him down, as if he had been standing still.

Viktor did have immunity and wouldn't be prosecuted, but he would be deported. More concerning was their failure. Directorate S tolerated no such mishaps, and Director Petrov would not appreciate the public display of incompetence. Victor's career had taken a serious turn for the worse, and Nikolai didn't want to join him. He carefully pulled into traffic and drove to the embassy. His report would take less than a minute, but Petrov's seething anger would last much longer.

CHAPTER TWENTY-THREE

Friday, March 20
3:28 p.m.

"Hopefully, that was our only excitement for the day, but I have to admit that the adrenaline rush relieved some tension. I can't believe how bold the Russians are. An attack against a Senatorial chief of staff on the Mall isn't an act of war, but it reeks of desperation."

"What do you think they're after?"

"Maybe they thought I carry a secret map showing the location of Mark's research in my purse."

"Is there a secret map in your purse?"

She peeked inside. "No, but I do have some mints. Want one?"

"Sure. You still wanna visit the site?"

"Yes, it's been a week, and I need some closure. Come on, it's just up ahead."

We arrived at the unremarkable entrance to the Smithsonian Metro Station. A sign rose ten feet from the concrete in front of two escalators leading underground. Tourists milled about, as the locals walked purposefully through them. Nothing revealed that a week ago, three men had lost their lives here.

Mac numbly stared at the scene, and I motioned her to an empty bench. She gingerly sat down, still staring at the ground in front of her.

"It's probably a crazy twin thing, but I can feel his presence."

"Definitely not crazy."

Her eyes watered. "He was the smartest person I've ever met, and he was a good man. He sought answers to questions that others didn't even think to ask. Everything he was ended here. Such a waste."

We sat in silence, and Mac idly rubbed Banshee's ears. Eventually, she stood and wandered, searching the ground, as if she could find her lost brother. She leaned over to place the roses on the ground near the entrance to the metro. I remained on the bench with Banshee. She stopped and slowly scanned the area, eying the buildings in the distance. She rejoined me on the bench.

"I was just telling you that Mark always asked questions no one else thought of, and I forgot to ask the most important question myself. Why was Mark here?"

I let her continue her thoughts uninterrupted.

"He knew he was in trouble. The security tapes from the metro make it clear that he knew he was being followed, and the flash drive in his pocket indicated he knew that he had to pass on his message. He knew his life was in danger, and he chose to come here. He could have stopped at a station where multiple lines converged and where police would be available. Instead, he chose this stop, which opens onto the Mall with only locals and tourists, which means he came here for a reason. It took me a week to ask the question, but now that I'm here, the answer is obvious."

"Care to enlighten me?"

"Remember the clock in the storage room?"

"Yeah, the time was set to 12:35, and you said that 1235 was the clue."

"Do you remember who made the clock?"

"Nope."

"Smith & Sons." She pointed to the northeast. "He was going to The Smithsonian. Come on, we need to find a 1235 inside."

She launched into a brisk walk, and Banshee and I rushed to catch up.

"What do you know about the Smithsonian Museum?" she asked.

"Not much."

"It's not just a single museum, but a complex of twenty-one museums, containing over 150 million specimens."

"Then it should be easy to find Mark's clue."

"Let's start with the The National Museum of Natural History. It contains the most displays, and Mark liked it best."

We passed through security and strode into the main hall. I stopped to appreciate the thirteen-foot tall African bush elephant displayed in the center of the lobby. The cavernous room dwarfed the massive beast. Three levels of balconies overlooked the lobby, illuminated by sunlight pouring in from arched windows surrounding the lobby. Although crowded with tourists, most of the foot traffic was leaving the museum for the day.

"My brother loved this place and visited often."

"Any particular display he favored?"

"Not really. He always wanted to learn something new. He spent so much time here that he befriended some of the researchers employed here."

"This is a research facility, too?"

"Scientists from all over the world come to study the collections. Only one percent of the collections are on display. The rest are in storage here and offsite. My brother spent hours exploring the lower levels of the museum."

"How many basement levels are there?"

"Three that they admit, but there are rumors of deeper levels."

"You believe that nonsense?"

"Would you have believed a week ago that there is a secret tunnel to escape from a secret office in the Senate building?"

"Good point."

"This town harbors layers of secrets. Let's sit over here for a minute, while I think about where to go first." Mac chose a bench facing a wide open exhibit area. Tired tourists herded hungry, exhausted children toward the exit, their patience for sightseeing fully expended.

"Evenings are the best time to be here. The crowd thins, and a quiet solitude settles in. I can almost feel him walking across this room, stopping to read the information signs, asking the employees questions about an exhibit, taking notes in one of his endless journals, and smiling at the families. I miss him."

"Are you sure that this was his intended destination last week?"

"Yes. Everything he did had a purpose. He got off the metro at that stop for a reason, and nothing else around here makes sense. Plus, he led us to the clock."

"Maybe he thought he could hide in the lower levels."

"Possibly, but he didn't act like he was running away. He acted like he was running toward something."

"There're about twenty million somethings in this building. How do you propose to find the relevant one?"

"Let's walk some more. We should go see the dinosaurs. They're my favorite part of the museum."

We ambled through three halls before beholding the dinosaurs. Banshee tensed, but I calmed him with a gentle touch. Mac and I split, as we wandered through the exhibits.

I approached a suzhousaurus, an ugly creature, and Banshee growled quietly. "Relax, boy. He hasn't been a threat for the last hundred million years." I read the informational placard, learning that the frightening beast had not been a meat eater. "I told you you're safe. This bad boy ate only trees, not dogs."

I turned to the next exhibit, when something registered in my mind. I returned to the placard, and in the bottom right hand corner, it read "Exhibit 19742" in tiny print, probably an internal tracking system. I moved to the next sign and saw "Exhibit 21373."

I motioned to Mac and pointed to the sign. "Each one of these exhibits has a number assigned to it."

Mac noted it and raced to the next two exhibits. A smile brightened her face. "It's so simple, it's brilliant."

"You think we need to find Exhibit 1235?"

"Absolutely."

"It doesn't seem like the exhibit numbers are in order."

"No, we're going to need help."

CHAPTER TWENTY-FOUR

Friday, March 20
4:13 p.m.

We found a curator in the lobby. Weary after a long day, he greeted us warmly. "Good afternoon, folks. How can I help you today?"

Mac noted his name tag. "Nice to meet you, Tim. I'm Mac, and these are my friends, Doc and Banshee. We have some questions about the numbering system used for the exhibits. We noticed the little numbers in the bottom corners of each sign."

"Those are internal labels, so we know where everything is."

"How are they assigned?"

"Randomly by when the exhibit is made public. When an exhibit is taken down, the number becomes available again. When an exhibit goes live, the next available number is assigned. That number will remain matched to that exhibit and location until it is taken down."

"So a specific exhibit number could be anywhere in the museum?"

"Correct. Is there something specific you are looking for?"

"We're looking for a specific exhibit number. How do we do that?"

"That information is not generally made available to the public, but if you tell me what is in the exhibit, I can guide you to the correct section."

"That's the problem, Tim. We don't know what's in the exhibit. We only have the number."

Although perplexed, Tim seemed happy to help with her unique question. "Let me make a call and see if Sue is still in the building. One moment, please."

Tim stepped aside and called on his radio.

"I think Tim likes you," I said.

"I'll like him better if he can track down that exhibit."

"You don't feel like spending the next month peering through crowds of school kids to look at a million different signs?"

"If I have to, I will, but I prefer to work smarter."

Tim motioned to Mac to join him. "What exhibit number are you looking for?"

"1235."

"A low number. Probably been on display a long time. Hold on."

He relayed the information over the radio, nodded, and thanked Sue before turning back to Mac.

"Exhibit 1235 is in our American History Museum next door. I can point you in the right direction."

"Thank you. Did Sue mention what the exhibit is?"

"Yes, a collection of early American journals."

Mac's eyes lit up, and we followed his directions outside to the Museum of American History next door. "If he somehow managed to do what I think he did, this will be Mark's best quest ever," Mac marveled.

"I'm guessing that he hid something in the exhibit."

"It makes sense. His information would be well protected."

I picked up a brochure. "This place has Dorothy's slippers from the Wizard of Oz, the original American flag, and Lincoln's top hat. A journal with national secrets would fit right in."

We wandered until something caught Mac's eye, and she sped toward an exhibit that contained the setting of an early office. The informational placard described artifacts from Ben Franklin's office, and the exhibit number at the bottom was 1235. Among the items scattered on the desk was a stack of seven journals. Elated, Mac kept moving.

"Where are we going?" I asked.

"We probably still have watchers, and I don't want to give anything away."

"Are you sure that's the right exhibit?"

"Definitely. Mark used only one kind of notebook with a red stripe on the binding. I recognized Mark's journal in that pile on the desk."

"Great. Now we just have to lose our followers, get past museum security, avoid all the cameras, get past the thick glass, and retrieve the journal without getting caught."

"When you say it like that, it sounds hard. Come on, let's lead our friends on a wild goose chase."

We roamed the museum, paying particular interest to various unrelated exhibits. Anyone watching us would be baffled by our random wandering. Tired of the game, we left the museum and returned to the bench next to the location of Mark's shooting.

"Are you really going to steal that journal?"

"Technically, it's not stealing. That journal was Mark's, and now that he's dead, it belongs to me. I'm only retrieving my own property."

"You won't consider just asking the museum to give it to us?"

"No. Homeland would grab it before we even got near it."

"What's your plan?"

"Still working on it."

"If Nicholas Cage can steal the Declaration of Independence, I'm sure you can figure out a way to get one little journal out of the museum unnoticed."

"Let me think, and I'll call you. Thanks for coming, and thank you, Banshee, for getting my purse back. I'm gonna grab an Uber and call it a night."

"Okay. Banshee and I are gonna walk home. Good night, Mac."

"Good night, Doc."

CHAPTER TWENTY-FIVE

Friday, March 20
5:08 p.m.

Agent Morozova watched them separate and decided to follow Mac. The tedious last hour of tracking them through the museum, staying out of sight and away from security cameras, and memorizing a list of exhibits where they had shown more interest, could lead to nothing. They may have merely distracted themselves with a visit to the museum.

Alina felt considerable pressure from the Director for results. Viktor's and Nikolai's failure to grab the purse, the simplest of tasks, had focused his angry expectations onto her. The Director had risked their exposure at a mere possibility of the acquisition of useful information, but so had she, when she shot the researcher.

Alina's rise in the Directorate had been improbable. Born in Murom, an unremarkable town outside of Moscow, to an unremarkable family, her father had labored in a factory, while her mother worked in food preparation for the State. Alina's physical and academic prowess was obvious at an early age, but Russia rewarded conformity over excellence. Alina, a strong willed child who refused to conform, eventually became a disciplinary problem at school.

Her life changed after her thirteenth birthday. Alina's maturing body caught an older boy's attention. When the seventeen-year-old tried to rape her, Alina fought. Using nothing but her hands and feet, she had beaten him to the point of hospitalization for multiple surgeries.

Unfortunately for Alina, he was the son of a minor Party official, who demanded punishment for Alina. If he had his way, she would have been sentenced to a harsh labor camp, where she would likely have died. In one of the only breaks in her difficult life, her case came to the attention of an SVR officer.

Lera Kozlova, one of the few women in the SVR, recruited girls with unusual intelligence, athleticism, and mental strength as young as ten years old to begin her training process. A thirteen-year-old who had beaten an older boy to within an inch of his life impressed her.

After an interview in Alina's holding cell, Kozlova attained her immediate release. She escorted her home, where she allowed fifteen minutes to collect her belongings and say goodbye with the clear expectation that she would never see her family again.

She took Alina to a facility where intense training began with other girls and young women. With no days off, the regimen challenged them academically and physically. She learned about reality, not the diluted facts the State shared with its citizens, but real facts about the West. Alina had been chosen to learn English with multiple dialects.

Self defense and weapons training occurred simultaneously, including fighting hand to hand and with knives, guns, and blunt objects. When she was sixteen, experts taught her how to use her body as a weapon by seducing men and women into sharing their secrets. Her mind and body became her most lethal weapons as she matured.

By age twenty, Alina was ready for her first assignment in the real world. Her youthful appearance and flawless English made her a valuable asset in the United States. She could escape notice and gather information through violence, stealth, and seduction. She had built her career with one success after another, and she was determined to continue the streak. Whatever it took, she would get that information.

.   .   .

Across the mall, DHS agents updated Agent Duff. "They spent over an hour in the museum, getting excited about random exhibits. Looked more like a nerd date than anything related to our investigation."

"What about the Russians?"

"That same woman is stalking them."

"Did she break any laws?"

"Nothing we noticed."

"Keep tabs on her, but don't intercept her, unless she interferes with our targets. The Russians are ballsy to let her keep tailing them after losing an agent earlier today."

"If the Ruskies were as smart as they are stubborn they'd be a worthy opponent."

"Don't underestimate them. She may have a part to play in this before the end."

Agent Duff ended the call and sat back in his chair. It had been a long and very frustrating week. It looked like Mac's search had stalled. Today's outing may indeed have been only a date. He organized his desk and left for the night. Hopefully, he would have a quiet weekend ahead to catch up on some much needed sleep.

.   .   .

Banshee and I arrived home focused on dinner, shredded chicken for him and grilled cheese for me. I had just finished, when John texted.

"It's started. Turn on the news."

I generally avoided news channels, but I turned it on to find a news anchor updating the top stories.

"In a bombshell, after hours report, Lana Hearns has made serious allegations against Prime Medical Partners, the leading provider of emergency room staffing across the country. Let's listen to her press conference."

Composed and indignant, Lana stood behind a podium loaded with microphones. "Today's report shines a light on a culture of deception at Prime Medical Partners that has corrupted the staffing of many of our emergency rooms around the country. These emergency rooms are our first line of defense in the case of major accidents and illnesses, and a primary healthcare resource for many of our most medically vulnerable citizens.

"For years, Prime Medical Partners has used offshore funds to bribe hospital officials around the country to secure lucrative contracts to staff emergency rooms. Despite worsening outcomes due to understaffing and pay cuts, they were able to maintain these contracts by bribing high ranking hospital officials.

"Their accounts were contained in a single bank in the Caymans, through a subsidiary company they created called SGITR, LLC. Ironically, SGITR stands for smartest guys in the room. They have violated tax and international money laws, and their corporate practice of medicine has endangered the lives of US citizens. I am calling on all relevant law enforcement agencies to begin an investigation of Prime Medical Partners. I am calling for the resignation and prosecution of all hospital officials who accepted bribes from Prime Medical Partners. It is time to get the dirty money out of medicine and return control of healthcare to medical professionals."

The screen cut to a live response from Don Prost at Prime Medical Partners headquarters. "We categorically deny all of these absurd allegations. Prime Medical Partners is a leader in the medical industry, and we hold ourselves to the highest ethical standards. We welcome a full and comprehensive investigation of these ridiculous allegations. Furthermore, we will be filing a defamation lawsuit against the reporter and all of those who provided her with this false information."

The screen cut back to the news desk. "Lana Hearns, who won a Pulitzer on her story about the bombings in Las Vegas, gave an explosive report today on widespread bribery that has threatened the quality of medical care in Hospital Emergency Rooms across the country. Prime Medical Partners suffered a 37% drop in stock value after Hearns's report. We'll keep you updated on new developments. In other news…."

I turned the TV off and snuggled Banshee. "Looks like we solved one problem this week. I think we've earned a good night's sleep."

Banshee's eyes fluttered closed.

CHAPTER TWENTY-SIX

Saturday, March 21
11:22 a.m

"How's your day going, Doc?" John's sunny voice lit up my cell phone.

"Pretty solid so far. What's the word on the street?"

"The PIMPS are getting destroyed on every channel. Seven senior healthcare executives have already resigned nationally with more expected."

"What about the hospitals? Are they taking it seriously?"

"Hell, yes. They are running fast from the PIMPS. I've already had three groups contact me this morning to inquire about how quickly we could take over their emergency room staffing. We have the infrastructure in place, so it would just be a matter of moving their doctors to our system. We may end up with 500% growth from this."

"That's fantastic news. I'm happy for you guys."

"Thank you for everything you did to make this possible."

"We should thank the PIMPS for running a dirty company and leaving a paper trail. It's always helpful when the bad guys are stupid and cocky at the same time."

"Amen to that. I gotta run. I need to make plans to hire some more folks to handle the new business. Have a good one, Doc."

"You, too, John."

I ended the call, and Mac texted that she would be over in an hour. She gave no details, but since our communications were likely monitored, I figured I would find out what the plan was in an hour. My phone rang again before I could put it down.

"Hey, beautiful. Taking time out from your Pulitzer Prize tour to call a lowly doctor?"

"It's important to stay humble. How are you doing, Doc?"

"Pretty good, but not as well as you. I can't turn on the TV without seeing another Lana interview. This story is taking off."

"That's an understatement. I'm booked solid all weekend. Thanks for the tip."

"Happy to share. I'm tired of these corporate assholes breaking all the rules and taking all the money."

"Can I quote you on that?"

"That was off the record, but you can attribute it to every damn doctor in the country. We all feel the same way. Any comments yet from Prime Medical Partners?"

"I reached out and their lawyer offered the usual denials and threatened to sue me for defamation and violation of proprietary financial information. He's kind of an asshole, and I could swear he called me a cunt under his breath as I was hanging up."

"Uh oh. Not a good career move for him. Where do you think all of this ends?"

"I think this is just the beginning. The PIMPS are facing possible jail time unless they flip on each other. My money is on the COO to cooperate first. That dude has no spine at all. Some hospital executives have lawyered up, but resignations and firings have already begun. A major change is a reevaluation of the way hospital contracts are awarded. It's going to be harder for corporate entities to win over physician-owned groups in the future. I've also got a whistleblower who wants to meet on Monday to share information about a large private equity firm providing radiology services nationally. If it pans out, another group may be going down."

"If they're cheating, I hope they get everything they've earned. How are you doing? I miss you."

"Miss you, too. I'm keeping busy in LA. You should visit sometime, and make sure to bring Banshee."

"That would be nice. I have some things to finish here, but I'll plan something in the next few weeks."

"Take care, Doc, and stay out of trouble."

"Who me? I never get into trouble. Go crush that next interview."

We disconnected. "What do you say, good boy? Do you want to visit California?"

Banshee tilted his head and stared into my soul.

· · ·

Mac arrived at my townhouse a little later dressed in black leggings, a long, soft, dark grey sweater, and black athletic shoes, as if ready for a relaxing, casual date, but also allowing for mobility, comfort, and an ability to blend into a crowd as well as into a shadowy museum. I had chosen dark grey, lightweight athletic pants with a black t-shirt.

She held a finger to her lips to silence me and pulled a small black box from her purse. She pushed its only button, and a light flashed green.

"Okay, it's safe to talk. How are you, Doc?"

"Fine, but really curious about what your fancy little black box does."

"I borrowed this from a friend. It emits a small electromagnetic field that disrupts electronics within a set radius. Right now, it's blocking signals to your phone and probably to your neighbors' as well. Tonight, it's going to help us get that journal back."

I looked at my phone and saw that no service was available. "How exactly is it going to do that?"

"We're going to hide in the museum, and after it closes, we're going to grab the journal. We'll spend the night in the museum and walk out in the morning. This little toy will block the camera signals, as we move through the museum."

"You think it will be that simple?"

"I hope so. The museum has a few guards at night, but relies on electronic surveillance to monitor the exhibits. The doors to the exterior would be hard to breach, but inside, nothing prevents us from moving around."

"Do I want to know where you got that toy?"

"It's from a friend from a previous life with access to the latest gadgets. I need to load a few things into Banshee's vest, if that's okay. It'll be easier to get it through security."

"Of course. Banshee is a willing accomplice to these sorts of activities."

After we loaded his vest, Mac turned off the black box, and we left the house.

.   .   .

Across the street, two DHS technicians furiously tried to reacquire the signals from the bugs they had left in the house.

"What the hell? The signal is back. We have good audio."

"How the hell did that happen?"

"No idea, but we're back online. How long were we down?"

"Almost seven minutes."

"Make a note in the log."

A young woman strolled by their van. Agent Morozova would not lose sight of her targets.

CHAPTER TWENTY-SEVEN

Saturday, March 21
12:57 p.m.

On that busy Saturday afternoon, we waited in a long line to enter the museum. Mac's bag passed through security without notice, and Banshee bypassed the metal detector after a few tricks for the security guards. No one thought to search his vest. We entered the crowded main hall, and Mac pointed toward the cafeteria.

"Let's get a good lunch and choose some food to go. It's gonna be a long night," she said.

"Are you sure it's crowded enough?"

"Enough not to raise suspicion that we plan to stay here all night."

We jostled through hungry tourists to buy lunch and a find a table. We bought bottled water and a couple of sandwiches for later.

"Are you sure about this? You have a lot to lose if you get caught," I said.

"Yes, I need that journal, and we won't get caught. We have a good plan."

"We have a simple one."

"Fewer things can go wrong with simple plans. Come on, let's go find a place to hide until the museum closes."

The crowd had thickened as we ate, and she pointed toward a door marked "Museum Personnel Only."

"Follow me, and act like you belong."

She removed her black box from Banshee's vest and pressed the button. The green light flashed, and all around us, several bewildered tourists noticed that their phones had lost service.

"You just transported these teenagers back to the Stone Age."

"They'll survive. Come on."

We approached the door with a blinking red light on the security pad. Mac pushed through the door, and no alarm sounded. Banshee and I followed, and the door closed quietly behind us. Mac walked down a set of stairs.

"Hopefully, no one noticed us. Let's go find somewhere to get comfortable," she said.

.   .   .

Upstairs, phones reconnected almost as quickly as they had fallen out of service. The teenagers had not only survived, but also had already forgotten the brief inconvenience along with everyone else, except Alina. She had noted their dark clothing, the large lunches they had eaten, the extra sandwiches and water they had purchased, and their use of some sort of device to enter a secure area of the museum. Taken together, she surmised that they planned to hide in the museum to recover something. Determined to find them, Alina would follow them and take whatever they recovered. The ceramic knife and composite gun she had worn through security would give her the advantage, if they put up a fight. She considered a museum employee with a badge she could steal to access the secure area to hunt them down. Enjoying the mere prospect, Alina had plenty of time to savor it. Hopefully, this project would end tonight, and she would have the information for the Director.

•   •   •

The two junior agents assigned to follow Doc and Mac didn't see them disappear into the authorized personnel area. All they knew was that one minute they were in the museum, and the next, they were gone.

They searched futilely for twenty minutes before heading to security to review their camera system's recordings. He found Doc and Mac on video, walking through the museum earlier, but the cameras failed to record their disappearance. State of the art facial recognition software allowed him to search all of the cameras in real time and found no sign of Doc, Mac, or Banshee. Somehow, they had disappeared again.

The call to Agent Duff went as expected, with yelling to emphasize his displeasure and frustration. A few more agents were assigned to help find the trail, and an electronic net was placed over the surrounding area. They had to show their faces to a camera eventually, and when they did, Duff would have them again.

•   •   •

Mac kept her magic box activated, as we descended to the third sublevel, figuring that the deeper we went, the less likely we were to encounter anyone, especially on a weekend. Her device temporarily disabled cameras as we passed, leaving us invisible to security. Mac stopped in front of a random locked door and knelt to inspect the lock.

"This should be easy. Hold my bag, please."

I watched, as she inserted the picks and opened the lock in seconds.

"Not bad. I didn't expect you to be a lock picking expert."

"I'm hardly an expert, but a little skill does come in handy sometimes."

I silently agreed. "Let's see what's inside."

We entered a large room with eight rows of steel shelves loaded with specimens. Everything from bones to pop culture outfits stretched into the distance.

"I wonder if anyone even knows this stuff exists. There must be five thousand items in this room alone," I said.

"At least. Let's find a place to get settled. We have a couple hours until the museum closes."

We chose a space on the floor in the back of the room that had empty shelving nearby. We hoped we could hide in there on the off chance that someone came into the room. Banshee wandered off to explore the new aromas.

"I didn't know this place had so many levels below ground," I said.

"It has at least three, but probably more. DC limits the heights of buildings, so the only choice is to go deeper. Plus, as you saw from my building, DC loves secret tunnels. This place is probably riddled with them."

"Since we have some time, how about you tell me what you did before you became a Chief of Staff in the Senate. I'm guessing most people in your position can't pick locks and access the latest electromagnetic technology."

"Most of what I did is still classified."

"Skip the details and give me an unclassified overview. Since we're about to steal something from the nation's most prestigious museum, I figure I have a right to know who my partner in crime really is."

"Fair enough. I grew up in a military family. My dad was a Navy Seal and absent most of the time. Luckily, he was based out of Coronado, so we didn't have to move as often as other military families did."

"So you grew up in Southern California?"

"Yeah, I learned to surf, and our dad brought us on base when he was in town and let us run the obstacle course. He made sure we knew basic self defense and how to handle various weapons. He was a great dad. Unfortunately, pancreatic cancer took him only one year into his retirement."

"What about your mom? Was she at home with you?"

"Most of the time. She was a teacher and a military wife, two difficult and thankless positions. I think the lifestyle was hard on her, but she cheerfully did her best. The hardest part for all of us was not knowing what was happening with dad. His job was so secretive, and he disappeared for weeks at a time. We jumped every time the doorbell rang, thinking that a military chaplain would be there to offer condolences, but he always came home so happy to see us."

"What does your mom do now?"

"She died of breast cancer a year after my father passed."

"I'm sorry. You've suffered through a lot of grief."

"Thanks. With Mark gone, I'm alone now."

"Your dad must have seen some interesting things during his career."

"I'm sure he did. I would love to know more about it."

"Is that why you joined the Defense Intelligence Agency?"

"Partly, I guess. He certainly instilled a sense of duty. The military didn't seem like a good fit for me, but the DIA seemed perfect. I could use my scientific background, as well as the things my dad had taught me, but in a smaller, more flexible setting. Not many people know that the DIA even exists, and they like it that way. We did important work but stayed out of the headlines."

"I'm sure your parents would be proud of everything you've accomplished."

"I hope so. What about your history? You've got a few skeletons in the closet."

"My life started simply enough. I grew up in the Midwest in a middle class house. My parents did their best, but passed away when I was in high school, and from then on I had to make my own way. I went to college at Notre Dame and chose Houston for medical school. They have the largest medical center in the world with multiple hospitals and plenty of trauma to fill the emergency rooms."

"Why did you choose emergency medicine?"

"Part of it is the challenge and adrenaline surges, but I think I like the chaos. You never know what will come through the door next. It could be someone with a splinter in their hand or someone with a knife in their chest. Every minute is a new experience, and every patient is a new adventure."

"Most people would find such chaos stressful."

"True, but the trick is to turn the chaos into order. You use your training and experience and your team to figure out what is wrong with your patient, and then try to solve their problems. Everyone enters the emergency room with questions and our job is to figure out the answers. It's satisfying when it's done right."

"What about all these side adventures you seem to have? I looked you up, and you've been involved with high profile cases involving organized crime, dirty cops and serial killers. Seems a little extreme, even for an emergency doctor."

"Maybe it is extreme, but I feel a sense of duty to my patients. I had never met your brother before that night, but the last words he spoke were a request for me to help him, and that means something to me. I wasn't about to give that flash drive to Agent Duff after your brother requested that I give it only to you."

"But your duty to him was complete when you gave the flash drive to me."

"Yes, but then you asked for my help, and I'm pretty sure Mark would have wanted me to see this through to the end, if he had had the strength to tell me. Besides, Agent Duff and the Russians are pissing me off, and this quest is interesting. I plan to see how this ends up, and make sure you find Mark's research."

"Thank you. Did you have anything to do with the news about that corporate group bribing hospitals for contracts?"

"You could say I'm involved."

"Why the national hysteria about the story?"

"Corporate involvement in medicine has been growing quietly over the last decade, but it's one of the largest threats to quality care today."

"I thought corporations were forbidden from owning medical companies."

"They are, but they get around the restrictions by owning a management company and running all the revenue through it. Basically, the company that provides medical care is just a shell and all the money passes through to the management company. It's a dangerous system, because corporations have shareholders and investors who expect to see profits. When they buy these companies, there is no way to increase prices, because those are controlled by insurance companies. They can try to increase the number of patients, but most of the time, that number has been maximized already. So the only way to increase profits is to decrease expenses, and the primary way to do that is to decrease staffing and salaries. For example, they replace nurses with medical assistants, doctors with physician assistants and nurse practitioners, and cut the staffing ratios. Now you're seeing the same number of patients with fewer resources, but there is no way you can provide the same level of care. The investors are happy, but the patients are often not. The business model is not the best way to deliver the highest quality of care."

"How do you fix it?"

"Under the current system, where insurance companies are a monopoly that controls the price of healthcare, a topic for another day, the only option is to restrict corporations from practicing medicine. Let them invest, but the businesses need to be majority owned and run by medical professionals. Until we do that, the corporations will bleed healthcare of every penny they can."

"It sounds depressing when you put it that way."

"It is. We go to school for twenty-five years to be able to practice medicine and some thirty-five-year old asshole in a suit driving a BMW tells us how many nurses we need to staff the emergency room on a weekend, when his only experience is visiting the emergency room after a drunk driving accident in college. We need to get rid of every one of those fools."

"Sounds like a fight for another day. Let's get some rest."

.   .   .

Alina quickly realized that a comprehensive search of the lower levels would be futile. She had easily stolen a badge from a guard she had asked for directions and entered the secure area without difficulty. The maze of hallways below consisted of three levels with thousands of doors to hide behind. It would take a whole team days to search everywhere. She decided to hide and wait for the museum to close, relying on a guess that Doc and Mac would wait a few hours after the museum closed before coming out of hiding. Alina would wait patiently for them to emerge and lead her to the treasure.

CHAPTER TWENTY-EIGHT

Saturday, March 21
8:02 p.m.

"Eight o'clock. Ready to go?" I asked.

"Now is as good a time as any, but my first stop needs to be a bathroom."

"I agree. Never commit a crime with a full bladder. It's too distracting."

"What about Banshee?"

"They have a service dog relief area upstairs."

Mac turned on her electromagnetic device, and we stepped outside our storage room. The widely spaced security lighting left most of the hallway in shadow.

"Not spooky at all," Mac said.

"Almost every horror movie features people sneaking through a dimly lit, deserted basement surrounded by dusty, dead artifacts with some evil presence stalking them. Let's get moving." My joking about our situation failed to alleviate my creepy sense of foreboding. Mac strutted down the hallway like she had worked there for decades, as did Banshee, so I tried to sweep the stems of anxiety from my mind.

We found the bathrooms and returned to the stairs that we had descended hours earlier. We moved quietly, but every sound echoed in the vast silence of the empty building. I had hoped that the main floor would feel less disquieting, but as we emerged from the stairwell, it felt more ominous. Dim lighting cast unidentifiable shadows from the exhibits, and large areas loomed in utter darkness.

We found the pet service area, and Banshee didn't need a command to make use of the facilities. We headed toward the early American history area, three halls away. I told Banshee to GUARD. I knew he would stay alert and let me know of any potential threat.

We proceeded with the staccato clicking of Banshee's nails across the hard floor the only sound breaking the heavy silence. I would need to remember to trim his nails before any subsequent robberies.

After only a few minutes, Mac shined a penlight on exhibit 1235 and whispered in my ear.

"It's there. See the notebook with the red stripe sticking out at the bottom of the pile? That's Mark's journal. Now I need to figure out the best way to get it."

Mac set her bag down to study the problem, and I whispered to Banshee, "GUARD, ALERT, GO."

Banshee slid silently into the shadows.

·   ·   ·

Alina predicted that they would use the same stairs and doorway to exit and had waited nearby. Even the dog walked right past her. With so many odors and people passing through the area earlier in the day, the dog's sense of smell may have been overwhelmed. She would still have to worry about his hearing and eyesight. Dogs, especially highly trained ones, could sense a presence with minimal sensory input.

She gave them a full minute's head start and smiled at the clicking of the dog's nails. In the dead silence of the closed museum, it provided her with a beacon to follow. Alina walked silently, stopping when they did and moving with the dog's clicking steps. Everything she carried was fastened tightly in her bag and pockets to prevent any noise that could reveal her presence. She was a deeper shadow moving among shadows.

Alina paused as she heard whispered conversation ahead and the sound of a bag set on the floor. They had reached their target, and the end was in sight. Alina crept forward ever so slowly until she could see them, but where was the damn dog?

·   ·   ·

Banshee flowed silently through the room, pausing to listen and sniff. Given his command to guard and alert, Banshee moved in expanding circles around his owner. The overpowering scents of thousands of visitors permeated the air. He listened and watched. Detecting no threat, he continued his rounds.

Alina held her breath, as a dark shadow roamed ten feet in front of her. The dog sniffed the air as he moved. The gun was in her hand, but she didn't want to reveal herself until she had to. She exhaled with relief, as the dog disappeared into the shadows ahead.

·   ·   ·

Mac pointed to the last panel of glass. "I think the easiest thing will be to remove that panel. It only has six screws."

"The easiest thing would be to throw a rock through the glass."

"Okay, a rock would be easier, but noisy and messy. The goal is to get it without anyone noticing that we were here."

Mac pulled a multi-tool out of her bag and easily loosened the screws. She removed the last one, and I helped her move the glass aside. She climbed into the exhibit and started searching the desk drawers.

"Just grab the journal, and let's go."

"I want to make sure he didn't leave anything else for me, unless you want to risk having to come back tomorrow."

"This place gives me the creeps."

"Scared of ghosts?"

"No, but prison terrifies me. I spent a few days in a cell once, and it was horrific."

"You'll have to tell me about that sometime." She glanced at me sideways.

"What do you make of this?" Mac shined her light through a crystal, and it refracted a golden glow in all directions.

"I don't think this belonged to Ben Franklin."

"Take it. If it's not Mark's, we can always give it back to the museum anonymously."

Mac stuck it into an invisible pocket in her leggings and turned her attention to the stack of journals. She glanced briefly at each one to see that the ink was clearly too old to be Mark's. She opened the journal with the red stripe and gasped.

"Everything okay?" I asked.

"Yes. It's just that Mark's handwriting is so distinctive. This is definitely his." Mac clutched the journal tightly to her chest, as tears threatened, but she quickly handed me the journal and finished her search, finding nothing else of interest. She stepped out of the exhibit and tucked the journal and the crystal into her bag.

"Let's put the glass back."

The distinct click of a hammer being pulled back on a gun preceded the sound of a feminine voice.

"Thank you for finding those notes for me. Hand them over, and you live. Challenge me, and you die. I get the notes either way. Call off your dog, or he dies, too."

I appraised the woman standing confidently fifteen feet away with her gun pointed at my chest.

"GUN," I uttered.

CHAPTER TWENTY-NINE

Saturday, March 21
8:38 p.m.

Banshee tensed to the sound of the new voice and halted on the far side of the exhibit. He crept low to stalk her, remaining invisible in shadow. The clear command GUN specified a task that he had trained well to perform. He saw Doc now and followed his gaze to a new person standing across the room with her arm outstretched. He recognized the black metal shape in her hand. Banshee remained in darkness, as he sped around the corner of the last exhibit with his target in sight. He launched, focused only on the hand that gripped the gun.

.   .   .

Even though I knew what would happen and had seen it before, the speed and violence of Banshee's attack shocked me. The woman had no chance. Banshee's jaws clamped her arm to send the weapon skittering across the floor, but not before a single shot shattered the silence of the museum. The force of the hit twisted her to the ground, where she gasped and clutched her wrist. Blood flowed through her fingers.

"Banshee, come here."

He ran to my side, retaining his protective pose. A growl rattled deep in his chest, as he watched the woman writhe on the bloody floor.

I grabbed Mac's hand. "We need to get out of here. Someone had to have heard that gunshot."

"What about her?" Mac asked, pointing at the injured woman.

"Leave her. She's hurt, and her gun flew off somewhere. Even if she manages to follow us, Banshee will protect us."

Mac grabbed her bag, and we hurried away. The woman glared at us with icy hatred. Evil really had been lurking in the museum.

.   .   .

Alina watched them run from the hall, then used her knife to cut a piece of her shirt to make a bandage for her wrist. It hurt like hell. She peered into the shadows where her gun had fallen and found it lying against a wall. She grabbed it with her left hand, not her best shooting hand, but more than adequate to kill both of them and that fucking dog. She could hear them running in the hallway and rushed after them.

The lone security guard three halls away startled when the gun fired. He had spent the last ten years on night duty, enjoying the serenity of the museum after hours, and knew every sound the old building emitted. The sounds of voices, followed by a gunshot and people running away punctuated his alarm. He activated his radio.

"This is Johnson. I've got intruders and a single gunshot in Hall B or C. Anything on camera?"

The two guards at the central monitoring office turned their attention to the appropriate monitors, but saw only fuzz.

"Negative. Cameras in that area are off line."

"Initiate lockdown and call backup."

The guards entered the appropriate command, and across the museum, lights came on, and an alarm blared. Security bolts thunked into place on all exterior doors, preventing anyone from leaving. In seconds, the building was secured.

The Office of Protective Services, responsible for the security of the Smithsonian, maintains a force of 850 officers to cover all Smithsonian properties. Only a skeleton crew worked nights, and most of those officers were assigned to other buildings. With a gunshot and possible theft, alerts spread immediately to the D.C. police, the FBI, and Homeland Security. Within thirty minutes, officers from various agencies swarmed the museum. Among those notified was Agent Duff, who met his team at the museum.

·   ·   ·

We were headed for the lobby when the lights and alarm came on.

"This is turning into a clusterfuck," I observed. "What now?"

"The doors will be locked down mechanically. Let's find a place to hide downstairs. Hopefully, they'll find that woman with the gun and won't search for us."

"Who is she?"

"No idea, but she had cold eyes and a distinct lack of compassion. Given our current situation, my best guess is that she's a Russian agent."

"It's a good bet she's a pissed off Russian agent now."

We took the stairs two at a time to the third subbasement and ran down a long hallway. Mac decisively shifted lefts and rights at intersecting hallways.

"Where are you headed?" I asked.

"No idea. I just want to distance ourselves from the shooting."

After a few minutes, she paused to take some deep breaths. "So much for our quiet robbery to leave no one the wiser," she said.

"I've done worse. I once was sneaking around a ranch and let a metal door slam shut, loud enough to wake the dead."

"What happened next?"

"I ran away, as two guards unloaded a couple hundred rounds in my general direction."

"You should have disclosed that you're a shitty thief."

"We were doing great until the witch showed up."

"True. We did get the journal and a bonus rock. Let's find a good place to hide. Look for a big room."

Large double doors in the next hallway led to a massive storage room stuffed with oversized exhibits. A wooly mammoth greeted us as we walked in, earning a startled snarl from Banshee.

"There's got to be a good place to hide in here. Look over there, and I'll check over here."

We split up to search the room, and Banshee separated from me to explore the new area. I was considering a promising area to hide, when Banshee growled with a single bark, followed by a human scream. Someone else hid in the room.

CHAPTER THIRTY

Saturday, March 21
8:51 p.m.

Alina knew the futility of her search, shortly after she entered the first level of the basement and discovered no sign of them. Rather than continue to look for Doc and Mac, she decided to hide. Self preservation took precedence over the hunt. She winced, as another bolt of pain shot through her wrist. She noted the blood trail she had left for the police to follow. She walked to a large storage room with an open door on the second basement level, making sure to leave a few drops of blood. Inside, she cut off another strip of her shirt to tighten the bandage on her wrist, stopping the flow of blood. She backtracked to the stairwell and climbed back up a level. With luck, the police would waste time searching for her in the storeroom below.

She chose a locked door at random, picked the lock, and entered another room similarly filled with random artifacts. She found a comparatively comfortable space between two stuffed crocodiles and settled in. She would wait until the museum opened in the morning and slip out with a group of tourists. Her arm throbbed, as she imagined different vengeful scenarios, until she fell into a fitful sleep.

. . .

I followed the low tones of Banshee's growling and a man's whimpering to find Banshee crouched in his attack stance, while the man in front of him seemed to try to back through the wall behind him. I commanded Banshee to relax and return to me.

The disheveled man with long, filthy hair and a scraggly beard was definitely not a security guard or employee of the museum. A faded, torn bath robe, possibly white originally, hung on his skinny frame, and frayed sandals adorned his dirty feet. His eyes contrasted with his chaotic general appearance. A clear, dark blue, they exuded intelligence and wisdom, as he now calmly evaluated Mac and me.

"What's the dog's name?" The man spoke in a quiet, confident voice without an accent.

"Banshee."

"He's a beautiful dog. Is it okay if I pet him?"

I commanded FRIEND, and gestured toward the man, honoring the odd request from one who had been so terrified of him moments before. Banshee relaxed and sat by the man, who slowly reached to pet him. A good scratch had Banshee leaning into his hand.

I glanced at Mac, who shrugged.

"Who are you?" I asked.

The man approached and offered to shake hands. "Apologies for my bad manners. I don't talk to people very often anymore. I go by Herodotus, but you can call me Doty. Herodotus is a mouthful."

"Nice to meet you, Doty. I'm Doc, and this is Mac." We shook hands and awkwardly stared at each other until Mac broke the silence.

"What are you doing in here, Doty?"

"I come here most nights. I like to study the exhibits. You wouldn't believe what they have down here. It's a shame they can't display everything. The public should be able to see this stuff."

"You don't work here, do you?"

Doty gestured to his outfit. "No. Apparently, my taste in fashion is not up to museum standards, although some of those guys are a bit grungy."

"Then how do you get to explore the halls at night?"

"I don't have permission to be here, but I don't bother anyone or steal anything. I just explore these storerooms. There's a lot to learn down here."

"Do you live in here?" I asked

He giggled. "No, that would be weird. I live in the tunnels and come here at night."

"Tunnels?"

"Yeah. There are miles of tunnels under these buildings. Looks like they were dug a hundred years ago. You can get most places in this city through the tunnels, if you want to."

"Doty, any chance you could show us how to get out of the building without anyone noticing?"

"Did you set off the alarms? Wait, are you robbing the museum? I don't want to help thieves."

Mac spoke gently to calm him. "We're not stealing anything. I work for a Senator, and Doc is an emergency physician. We came in to retrieve a notebook my brother hid in here with important information in it, and a woman tried to steal it from us at gun point. We just need to escape."

Doty pondered the story for only a moment before deeming it plausible. "Sure. Follow me, but it has to be our secret."

"Thank you. Your secret is safe with us. Please lead the way."

Banshee strolled beside him, and Mac leaned in to whisper to me as we followed.

"Are we really gonna trust this guy?"

"We have no better option."

"You think he could be dangerous?"

"I doubt it. He seems fairly stable and clear headed, in that he seems to want to connect with us, even though he has chosen a unique lifestyle. Let's see where he takes us."

Up ahead, Doty continued his animated walk with occasional skips and frequent looks back to make sure we were following. He moved confidently through the hallways and stopped in front of a room labeled as a janitor's closet. He proudly pointed at the door, as if welcoming us to a mansion. He opened the door with a flourish to reveal a standard eight-by-eight-foot janitor's room.

"What do you think?" he asked.

I took in the shelves of cleaning supplies, mops, buckets, brooms, and an oversized sink that crammed the small room. "It's a very nice janitor's room," I offered.

"Yes, but it's also a portal to another world. Come on, I'll show you."

Doty pushed to the back of the room and pointed to a vent about five feet above the floor. "The portal. Come on. Let's go."

Mac looked at me dubiously, as Herodotus loosened the latch that held the grate in place. He set it on the ground and motioned for us to enter. Mac pulled out her flashlight and shined it down the tunnel, about four feet wide and tall, too small to walk in, but not too claustrophobic.

"It looks like a bigger room after about ten feet," she said, as she crawled into the tunnel.

Banshee leapt after her, and I followed. The tunnel was formed of packed, dry dirt, smooth from passages over time, I imagined. Behind me, I heard Doty climb in and reset the grate. A short crawl later, I jumped into a large open area. Mac shined the light around, as Banshee explored. Artwork in geometric designs and intricate patterns covered most of the walls. It must have taken thousands of hours to paint the detail.

Doty hopped down from the tunnel and picked up a flashlight from a ledge nearby. "Do you like it? I call this room The Cathedral."

"It's beautiful. Did you do all this?" Mac asked.

"Yeah. I like to paint in my free time. Helps me think."

"Where do you get the supplies?"

"I borrow some from the museum. Their conservation room has thousands of gallons of paint. I figured they wouldn't miss a few cans."

"Do you ever take the exhibits?"

"No. Never. Those are treasures. I study them, but I never take them. I take only supplies I need to survive, food and batteries, the occasional can of paint or piece of abandoned clothing. Never anything valuable. Come on, let me show you the rest of the place."

CHAPTER THIRTY-ONE

Saturday, March 21
10:03 p.m.

Upstairs, Agent Duff restored order by sharing enough details to convince the other agencies of his ongoing investigation. They agreed that the Office of Protective Services would lead the investigation and that officers from Homeland would provide support. Agent Duff met his team in the early American History hall.

"What do we know?" he asked.

"Looks like someone broke into this exhibit. We've reached a curator to discover what's missing. We should have an answer in a few minutes. An altercation of some kind happened over here. You can see the blood trail that we're tracking and where the single gunshot struck that exhibit over there."

"Conclusions?"

"Someone broke into this exhibit, where a fight with a gunshot ensued, and at least one person is injured. No idea how many people were involved."

"What about the cameras?"

"They conveniently malfunctioned during the critical time. We assume someone had a local electromagnetic blocker, which implies sophistication."

"I know Mac and Doc were involved, and they may be injured."

The curator arrived with a list of the exhibit's contents. After a tedious examination of the exhibit, he confirmed that nothing was missing.

Agent Duff shook his head. "Why the hell would they break in and not take anything?"

"Maybe they were interrupted before they could."

"It's possible. Let's move every piece of this exhibit to our labs for processing."

"That's gonna piss off some museum people."

"They'll get it all back. I want every page of every journal scanned for messages from Mark. Let's get to work."

Agent Duff stormed off to check on the blood trail.

.   .   .

Doty led us through a tunnel lined with ancient brick and stone, crumbling in places, but seemingly sturdy. The complex patterns covered every reachable surface. The tunnel terminated in another room, clearly his living quarters, with a gray mattress in the corner covered by a thin, brown blanket. The neatly made bed had two stained pillows in a straight line along the top. A few dishes and food supplies sat neatly stacked on a shelf next to the bed.

A small desk and chair occupied the opposite corner. Next to it, hundreds of books crammed a sagging wood shelving unit. I approached to read the titles, all history books, many of them well perused. Doty lit candles scattered around the room as he talked.

"Make yourself at home. I'd offer you something to eat, but I'm a little low on food at the moment."

"Thank you. This is a pretty impressive setup. How long have you been down here?"

"No idea. I don't worry about time these days."

We sat on the floor, and Mac pulled our sandwiches from her bag, handing one to Doty, while she and I shared the other. He happily accepted the offering and sat down across from us. Banshee curled up beside him, and he gently pet him, as he ate the sandwich.

"Doty, how did you end up here?" I asked.

He finished his sandwich before answering. "I used to be a history professor at Georgetown on track for tenure. My area of expertise was early American history, focusing on government formation after the revolution. Most school books have it all wrong. They tell a story of a bunch of geniuses forming the perfect system, but the truth is messier. They were neither geniuses nor heroes. Hell, some weren't even good men, but their system worked.

"Life was great. My classes were full; my colleagues respected me; and at home, I had the most beautiful, intelligent wife any man could wish for. Paula was perfect. She was a grade school teacher, kind, loved kids, and pregnant with our first child."

Fog seemed to spread across Doty's eyes. "Toilet paper. It all changed because of so trivial a thing as toilet paper. We ran out, and Paula went to the store only two blocks away. We had perfect weather that day, so she decided to walk."

"An SUV ran a red light and plowed over her on the crosswalk. Security camera footage showed that it never even slowed down. He may not have even realized that he'd hit her. He totaled the car three blocks later, and his lab tests came back full of cocaine, methamphetamines, and alcohol. He suffered only a broken wrist."

"He left my perfect Paula broken on the pavement. In only an instant, our lives were shattered, because of a crackhead and an empty toilet paper roll. I can't remember the funeral. I fell apart. I stopped going to work and answering the phone. Eventually, I lost our house and lived one breath at a time on the streets. I learned about the tunnels and found this little hideaway. Later, I discovered the entrance to the museum, and its history drew me in. I found their reference book section and slowly acquired my little library over there. Now I escape in them here in peace and quiet."

"I'm so sorry. Thank you for sharing your story," Mac said.

"Thanks. I went through some dark times," he mused.

"How did you come up with the name Herodotus?"

"He's a hero of mine and widely considered the father of history. He was the first to document the histories of Greece, Western Asia, and Egypt about three thousand years ago."

"Do you ever go outside?"

"Of course. I enjoy fresh air and sunshine on nice days, but I can do without people, too many tourists, and too much noise. I've found serenity down here. Now, how did you guys end up down here?"

"That's a long story," Mac said.

"Fortunately, I have enough free time to hear it."

Mac began with the death of her brother and engaged in a detailed description of what had led us to this point. I sat in the scarred, wooden chair at his desk and noticed the papers and notebooks arranged neatly on the surface. Doty nodded his assent for me to peruse them, as he listened to Mac.

The notes in his neat, crisp handwriting clearly referenced his source material. They covered a variety of topics related to the early formation of the American government. I knew little about the subject, but I did know something about research. His high quality, well-organized notes allowed me to glimpse the collegiate professor he had been. I returned the notebooks to their neat stacks on the desk, as Mac finished her tale.

"Damn, that's the most interesting story I've heard in a while. Tangles with DARPA, Russian agents, DHS agents, and national secrets led to a secret notebook and a rock hidden in the Smithsonian. What's your next step?"

"I need to sleep, and then I need to see what's in the notebook."

"You're welcome to rest here, if you want. I was gonna do some more painting. It calms me and helps me think. No one will bother you here."

Doty wandered away, and Mac turned to me. "This is surreal, hanging out in secret tunnels with the smartest homeless man in America. Am I dreaming?"

"Not yet. Let's get some sleep while we can and evaluate what Mark left you in the morning. Banshee will watch over us."

Mac grabbed one pillow, and I took the other, as we sought comfort on the mattress. We ended up back to back, and exhaustion overwhelmed our awkward discomfort, as we both fell asleep. I knew that Banshee would rest at the foot of the bed with both ears perked up.

CHAPTER THIRTY-TWO

Sunday, March 22
8:11 a.m.

I awoke disoriented an unknown time later, feeling Mac's warmth still snuggled against my back. With grogginess like heavy fog persisting in my mind, I looked around to discover the source of rustling noises to see Mac seated at the desk, absorbed in the journal by candlelight, which made no sense, as she felt so warm against me. Comprehension crept through my sleepy brain. I hoped to find Banshee, but a glance over my shoulder confirmed Doty's peaceful slumber next to me. I extricated myself from the blanket and joined Mac.

"You two were so cute together. I didn't want to wake you," she whispered.

"Thanks. Spooning with a guy named Herodotus was not on my bingo card for the year. Have you learned anything?"

"I figured out what Mark was up to. This journal documents his thoughts on the project over the last three years. It contains no actual research, only his personal notes of his journey. It all started about ten million years ago, when this gal fell into some amber."

Mac held the amber close to a flame, and light flickered through the faceted stone, sending golden patterns across the room. The stone encased the perfectly preserved body of an insect.

"Meet Tammy, a queen among her colony at the time. She is a member of a termite species that has survived intact over the last ten million years. Most importantly, Tammy carried some eggs when she fell into the amber."

"Why is that so important?"

"Because Mark figured out a way to extract DNA from her eggs."

"Mark collected ten-million-year-old DNA from a termite queen?"

"Yep. Through a complicated process not documented here, he isolated a complete set of DNA from the specimen. He used a laser to access it. You can see the hole here, if you look closely."

She rotated the amber and pointed to a tiny scratch on its surface. Peering more closely, I could be convinced of a hole, but I never would have noticed it on my own.

"Okay, so your brother was able to isolate ten-million-year-old DNA from Queen Tammy. Was he planning to bring her back to life to terrorize the world?"

"No. You've been watching too much bad science fiction. Besides, there's no need for that. Tammy's species still thrives in the Dominican Republic."

"I have to ask. Why are we being hunted by Russians and DHS agents for Tammy's DNA?"

"It's what he did with it that's cool. He compared it to a sample from a modern queen and studied exactly how they evolved over about a quarter million generations. Evolution is constant, but we need multiple generations to see its effects. Ten million years is the largest sample size ever collected in terms of number of generations and time between samples, truly a unique opportunity to discover evolution."

"I thought Darwin discovered evolution."

"Let me clarify. Darwin first described evolution, but Mark took it a step further to quantify evolution. He reduced the changes in the genome over time to a complex mathematical formula. Don't you see what he did?"

Her excited eyes flashed. "I'm just a doctor. What am I missing?"

"These formulas he discovered define DNA changes over time. Although he discovered them from past samples, the formula could be applied to future ones. Right now, gene therapy is limited to adding and deleting genes from the genome. This formula would allow someone to evolve genes manually thousands or even millions of generations into the future. We could make changes in a lab that would take Mother Nature millions of years. We could modify any gene and reinsert it into the genome via a viral vector."

The implications dawned on me. "You're talking about gene modification on a scale never before conceived. We could use this to cure genetic diseases. This could be the greatest medical advancement ever. We could eliminate most cancers and autoimmune diseases."

"True, but we could also evolve genes to make them more malignant and release it via a viral vector, too. If that gene were specific to a particular racial or ethnic group, it would affect only that population. Entire groups of people could be wiped out with this technology."

"You're talking about biological genocide."

"Yes. You could also dramatically evolve a human to give that person exceptional strength and intelligence. You could create an army of super humans that would dominate existing people. The potential weaponization of his research terrified Mark, which is why he kept it so secret."

"That's why the Russians and DHS are so desperate to have it. Whoever controls it would have a huge strategic advantage. They could evolve a gene to kill their enemies, and let them know about it. The mere threat of releasing it would ensure compliance. It would be the ultimate weapon. So where is his research?"

"He left me another clue at the end of his journal."

I held the amber against a candle's flame. "Who would have guessed that clumsy Queen Tammy's falling into amber ten million years ago would lead to this extraordinary problem. Why did he name her Tammy, anyway?"

"It's short for Timeless Across Many Million Years. He had only one chance at obtaining the sample. The process to remove it destroyed any remaining DNA. Now, it's just a pretty paper weight."

"What are you going to do?"

"Solve his final clue. Here, look at the last page."

She passed the journal to me. The neat handwriting said, "Last clue, I promise. Good luck and luv ya," followed by two numbers:

125638742048903125

4665631251438742049

"How do we know this is really the last clue?" I asked.

"Rules of the game. Mark always announced the last clue and never cheated on it."

"Any ideas on this one?"

"The math is clear, but the meaning confuses me."

"Care to explain the math clue to the simpletons in the room?"

"Sure. It's a substitution code. One to the first power is one. Two squared is two times two, which equals four. Three cubed is three times three times three, which equals 27. We just break down the code to the base numbers. Here is the first number."

She grabbed a piece of blank paper and wrote out the numbers as she explained.

$1 = 1$

$256 = 4$ to the fourth power

$387420489 = 9$ to the ninth power

$0 = 0$

$3125 = 5$ to the fifth power

"So the first number is 14905."

"The lady is pretty smart." Doty's voice startled us. He had crept up behind us while Mac explained.

"How much of our conversation did you overhear?" Mac asked.

"All of it, I think. These stone walls don't exactly absorb sound. Your brother figured out how to quantify evolution from a ten-million-year-old termite named Queen Tammy, and now you got the Feds and the Russkies after you, and your brother did some fancy math for a final clue. Did I miss anything?"

"No. That about sums it up."

"Back to the clue," I refocused. "You explained the first number. What about the second number?"

"Do the math and you come up with 65129."

"Okay, so now we have 14905 and 65129. What do those mean?"

"They're ordinary numbers with no special properties. I have no idea what they mean."

"What's the next step?" I asked.

"We need to get topside, and I need a long, hot shower and a change of clothes. I'll figure it out eventually."

I'm getting a bit ripe myself. "What do we do with the journal?"

Mac clutched the journal lovingly and turned to Doty. "Can I trust you with this? It's one of the last things my brother left me. I would like it back when this is all over."

"You can trust me. I'll take care of it."

"How will I contact you to get it back?"

"I'm usually outside when the weather is good, especially in the morning. I'll show you where to look for me when we leave the tunnels."

"Speaking of which, we should get going. The Feds are gonna want to know where we were last night." I pointed out.

Mac thought for a moment. "Lets tell them the truth. We spent the night together. C'mon, let's move."

Mac dropped the amber into her purse, and Doty led us to what appeared to be a dead end and motioned us to be silent and to turn off our lights. He slid aside a pile of rubble which turned out to be on surprisingly silent rails, and we slipped through the opening. He slid the rail back, and the rubble looked like the other piles of debris in the larger tunnel. He secured a latch at the bottom of the pile.

"Clever," I said.

"Took a while to build, but worth the effort. I can latch it from either side, so it stays locked all the time. It gives me some privacy and security. This way."

Doty confidently led us through the tunnel. We passed a few people sprawled along the sides, but they ignored us. "People down here keep to themselves," he said.

After a few minutes, we arrived at a door with a disabled lock. Doty pushed through the door to a service tunnel that connected to the metro station. Mac turned on her electromagnetic blocker to disable any cameras in the station. A short walk later, we stood on the platform of the Smithsonian Metro station. Doty took the escalator with us to the National Mall.

"I can't thank you enough for everything you did for us. You probably saved our lives, or at least, kept us from getting arrested. If there's ever anything I can do for you, please let me know," Mac said.

"I'm grateful for the opportunity to help. Last night was the most interesting I've experienced in a while. Take care of yourselves. Look for me up here when you want your journal back. I'll keep it safe."

We watched him thoughtfully stroll toward the Lincoln Memorial.

"If I didn't have Queen Tammy in my purse, I'd think this whole thing was a dream."

"It'll become a nightmare as soon as our phones are back in service. Agent Duff will be all over us. Do you think over or under ten minutes until he finds us after we turn our phones back on?"

"I'll take the under. He's probably anxious about our falling off the grid last night."

We bought breakfast tacos and coffee for her and a Diet Coke for me from a food truck, and rested on a bench to enjoy them. Mac pulled our phones out of the Faraday bag and turned them on. She set her timer and bit into her second taco.

CHAPTER THIRTY-THREE

Sunday, March 22
8:57 a.m.

The technician immediately noticed the phone on his priority watchlist going live with another phone hitting two seconds later. He promptly alerted Agent Duff with location data. The closest units scrambled against light Sunday morning traffic to find the subjects. In his car with lights flashing, Duff felt angrily determined to reach the Mall before they disappeared. They had been completely off the grid for over eighteen hours, which was nearly impossible in a town with as many cameras as Washington.

The first agents had eyes on the subjects within five minutes and reported their leisurely breakfast on the Mall, as they laughed on a bench with the dog stretched out at their feet. Duff turned off his lights, double parked, and rushed across the dewy grass to stand in front of them. Mac stopped her timer and held up her phone.

"Eleven minutes. I'm disappointed. I bet that you would be here in less than ten," Mac informed him.

Sighing, Agent Duff sat down at the other end of the bench. "If it's any consolation, my guys had you in about five minutes."

"That's solid work. What can I do for you, Agent Duff, breakfast taco?"

"Don't mind if I do, thank you. We had a long night looking for you two. I don't suppose you want to let me in on what you were up to?"

"Doc and I wanted some quiet time together, so we went to the museum and then spent the night together. We turned off our phones for privacy and found a quiet hotel."

"I don't suppose you remember the name of the hotel?"

"I can't recall. It was a spontaneous choice."

He looked at our rumpled clothing and made a show of looking under the bench. "Forget your overnight bags?"

"As I said, it was spontaneous. We didn't pack anything."

Agent Duff wiped sauce from his upper lip and stared at us. "Really strange. Yesterday, we had you at the museum, but then you disappeared at the same time the cameras went offline, coincidentally."

"That is odd. I hope their system is working again."

"That brings me to another strange story. Last night after hours, someone broke into the museum, right where you two disappeared the day before."

"That's awful. I hope nothing was taken."

"Someone broke into a specific exhibit, but nothing is missing."

"I guess it's not technically a robbery if nothing is missing," I observed.

"Shut up, dipshit. I'm about to search you right here on the Mall."

"What exactly would you be looking for, Agent Duff? The objects that weren't stolen?" Mac asked.

Agent Duff seethed behind his intense gaze. "Museum security reported a gunshot, and we found blood at the scene. You wouldn't know anything about that would you?"

"I'm sure I would remember a shooting. As I said, we enjoyed a quiet evening together last night."

He watched us intently, as he finished the taco. "Let's cut the bullshit. I don't know how you did it, but you were in that museum last night, and I'm pretty sure you found something related to Mark's research. Given the gunshot and blood, and that none of my people were there, our Russian friends must have caught up with you. You need to come clean with me before more people die, specifically you. Tell me what you know."

Mac held his gaze. "Sorry we can't help. We don't know anything about malfunctioning security cameras, museum robberies, or gunfights. We had a quiet night together and breakfast here on the Mall."

Agent Duff stood and threw his taco wrapper in the trash can. "Dangerous people are after that information, and I can't protect you when you disappear like that. I'm not gonna waste time proving that your story about last night is bullshit. We both know you were in the museum last night. After this is all over, I'd appreciate your explanation. For now, watch your back. Thanks for breakfast."

He stormed off without a glance back. "That went well, but we learned nothing new," I observed.

"We learned that the Russian woman got away last night. They didn't find her."

"True. I hope she had a miserable night."

.   .   .

Alina's night had indeed been miserable. She had curled up behind the stuffed crocodiles and fell into a fitful sleep. A few hours later, two security guards cursorily searched the room, walking down each aisle with their flashlights. They overlooked her among the thousands of exhibits and cleared the room after only a few minutes. Alina managed to fall back into a restless sleep.

She had awakened stiff and thoroughly annoyed. Her back had not appreciated the hard surface, and her wrist throbbed painfully. She could only imagine the bacteria crawling through the wound. She needed to get it cleaned and begin antibiotics before her hand started to rot. She hated dogs.

Her departure had been unremarkable. She found a break room down the hall, donned an abandoned white coat, and swiped a clipboard. No one she passed took notice of her, as she flashed friendly smiles and brief greetings. She found a stairwell and climbed to the main level, dropped the coat and clipboard in the stairwell, and walked into the main hall to mingle with tourists. A few minutes later, she stepped out the front door and hailed a taxi. She would see a doctor first and deal with the director. Then she would handle Doc, Mac, and that fucking dog.

CHAPTER THIRTY-FOUR

Sunday, March 22
11:22 a.m.

Mac felt renewed after a shower. She dressed in a casual sweater and slacks for a weekend visit to her office. She had nothing scheduled, but she was sure to have messages and emails to address and wanted to get a head start on her work week.

Only a few staffers occupied the relatively quiet halls of the Hart Building. Mac unlocked the Senators' office, finding it blissfully vacant and silent. She locked the door behind her, started a pot of coffee, and began to dispense with her emails. She hoped to catch up on them within a couple hours.

An hour into her work, a key turned in the lock, and the Senator stepped in. Like Mac, she had dressed casually in jeans and a sweatshirt bearing the California state flag.

Mac stood to greet her. "Senator, I didn't expect you in today."

The Senator waved her to her seat. "Relax. I was in the area and just need to grab a file. What are you working on?"

"Catching up on messages and emails to clear them before tomorrow."

"Efficient, as always. I heard you had some excitement on the Mall yesterday."

"Not much. Someone grabbed my purse, but we got it back."

The Senator focused on Mac before sitting across from her. "A Russian agent with diplomatic immunity took off with a Senatorial Chief of Staff's purse on the Mall, and your friend's police dog stopped him. Seems awfully drastic, don't you think?"

"I was certainly surprised."

"Would the Russians have found anything interesting in your purse or phone?"

"I doubt it, unless they care what lipstick I use. I carry nothing important in my purse."

The Senator's eyes intensified to a withering look that made most people nervous, but Mac steadily returned her gaze. "Mac, you know it's critical for us to find Mark's work before the Russians do, and it's important that I get it before those idiots at Homeland. I can make sure it gets into the right hands."

Mac summoned her courage. "Who are the right people, Senator? Why do you want it before Homeland?"

The Senator leaned back composedly, although momentarily shocked by Mac's unprecedented challenge. "I know this is personal, as it is your brother's life's work, but it could change the world. If it gets to the right people, it can change society for the better, and that's of course what I want. Now, what have you learned? Do you know where we can find it?"

Mac had never withheld information from the Senator, but something was off. For the first time, the Senator appeared desperate, which Mac had never seen from her. "I'm sorry, Senator. I still have no idea what he was working on or where his research is."

"What about these clues he left you?"

"All dead ends so far. I'm still at square one."

The Senator appraised her for a few moments before standing. "I hope it is clear how important this is. I expect immediate updates on any developments, and I will not tolerate disloyalty. If you want to continue in this office, you will get that information for me."

The Senator swiped a file from her desk and left without another glance at Mac, who stared in disbelief at the retreating figure. They had worked together for years on many stressful projects, but she had never seen the Senator act like this and certainly had never had her job threatened. Of course, she had never openly lied to the Senator, either. Mac went back to work, but her thoughts kept returning to the Senator.

·   ·   ·

Alina stood at attention before Director Petrov. Unlike Mac, she left nothing out. The penalty for withholding information from the Director would be much greater than the loss of her job. She stood silently and awaited his response.

"This operation is of utmost importance, and we are failing. This is unacceptable. Nikolai failed to obtain her purse, and you, an armed agent of Directorate S, were unable to subdue two civilians and a dog. This is an embarrassment to this department and to Russia. Your incompetence cannot be tolerated."

The Director pondered his options for a full long minute. Finally, he reached in a drawer and pulled out a single bullet that he placed upright on the middle of his desk. "You have one more chance, Alina. I want that information on my desk within forty-eight hours. If you fail, I will personally fire this bullet into the back of your head. Dismissed."

Alina exhaled a sigh of relief, as she walked out of the office. She had a bullet with her name on it, but she had been given time to resolve the issue. She would not fail again.

·   ·   ·

After a shower and lunch, Banshee and I ambled to the emergency room, enjoying the beautiful weather. I looked forward to seeing how

John was doing and found him speaking with a patient in the Doctor's area of the emergency room.

"Dr. Pastone, I don't think it's safe to take this antibiotic with my cholesterol medication."

"It's perfectly safe. They don't interact with each other."

"That's not what I heard. Someone on my Facebook group had a friend who took antibiotics and a cholesterol pill, and he had a heart attack and died."

I waited for John's head to explode, but to his credit, his voice remained calm. "Sir, I'm sorry that a friend of someone in your Facebook group died of a heart attack. He may have been taking antibiotics and cholesterol pills, but that doesn't mean that they caused his heart attack. He may have had chicken for dinner. Do you think that caused his heart attack?"

"Are you saying this medicine isn't safe to take with chicken?"

I hurried away before I burst out in laughter. Shaking his head, John sat next to me a few minutes later.

"Is he going to take the antibiotics?" I asked.

"He decided it was probably safe, as long as he took them two hours apart with a dose of Echinacea in between, but he wants to confirm the plan with his Facebook group first."

"What the hell will the Echinacea do?"

"It won't do a damn thing, but if it gets him to take the antibiotic, then he can bathe in the stuff for all I care. Natural herbs and Facebook groups are gonna drive me to early retirement."

"How goes it on the business front?"

"Couldn't be better. I'm talking to seven different hospitals that want to move away from their current contracts. By next week, we could be one of the ten largest emergency medicine staffing companies in the country."

"Just make sure not to open up any extra bank accounts in The Caymans. I don't want to hear about your group on the news in the future."

"No worries there. We're gonna keep it clean and do it right, although I am taking one idea from their business model."

"Really?"

"Yep. Gonna name my new management company DGITR, LLC."

"Please tell me that stands for dumbest guys in the room."

A huge smile spread across his face. "Yes, sir. It'll be a reminder of how we got here. Thanks, again, for your help. We wouldn't even have this contract without your connections."

"I'm happy to help and glad that I have met a few interesting people along the way. Run the business well and that will be thanks enough for me."

"Excuse me, Doctor. Thanks for fixing me," a young girl smiled at John from the other side of the desk.

"Of course, Lola. I didn't need to fix anything. This is my friend, Doc. Show him why you're here today."

Lola opened her mouth and stuck out her tongue, revealing a pattern of smooth, red islands on the surface of the tongue.

"That's impressive. What did Dr. John tell you about that?"

"He told me it's called a geographic tongue, and no one knows what causes it, but it's not serious, and I don't need any medicine or shots. He said it makes ice cream taste better."

"I'm not sure about that last bit, but ice cream won't hurt it. Just to be on the safe side, I would try some ice cream today if I were you."

"Okay. Thank you. Bye!" Lola skipped down the hallway with a relieved dad in tow.

"For all the crazy and stressful shit we see in here, sometimes it's nice to tell a family that what they have is harmless and doesn't need treatment," John said.

"Agreed. I love prescribing ice cream. I'll let you get back to work. I'm gonna close out some charts before admin tracks me down, and then I'm out of here."

CHAPTER THIRTY-FIVE

Sunday, March 22
6:31 p.m.

Mac headed home, exhausted from the events of the weekend. She threw a frozen lasagna into the microwave and changed into sweatpants and an old, grey t-shirt, impossibly soft after years of wear. She curled up on the couch with her dinner and a glass of Chardonnay and contemplated her brother's last clue.

She still liked to pretend that Mark was alive and well. His journal and the clues he had left for her made her feel like he had been watching her, as she played his game, and she mentally pleaded with him to give her a hint. Two ordinary five-digit numbers led her nowhere.

She let the clue bounce around inside her head, as she sipped her wine. She knew that something would trigger the answer eventually and that she couldn't force it. She stretched out under a blanket with a good book and read until exhaustion overcame her. She dreamed of numbers with no answers.

.   .   .

Banshee noisily chewed a braided rawhide bone, as I climbed into bed. It had been a crazy ten days since Mark had whispered his last words to me. I wished I had known him at his best. People like him solved problems that the rest of us weren't even aware of. His use of ten-million-year-old termite DNA to cure cancer certainly qualified as thinking outside the box. His reduction of evolution to a mathematical formula seemed impossible to me. Then again, Einstein reduced the relationship between mass and energy to a simple formula.

I opened my book. Nothing clears my mind like an escape into a good thriller, and I was soon lost in a fictional world where anything is possible. I laughed at the main character's use of a flip phone to call his boss. Technology advanced quickly, and all books dated themselves when once new technology reached obsolescence. I finished a chapter and turned back to the title page to note the publication date of 1999. I set the book on my nightstand and turned off the lamp. In 1999, I had been in college trying to get into medical school and deciding which twenty contacts to store in my flip phone. Times had changed.

I closed my eyes and cleared my mind to enter that peaceful moment of semi-consciousness before sleep, the only time when active thought left me, and my brain could freely emit suppressed ideas. Dimly aware of a concept fighting its way to awareness, I allowed it to strengthen and burst forth, causing me to sit up and gasp.

Banshee, asleep on the floor beside the bed, sprung to his feet and growled, searching in vain for a threat.

"Relax, boy. Nothing's wrong. Come on up here."

Banshee hopped on the bed and lay next to me, still wary. I pet him and calmed him. "Relax. Everything's okay. I may have figured out the last clue. We'll check it tomorrow on a clean phone."

Banshee and I slept deeply throughout the night.

CHAPTER THIRTY-SIX

Monday, March 23
6:48 a.m.

I woke up early and went for a four-mile jog with Banshee. On the way home, I stopped at the hospital. I had a theory and couldn't trust my own electronic devices with the DHS and Russians monitoring me. I ran into Greg, a nurse starting his shift.

"Morning, Doc. You here on business or pleasure?"

"Just out for a jog. Mind if I borrow your phone? My battery died."

"Sure thing. Here you go."

I opened a browser and entered the information I had figured out last night. On the fourth try, the answer popped up, and I silently cheered, as I closed the browser and returned the phone.

"You seem happy. You get some good news from my phone, Doc?"

"I did, Greg. Thanks for letting me use it. Have a good shift."

I walked outside and called Mac on my phone, which did not have a battery problem.

"Morning, Doc. What's got you calling so early?"

"I wanted to see if you were free for lunch."

"I don't know. Mondays are crazy around here. Can it wait?"

"Yes, but I'm pretty sure you'll want to see me today."

"Can you give me a hint?"

"Not on a party line."

"Okay. I'll meet you out front of the Hart Building at 11:30. Gotta run."

I ended the call and jogged home with Banshee, wondering how many others would join us for lunch.

·   ·   ·

Alerted to the call, Agent Duff lined up a team to follow them. At the Russian embassy, Alina learned about the call a few minutes later. She planned to follow them, too, while avoiding the DHS agents sure to be nearby. She donned a new look for the meeting.

·   ·   ·

A few minutes late, Mac found Banshee and I resting on a bench under a humid, sunny sky. Mac sat beside me and showered Banshee with praise and ear scratches. He leaned into her.

"What's the big mystery, Doc?"

I handed her my phone and pointed to her bag. She placed it in her Faraday bag next to her own, sealed it, and turned to me, raising her eyebrows.

"I solved the last clue."

"How the fuck did you manage that?" I don't think the competitive side of Mac was used to coming in second.

"On a whim, I checked the publication date on a book I was reading last night. I turned off the light, and it hit me. Right below the publication date is the book's ID number."

"The International Standard Book Number," Mac breathed.

"That's it. The ISBN number, a ten-digit unique identifier of each book."

"So now we just need to look up the ISBN number."

"First, I combined the two numbers, and no book is associated with 1490565129, but if you reverse the second number, you get 1490592156, which does correspond to a book. Want to take a guess which one?"

"Not *Charlotte's Web*?"

"A great book, but no, it's the *Principia* by Sir Isaac Newton."

Mac sighed with a laugh. "Of course it is. Mark was always a fan of historical mathematicians, and Isaac Newton was a favorite. I'm not surprised that he chose the *Principia*, one of the most important books on math ever written."

"I'll have to trust you on that one. My reading list skipped over great math books."

"Surely you had to learn some math to be a doctor."

"Of course. I can convert pounds to kilograms."

"That puts you ahead of most Americans."

"Good to know. Now we just need to figure out what's in the book that's so important."

"I don't think the clue wants us to look at the writings of Isaac Newton. I think Mark wants us to look at a very specific copy of the *Principia*."

"How do we figure out which copy?"

"We walk about ten minutes in that direction. Come on."

Banshee leapt between us, as Mac abruptly started walking toward the Supreme Court Building. "As a tenacious researcher, Mark often consulted obscure texts. Luckily, we're right next to the largest library on the world, The Library of Congress."

We rounded the front of the Supreme Court Building, and I got my first look at the Library of Congress, and I stopped to admire the details as Mac assumed her role as tour guide. "This is one of three buildings on Capitol Hill, the Thomas Jefferson Building. At the foot of the stairs you have a fountain showing King Neptune, the Roman god of the sea, and his court. Above the first floor window you see thirty-three ethnological heads carved above each window. These represent different ethnic races, from Arab to Zulu. Above the second floor windows are the busts of nine great men chosen by the first librarian. My favorite is the bust of Dante."

"It's appropriate for Dante to be here. This quest has visited some of the circles of hell."

"Hopefully we won't visit all the way to the ninth level."

"Won't the agents be following us?" I asked.

"Yes, but there's a separate entrance for researchers, and I'm betting they don't have access. I do. We can get in quickly and lose them inside. The place is a giant maze."

We wove through the tourists mingling on the patio in front of the building to a small door labeled Authorized Personnel Only. I followed Mac inside to face a security guard and a metal detector. He asked for her pass, and the lights turned green after he scanned it. He gave it back to her and asked for my ID, which he scanned into the system. My license resulted in no green lights, but he printed badges for both of us authorizing access to the library.

"What's with the dog? Only service dogs are allowed in the library."

"He is a service dog."

"Looks more like a guard dog, but he's fine to go through. Just keep him on a leash."

We passed through the metal detector and entered the library.

CHAPTER THIRTY-SEVEN

Monday, March 23
11:57 a.m.

Outside, DHS agents huddled together to form a plan. The move to access the Library had surprised them. They decided two agents would follow through the employee door, but they would wait a few minutes to escape the notice of Doc and Mac. The other two agents would use the main door and try to locate them. Once inside, everyone would split up to search for them, maintaining contact by radio.

Nearby, a frustrated Alina clenched her teeth, as she watched them enter the Library through the restricted door. She would have to enter through the main doors and search for them. Dressed as a tourist, she scanned the crowd for a victim, choosing a woman who showed her pass to her friends before tucking it back into her purse, which she failed to close. After a mild bump and a mumbled "excuse me," Alina obtained a pass to enter the Library.

• • •

I stood in awe as I looked up at the domed ceiling of the main reading room, impossibly large and far away. Eight giant marble columns around the room supported ten-foot-high female figures representing the characteristic features of civilized life and thought. Sixteen bronze statues lined the balustrade of the galleries, memorializing men whose lives epitomized the thought and activity represented by the larger statues. Reading stations lined the floor in a circular pattern, half of them occupied.

Mac smiled as she watched my reaction. "It can be a bit overwhelming at first."

"These statues are incredible."

"If you look up there, you will see our old friend Herodotus, commemorating the field of history."

"I want to grab a book, curl up in one of those chairs and just read for a day."

"I can arrange that, but we probably need to keep moving. Our friends are going to catch up to us soon."

Mac walked directly to the information desk and showed her pass. "Would you help me, please? I'm from Senator Whiteside's office and would like to see Newton's *Principia*."

"We are always happy to help. It's located in section QA803.A45, part of our rare book and special collections area. It's on the second floor."

Mac led the way upstairs, picking up her pace as she neared her goal. I struggled to keep up, as I looked at wonders in every direction. A glance out of one of the balconies overlooking the main reading room showed two of our agent friends scurrying across the floor. I hustled to catch up to Mac, who scanned the books to her left, as she walked down an aisle of bookshelves. She turned to me with a triumphant smile, as she reverently removed a book from the shelf.

"Here it is. Let's see what Mark left for me."

.   .   .

Alina slipped through security with her ceramic knife overlooked. She stopped to marvel at the voluminous books and shelves surrounding her and approached an information desk with her friendliest smile.

"Hi, I'm a math teacher from Iowa. Could you please point me in the direction of your famous math texts?" She planned to search Lawton's area of expertise first.

"Our math and science texts are located in that area." The librarian gestured toward a large wing full of books.

"Thank you so much. Where would the most famous ones by the greatest mathematicians be?"

"The second level."

Alina was already moving toward her prey.

.　　.　　.

Mac gently set the book down on the nearest table.

"That's a pretty big book. I hope we don't have to read the whole thing to find another clue," I said.

Mac pursed her lips and stared thoughtfully at the book. She gently turned pages, scanning the yellowed paper covered with words and diagrams. She turned to the final page and noted the number 590. With almost 600 pages of text and diagrams to review, she closed the book and stared at it, willing an answer.

"I guess we could start reading," I suggested.

"No. I've read it before. Newton didn't know anything about evolution when he wrote it, so the clue is not in his writing. It must be something hidden in the book." Mac checked the cover inside and out but noticed nothing unusual. "I guess we'll do it the hard way." She sat down and carefully turned each page after scanning the text. I sat down next to her, and Banshee sensed that we were staying awhile and collapsed under the table at my feet.

.　　.　　.

Alina had grown concerned that she had guessed the wrong area, when she heard voices quietly discussing a book. She peered around a corner to see Mac and Doc seated at a long table with a large, old book open in front of them. Mac slowly scanned each page. Alina wanted a closer look. She settled into the guise of an Iowan and strolled down the aisle, looking in wonder at all of the books on each side of her.

Doc briefly glanced at her with a polite nod and no hint of recognition. When he turned away, she focused on the book to read the title before continuing down the aisle and disappearing around a corner. She decided to wait until they found something before confronting them.

·   ·   ·

My attention wandered, as Mac continued her study of each page. I noticed a woman either from Iowa or who loved the state emblazoned across her sweatshirt. She smiled politely, as she passed, gazing in awe at all the books surrounding her.

Banshee tensed at her approach and growled. I reached down to calm him. Trained to ignore people, Banshee alarmed me, and we both watched the tourist disappear around a tall, loaded bookshelf. He laid his head back down, but kept staring in her direction.

"What's the matter, boy? You don't like the way people from Iowa smell?"

Banshee ignored me and repositioned himself to face the direction the tourist had gone. He laid his head back down, but his ears were perked up, watching for any sign of danger.

Mac inhaled sharply, hurriedly closed the book, and turned to me with radiant eyes. She leaned to whisper to me. "Mark left his final message within these pages."

She gave me a brief side hug. "We only have one shot at this. Mark liked to write clues in light sensitive, disappearing ink. I think he used that ink here."

"Can't you just take a picture of it?"

"Not with our compromised phones. I'll memorize it before it disappears."

"Can you do that?"

Mac flashed a killer smile. "I wasn't as smart as Mark, but I can do it. After I open it, please don't distract me."

Mac found the page and opened the book. Over her shoulder, I saw a piece of paper tucked into the binding over the original page. The handwriting at the top read, "Mac, If you're reading this, something terrible has happened. It's up to you to decide what to do with this information. Love, Mark."

The rest of his message contained ten lines of complex mathematical sentences. Mac intensely focused on the equations, as I watched her.

· · ·

Alina couldn't decipher what they said, but their excited whispers sounded like they had found something. She watched them, hunched over the book. She slid the ceramic knife from her waistband and treaded silently to the end of the row of shelves. Adopting an air of indifference, she sauntered to within a few feet of them, lunged at Mac, pressed the knife to her throat, and whispered, "Stay quiet, or she dies."

CHAPTER THIRTY-EIGHT

Monday, March 23
12:36 p.m.

Banshee growled, but I reacted too late. The friendly tourist from Iowa held a knife to Mac's throat.

"Stay quiet, or she dies."

I held up my hands in surrender. Beside me, Mac slowly closed the book in front of her and laid her hands on the table. Still growling, Banshee stood next to me, calm but focused on high alert.

"I want to thank you two for finding this book for me. It's been a long chase."

"You plan to walk out of here with that book?" I asked.

"No, the princess will carry it out for me while you and your pet wait here. My knife will be against her liver. I already killed her brother. I have no qualms about sending her to join him. Stand up."

Mac stood slowly, furiously trembling in such close proximity to the demon who had murdered her twin. The woman expertly shifted the knife from her throat to her back and ordered Mac to pick up the book. Mac met my eyes with hopeful reassurance before looking at Banshee, who fixated on her, as she tapped her left forearm with three of her right fingers.

Banshee ferociously barked, shattering the silence of the library. His roar echoed off the vaulted ceiling and reverberated throughout the library, sounding as if an army of wild animals had conquered the building.

At the first instant of Banshee's scream, Mac, prepared for the startling cacophony, stomped her heel into the sensitive instep of her attacker and spun so quickly that the knife-wielding tourist had no time to react. Mac grabbed her wrist with the knife and threw two powerful punches into the woman's sternum. The woman dropped the knife and struggled to breathe. Mac kneed her chest, and she doubled over. In a blur of motion, Mac grabbed the back of her head and slammed it on her rising knee. Her grief and fury channeled her strength and crushed the woman's nose. Semiconscious, the attacker collapsed on the floor.

Mac's hands wrapped around her neck and squeezed. The now helpless woman's eyes widened in shock and fear.

Stunned much more by Mac's explosive violence than by Banshee's howls, I commanded his silence, though echoes continued to resonate. I reached out to Mac, gripping her upper arm and pulling her back.

"Mac, don't do this. It's not who you are."

"She killed Mark."

"She will face justice for that. Let go."

Mac regained control of herself and finally released her. Mark's killer drew a deep breath and started to sit up, but I pushed her back. "Sit still until the authorities come. GUARD."

Banshee towered over her with teeth bared over a low growl. "If you sit still, he won't attack. If you try to get up, he will subdue you." I turned away from her and kicked the knife under the table. The woman stared at the snarling beast inches from her face.

"Are you okay?" I asked Mac.

"I think so."

"Let me take a look at your side. You have some bleeding there."

Surprised to see the spreading blood stain on her shirt, Mac said she hadn't even noticed the wound.

"Under stress, your body releases adrenaline, which masks pain. Nice move with Banshee. His barking startled even me."

"I remembered the command and hoped he would obey it coming from me."

"That means he trusts you. Congrats, you're part of his pack." I lifted the back of her shirt to inspect the wound. "Nothing serious. You have about a one-inch, clean cut, nothing a few stitches can't repair, and you'll have a little scar to commemorate this day." I put some pressure on the wound with the loose fabric of her shirt to slow the bleeding.

"Thanks for pulling me off her. I would have killed her. Not that she doesn't deserve it, but I'm glad I didn't. Her casual admission that she killed Mark sparked a fire that engulfed me. I couldn't think straight." Mac, shaken by her own behavior, sat down in the nearest chair.

"Sit tight. I think a lot of people will be here momentarily."

·   ·   ·

The Library had frozen at the sounds of Banshee's barking, but after several seconds, visitors streamed for the exits, and employees and security converged on the disturbance. DHS agents, among the first to arrive, found Banshee standing over a bloodied woman, while Mac sat exhausted in her bloody blouse. I addressed the agents with my hands clearly open in front of me.

"You can put the guns down. The woman on the ground admitted her responsibility for the murder of Mark Lawton and threatened to kill Mac. Please call Agent Duff to help us out."

The agent seemed happy to pass the mess up the chain of command. He briefly summarized our situation on his radio. "Duff said he'll be here in fifteen minutes. No one leaves before then." The DHS agents pushed back staff and other onlookers. I called Banshee to my side, and he sat between me and Mac.

The DHS agents sat our attacker up and cuffed her. With their permission, I approached to check on her before an ambulance arrived.

"My name's Doc, and I'm gonna take a quick look at your face, if that's all right."

"I know who you are. I am Alina Morozova, and I have diplomatic immunity."

"Congrats on the immunity. I want to make sure you are stable for transport to the hospital." She was neurologically intact and not at risk of losing her airway. She probably had some fractured ribs and possibly a broken foot, and her face required surgery, but she was not in imminent danger. I wondered at her history, given her calm ability to take that kind of beating.

I sat down at the table next to Mac, and she quietly opened the book and perused Mark's note. She held my hand under the table and squeezed it, as she stared at the equations. I watched the ink fade into disappearance, and Mac serenely closed the book.

As we awkwardly awaited Agent Duff, an eerie silence enveloped us, broken only by Alina's noisy breathing through her mouth and Banshee's contented panting.

Agent Duff interrupted our individual reveries with six more agents behind him. One was a medic who began a more thorough assessment of Alina, as Agent Duff sat across from us. "Looks like the two of you had quite the morning. Care to explain all of this?"

I looked at Mac, and she nodded for me to share the whole story. When I mentioned that the book contained the final clue, Agent Duff interrupted.

"You're saying Mark wrote his equations in that book? Show me."

Mac opened the book and turned it toward him. He stared in confusion. "What the fuck is this? It's a blank page."

Mac continued the story. "Mark used an ink that fades with exposure to light. The longer the exposure, the more it fades."

"Please tell me you got a picture of the message before it disappeared."

"Unfortunately, no. Since certain government agencies have tapped into our phones, I didn't think it was safe to take a picture."

"What did the message say?"

"Mark said it was up to me what to do with his research, and then he listed his calculations. Unfortunately, that Russian witch over there interrupted us, and I didn't get a chance to copy them. I'm afraid the research is gone."

Agent Duff simmered. "It can't be gone. Surely you can duplicate his work. I need that information."

"Agent Duff, it took Mark years to unveil his discovery. I doubt I could recreate his work, even if I had decades to try. I'm not sure humanity could be trusted with it, anyway. Regardless of our philosophies, this matter is concluded, except for her prosecution for the murder of my brother."

Agent Duff fumed, staring helplessly at the blank page. He slammed the book shut and turned to Alina. The medics had cleaned the blood from her face to reveal her confident sneer.

"Alina, is it? I have you on the assault of Ms. Lawton, and I'm pretty sure your blood will place you at the Smithsonian the other night. I don't have you on Mark's murder yet, but I'm sure we can get there. Do you have anything to say for yourself?" Agent Duff asked.

"I am Alina Morozova, citizen of Russia, and I have diplomatic immunity. I demand to be released to my embassy immediately."

"Do you have a diplomatic passport on your person?"

"No."

"Then sit tight while I make a call."

He called the Russian Embassy. "This is Agent Duff with the Department of Homeland Security. We have a woman in custody who claims diplomatic immunity, but she has no identification. She gave the name Alina Morozova. Please connect me with someone who can confirm or deny her legal status."

On hold to the accompaniment of a bad Tchaikovsky recording, a gruff voice came on the line. "How can I help you, Agent Duff?"

"To whom am I speaking, please?"

"This is Dmitry Petrov, legal attaché for the embassy. I understand you have one of our citizens in your custody, Ms. Alina Morozova."

Director Petrov used the cover of a legal attaché, but Agent Duff knew that he was speaking to the highest ranking Russian spy in the United States. "That is correct. She is claiming diplomatic immunity."

"May I inquire as to the reason she is in custody?"

"She used a knife to assaulted and threaten the life a senior congressional staffer to steal information vital to our national security."

"I am told she is a secretary for one of our trade ministers."

"Does she have diplomatic immunity?"

"Absolutely not. I am shocked to learn of these illegal actions she has perpetrated against a citizen of your country. I will leave her to your legal system. Please tell her that she left something on my desk, and if I ever see her again, I will make sure to give it to her."

"I'll pass on your message, and I hope that we can consider this matter closed."

"It would be best for both of our countries to move on from this misadventure. I will consider the matter of Comrade Morozova to be closed. Good day, Agent Duff."

He stood in front of Alina. "Director Petrov says that you are a secretary with no diplomatic immunity. He also said that he would not interfere with our prosecution of your crimes. He wants you to know that the last time you talked, you left something on his desk, and if he ever sees you again, he will be sure to give it to you."

Color drained from Alina's face, as she recalled the bullet. "I would like to speak with a lawyer."

"I am sure you would, but that right is guaranteed to American citizens, not to foreign nationals who attack them. Your activities, sanctioned or not, constitute a national security threat to this country, and therefore, you will be held and tried as a terrorist."

Alina continued to plead for immunity, as the agents led her from the library.

CHAPTER THIRTY-NINE

Monday, March 23
1:45 p.m.

"What will happen to her?" Mac asked Duff.

"We'll question her, and she can trade information for privileges, like outdoor exercise, but she'll be our guest for the rest of her life."

"Could she be swapped in a prisoner exchange and get away with Mark's murder?"

"I don't think so. The Russian on the phone is the senior spook in Washington, and he completely disavowed her and promised to execute her, if he gets the chance. Failure carries severe consequences in Russia."

"They can just send someone else after us," I pointed out.

"I don't think you have to worry about that. They tried and failed, well aware that Homeland has recovered whatever Alina fought to take. They're more likely to cut their losses, because from their perspective, our government got the information before their agent could. You have nothing more to offer them, which brings me to the question of what to do with you two."

"We have done nothing wrong," Mac asserted.

"You've been hiding information from me since the beginning."

"Agent Duff, I followed messages left by my brother per his dying wish. They were personal messages to me, and the government has no right to them. Besides, you would never have solved any of the clues, anyway. The only reason you know about this book is because we found it for you."

"Show me the page again."

Mac opened the book, and we stared at the blank page tucked inside. Agent Duff looked closely at it from different angles, but could not see even a hint of writing. "Please write down exactly what was on this page, every detail you can remember."

Mac recreated the note to the best of her ability. She completed the words at the top, but struggled with recalling the equations. She produced three lines of numbers, and those looked incomplete. She handed it to Duff with an apology.

"Sorry, that's all I can remember."

Duff looked at the symbols and shook his head. He had no idea what they meant, but strongly suspected their uselessness. "What about you, Doc? Remember anything Ms. Lawton doesn't?"

I didn't even have to lie. "I briefly saw the message, and the only numbers I understand in that book are the page numbers."

"We'll take the book back to the lab and see what the technicians can find."

"Stop right there, Mister. That book is not leaving this library." We all turned to face the speaker, a petite white-haired woman who tolerated no nonsense. She pushed her way through a couple of agents to face Agent Duff. Actually, she got into his chest as she stood barely five feet tall, but her finger was up in his face.

Agent Duff took a step back. "Who are you, ma'am?"

"I am Dr. Paolini, the head librarian here, and that book is under my care."

"Dr. Paolini, I understand that the book is important, but information with national security implications has been added to it."

Dr. Paolini turned her attention to the book and looked apoplectic. "Who marred this page in our book?"

"My brother did, to hide critical information. He was shot and killed over it."

"I'm sorry for your loss, but that is no excuse to insert a blank page into the old binding of an irreplaceable treasure."

"It wasn't blank, initially. The ink was designed to fade with exposure to light. We don't need the whole book, only that page," Agent Duff offered.

Dr. Paolini boiled over. "I have worked in this Library for forty years, and we have never endured a knife fight in the middle of our precious book stacks with people bleeding everywhere and with a wild beast screeching like peace will never reign again. And I've never let the government confiscate or deface one of my books. No one touches that book without my head conservator present."

"Dr. Paolini, my technical people will take all precautions to minimize damage to the book."

"My conservators are the best in the world."

I admired the spunky academic's putting Agent Duff in his place, but tuned them out as they argued. "How's your back feeling?" I asked Mac.

"It's hurting. I think the pain-killing adrenaline has worn off."

"We can numb it in the ER and close the wound. If you want, we can use staples, and you can tell everyone that a shark bite caused it."

Mac's discomfort curtailed her laugh, but at least I could distract her momentarily. "I prefer a minimal scar, thank you."

"We can do that, too. Let's get out of here."

Agent Duff and Dr. Paolini had reached a truce, where the head conservator would remove the page with minimal damage to the binding under the watchful eyes of DHS technical experts. I approached Agent Duff.

"Are we done here? I need to get Mac to the ER."

"We're not even close to done."

"Okay, but can we get her fixed up before the interrogations continue? She might be more cooperative if she's not bleeding and in pain."

"One of my agents will drive and stay with you. After she's treated, you'll both be brought back to my office. No bullshit, or you'll be locked up until you qualify for social security."

"We'll get her fixed up, and we promise not to flee."

I helped Mac stand and supported her as she gingerly walked to the exit, escorted by Banshee and two agents.

In the middle of a now empty main reading room, I asked everyone to pause for a moment and gave Banshee a command. "BARK."

Banshee howled at the statues lining the room, the echo intensified by the dome above. I motioned him to silence, but the sound continued to reverberate from all directions as we exited the building.

CHAPTER FORTY

Monday, March 23
3:20 p.m.

Soon after an uneventful escort to the ER, I secured a room for Mac, who carefully stepped onto the exam table and turned over on her stomach.

"I need a nap," she sighed.

"Feel free to doze. Want me to get one of my colleagues or fix it myself?"

"You do it. I trust you, especially after everything that's happened."

I gathered my supplies, rolled Mac's shirt up and removed the bandage. A quick inspection confirmed that the knife had penetrated the skin and fat layers and part of the muscle. I drew some lidocaine and added some bicarbonate to minimize the burn.

"Hold still, this part stings a little, but then you won't feel anything."

I slid the needle into the wound under the edge of the skin and slowly injected the lidocaine. Most people hate needles, but the sting from the medicine actually causes the pain. With a slow injection, even that is minimal. Mac tensed as I started, but quickly relaxed.

"The painful part is over. I'll rinse it out to prevent infection." I irrigated the wound with a liter of fluid under high pressure, making a little bit of a mess, but cleaning away any debris. An inspection post cleaning verified straight edges without much tension.

"Last chance. Do you want a pretty scar or a badass shark bite?"

"I may regret this some day, but let's go with pretty."

"Yes, ma'am. I'm stitching a deep layer that will pull all the tissue together, and then I'll close the top layer with skin glue. You're actually lucky. The wound has clean edges, follows the natural skin lines, and is not under tension. She couldn't have cut you in a better place for repair."

"I'll be sure to thank her for stabbing me in a convenient area."

"I doubt we'll see her again."

"She'll still haunt my nightmares. What an evil bitch. I lost my senses at the way she so casually mentioned killing Mark. I'm glad you stopped me. I'm not sure I could have recovered well if I had killed someone like that."

"Unfortunately, I have some experience with that. When I tracked down some bad people in Houston, I ended up locked in a room with a crazy man who planned to torture me to death. I was able to surprise him and got him in a chokehold. He passed out in about fifteen seconds, but I held the choke hold for four long minutes to make sure that he would die."

"Does it still bother you?"

"Yes and no. He was a horrible person who enjoyed hurting people and who deserved the death penalty for his crimes, anyway, and I had to kill him to survive. I could not escape and could not beat him in a fair fight, had he regained consciousness. I don't like that I did it, but I know I would do it again. I probably saved lives by preventing his future crimes."

"Self-defense is different, Doc. I had chosen to kill her after I neutralized her threat."

Left to our own thoughts, I finished the repair in silence and focused on the perfect alignment of the edges of the cut. I took a picture to show Mac.

"What do you think?"

"Looks good. Thanks, Doc."

"Keep it clean, blot dry, and don't pick at the glue. It will wear off by itself in seven to ten days. You can shower, but don't scrub. If it gets red, hot, swollen, tender, or starts leaking fluid, it's probably infected. Call me, and I'll take care of it. Any questions?"

"No, but I'm not looking forward to seeing Agent Duff."

"Sit tight. I'll have someone bring you a clean shirt, and we can go face his questions together."

.   .   .

Our professional, unfriendly DHS agents drove us back to their headquarters and deposited us into a conference room. They left the door open, but an agent stood outside. A refreshment bar sparked my interest. I headed straight for the drinks and snacks.

"Would you like something? These guys have a nice arrangement."

"Water and some chocolate, please."

"Anything specific?"

"You choose."

I chose M&M's for her and peanut butter cups and a Diet Coke for myself. As I sat down beside her, she smoothly slid her candy toward me and took the peanut butter cups. We freely enjoyed our snacks until Agent Duff arrived, followed by five other agents in suits.

"I see you made yourselves at home."

I held up the candy. "I figured this had been purchased with tax dollars, so technically, it's partly mine already. Please help yourselves, if you want something."

"Okay, smart-ass, here's the deal. You come clean right here, right now, with everything you know, and no charges will be filed, but if you hold back on me, I'll make your lives miserable."

"I understand. Are you gonna introduce the others in the room?"

"They're my colleagues."

"Do they have names?"

Agent Duff pointed to each. "Let me introduce you to Agent Smith, Agent Smith, Agent Smith, Agent Smith, and Agent Smith. Satisfied?"

"I'm sorry. I didn't catch the name of the fourth agent."

Mac put a hand on me before I got myself arrested. "Agent Duff, I'm ready to tell the whole story, and you're going to hear about a journal my brother kept. It contains his thoughts and one of his clues, but no actual research or anything that would allow someone to replicate it. I understand that you will want to review it, but after you do, I would like the original returned to me. Deal?"

"Fair enough. As long as it has nothing to do with national security, I will return the journal to you."

Mac began with our first meeting in the hospital ten days ago. She articulated a clear, concise summary of our investigations, omitting nothing. The Agents Smith took notes in addition to their recording, and Agent Duff interrupted only for occasional clarification. Mac concluded with the events in the Library.

"That is quite the adventure, but I'm confused. Given that your brother knew that the ink would disappear, how did he expect you to save the information?"

"I'm sure he did it as a precaution to prevent malicious people from obtaining it. He knew I would be aware of the time constraints he imposed and probably expected me to take a picture before the message disappeared forever, but I couldn't do that safely, because I knew that my phone had been compromised by you, so probably by the Russians as well. I trusted his judgment, so I let the ink vanish."

"You had no problem with watching your brother's life's work disappear?"

"I chose obliteration over its weaponization. Letting it disappear doesn't diminish Mark's brilliance, but does make the world a safer place."

"We could have done a lot of good with his discoveries."

"You could do even greater harm."

"You compromised national security by letting that information go."

Mac leaned forward and steeled her voice. "Agent Duff, I have taken an oath to protect this country and have served with honor. I compromised nothing. If I had let the Russians get it, then you could accuse me, but I let it destroy itself rather than let our enemies take it. I fulfilled my patriotic duty."

Agent Duff leaned back. "You know someone else is going to recreate his research."

Mac laughed. "Good luck with that. Mark was a unique, generational talent. If you think you can find someone on LinkedIn to replace him, then you'll be disappointed."

"Last issue is the journal. How do we find this Herodotus?" Agent Duff asked.

"You don't," I said. "You wait for him to come out of the tunnels, and we can ask him. He's a fragile personality and more than a little paranoid. You won't get it by force, but he likes Mac and will bring it to her."

We arranged to watch for him on the Mall the following day, and we signed secrecy agreements that promised all sorts of hardship if we were ever to disclose anything.

Agent Duff walked us to the door. "You get me that journal and stay quiet, and this thing is over. Thank you for cooperating. Now, get out of here."

An agent drove us to the Capitol, where Mac hugged me goodbye. She wanted to check her office and take the metro home. The agent then took Banshee and me home, and I settled into the couch to watch some basketball.

CHAPTER FORTY-ONE

Monday, March 23
6:58 p.m.

Mac cleared security with expressions of concern given her scrub top and disheveled appearance, not her typical Washington power outfit, even after hours. She unlocked the office and abruptly faced the Senator, standing in front of the open door blankly staring at her.

"Senator, you startled me. I didn't expect anyone to be here this late."

"I hoped you would stop by. I hear you had an adventurous day." The Senator pulled a chair from the conference table and motioned to Mac to sit across from her. Mac flopped into the chair.

"I apologize for being out of contact this afternoon. I expected only to meet Doc for lunch, but he guessed that the Library of Congress held Mark's last clue. We decided to check it out, and that Russian witch showed up and stabbed me."

"I heard that you were injured. I hope not seriously."

"I needed ten stitches in my back, but it will heal. Mac managed a brief smile. "I fought her off. I'm pretty sure I broke her nose."

"Really? I hadn't heard that."

Mac summarized the altercation, and the Senator redirected the conversation. "Let's get back to the message that Mark left. What exactly did it say?"

"I'm paraphrasing, but it said that something had happened to him for me to receive his message and that it was up to me to decide what to do with it."

"What do you think he meant by that?"

"It's no secret that Mark struggled with second thoughts about his discovery. It offered potential for profound medical advancement, but also for horrific weaponization. He knew it could kill millions and alter the balance of world power. I think he felt that the risks of his discovery outweighed the benefits."

"And what do you think?"

"I've had a few days to process it, and I'm convinced that Mark was right. His discovery is too dangerous for humanity. The Russians' violent desperation to obtain it proves the point."

"I understand that Mark wrote several lines of equations in disappearing ink. Tell me about those."

"You are well informed, Senator."

"It's my job to be informed. Now tell me about the equations, please." Her superficial politeness radiated menace. Mac had known the Senator long enough to recognize that she was about to lose her temper.

"He listed ten or twelve lines of complex equations. I had only a moment to look at them before the Russian attacked me. By the time I turned back to the book, the ink had faded to illegibility. I'm afraid the information is gone."

The Senator routinely evaluated lies, a required political skill. She read Mac's expressions closely, but couldn't determine the veracity of her assertions. The fact that Mac might be withholding information from her ignited major concern.

"Mac, I've witnessed personally how quickly you absorb information, and while your memory may not be photographic, it's damn close. I find it almost impossible to believe that you didn't memorize those equations."

"Ordinarily, I would agree with you, but with the shock of finding it and then of being held at knifepoint and forced to fight for my life, I couldn't focus on it. The ink had vanished before I could memorize it."

"And you expect me to believe that Mark was willing to let his greatest discovery disappear forever after only a few minutes?"

"Mark preferred its destruction to its misuse. He wouldn't have worried about its disappearance as long as he lived. He could have recreated his own equations from memory. Sensing the threat to his life, he would have perceived a high probability of malicious intent, so his willingness to destroy it in the event of his death makes perfect sense."

"Perhaps the agents will be able to salvage the information from the paper."

"Maybe, but Mark assured me that after ink disappeared, it was gone forever."

The Senator stood and paced behind the table, a habit that revealed rare anxiety. "Mac, you've never failed me before. I'm disappointed in you. I have assured important people that you would get the information and that I would make sure it got into the right hands."

"Who exactly has the right hands?"

"Powerful people who would protect the technology and use it correctly."

"What are their names?"

The Senator ignored her question. "I'm sure you're tired. Go home. Think hard about what you saw on that paper. If you can remember, it would assure the continued growth of your career."

"And if I cant remember?"

The Senator grabbed her bag and opened the door. "Goodbye, Mac."

The door closed softly, leaving her stunned that the Senator had threatened her. Mac had been adamant with everyone that she didn't have time to memorize the equations. She thought she had been convincing, but the Senator clearly felt that she was lying. Mac shuddered. She idly ran her fingers over the table, recreating Mark's equations. She envisioned a perfect image of the page and could easily transcribe the work if she chose. She marveled at the brilliance and simplicity of his discovery. She would not share it with anyone, ever.

CHAPTER FORTY-TWO

Tuesday, March 24
11:47 a.m.

Mac met me and Banshee near the Metro stop at lunchtime. She sat next to me and stroked Banshee's ears. She looked weary and stressed. "Did you get any sleep?" I ventured.

"Not much. I couldn't stop thinking about what the Senator said to me last night. She implicitly threatened me to reveal Mark's secret."

"What did you tell her?"

"I told her I didn't have time to study and memorize the formula."

"Did she believe you?"

"Do you?"

"What I think doesn't matter, because I don't want it, and I couldn't understand it if I had it. You either don't know the formula, or you do and choose not to share it. Either is fine with me."

Mac snuggled into my arm. "Thanks. I think you're the only one who really understands what I'm going through." We sat quietly in the cool sunlight until a familiar figure arose from the metro stairway.

"Here comes Doty for some fresh air," I waved, and he smiled warmly, as he joined us.

"Long time, no see. How are things up above?"

"More exciting than we prefer," Mac gave him an overview of our recent adventures. "I wanted to see if you could return my brother's journal."

"Of course. It's sitting on my desk where you left it. Is it okay if I bring it tomorrow? I have some things to do this afternoon."

"Is everything okay?" I asked.

His eyes intensified. "Yeah. Can I meet you here tomorrow about the same time?"

"We'll see you then. Take care."

Doty nodded and wandered through groups of tourists.

"What do you think is keeping him busy this afternoon?"

"No idea. Hard to predict the activities of a brilliant, reclusive historian who lives underground. What are you doing this afternoon?"

"Let's go watch the PIMPS testify before Congress. Want to catch some of it?" Mac suggested.

"Can we get in?"

Mac held up her badge. "Yes, I'm pretty sure we can find a seat with this."

"Nice to know an important person."

"I think my days in the Senator's office are numbered."

"You really think she would fire you?"

"I don't know, but I'm not sure I want to stay with her. I think it's time for a new opportunity and a fresh start."

"What will you do?"

"No idea. Come on."

.   .   .

The hearing, held in one of the larger committee rooms, was packed with people. Mac's ID accessed reserved seating in the front. The Senate couldn't seem to agree on much, but bribing hospital officials to provide substandard medical care apparently concerned both parties.

The three officers from Prime Medical Partners sat at a table facing twenty-one irate Senators, who lobbed accusations and difficult questions, hoping for the lead sound bite on the evening news. Hopefully, they genuinely cared about quality healthcare as much as they did about their next election.

"Mr. Prost, in your capacity as lead attorney for Prime Medical Partners, I assume you are aware that bribing a hospital administrator to get a contract is illegal. Is that correct?"

"Yes, Senator."

"Then can you please explain to me why, under your watch, no less than thirty-seven executives were bribed?"

Don's own attorney leaned over and whispered in his ear. "On the advice of counsel, I plead the fifth."

"Tell me, Mr. Prost, were you aware of the bank account in The Caymans that made these illegal payments?"

"On the advice of my counsel, I am pleading the Fifth."

"That is certainly your right to do so, Mr. Prost, but your fear of the question speaks volumes. Now, let's turn our attention to..."

The hearing continued for another fifty minutes with tough questions from the panel followed by weak denials or refusals to answer from the executives.

"It doesn't seem like they accomplished anything," I observed.

"Those guys were under oath, so if they change their stories, they can be charged with perjury. Also, their refusal to answer basic questions is a public relations nightmare. These guys are done for good in medicine."

We were funneled out of the room with the rest of the crowd, when a heavy hand perched on my shoulder and spun me around. Banshee growled, as I looked into Don Prost's wild eyes. He leaned to whisper in my ear.

"You did this, you little fuck. You ruined this company, and I'm gonna make it my mission to fuck up your life."

"Good luck orchestrating that from jail."

Don pushed me backward and pulled back his fist, and Banshee leapt straight up between us and barked in his face. Don recoiled, and the commotion drew the attention of a Capitol policeman.

"What's going on here?" he asked.

I calmed Banshee, as Mac stepped forward with her Senatorial identification.

"Officer, Mr. Prost approached my friend, threatened him, pushed him, and was ready to throw a punch before the dog barked at him."

The officer turned to me. "Is that what happened?"

Flushed and sweating profusely, Prost's dilated eyes blazed, and the blood vessels in his neck pulsed with an unnatural rhythm. "Yes, Officer. As a physician, I'm concerned that Mr. Prost exhibits signs of cocaine use."

Prost exploded and would have attacked again, if his coworkers hadn't restrained him. The officer turned to him. "Sir, are you under the influence of any illegal drugs?"

"No, and that man attacked me first. He's been lying to ruin our company. I want to press charges."

"Officer, I have the whole episode on camera, if you want to see what happened," a news reporter offered.

The officer reviewed the footage. "Sir, turn around and put your hands behind your back."

Prost protested, but three more officers had arrived to cuff him quickly. As they left, I asked the officers to wait a moment. "DRUGS," I pointed to Prost. Banshee approached, sniffed, and quickly focused on the front right pocket of his pants. Banshee nudged it and sat.

"Officer, he's a trained police dog. I suspect you will find drugs in his pocket."

The officer reached into it and pulled out a glass vial of white powder. He held it up to the light while reporters' cameras captured the moment. They led Prost away, trailed by the group of reporters.

"That was unexpected," Mac said.

"I noticed his addiction the first time we met. He was headed to prison anyway, but now he won't be able to take another hit that could induce additional violence. Let's call it a day."

"You can call it a day. I have to get back to work. See you tomorrow."

·   ·   ·

Mac returned to the office, bustling with activity. She quickly scanned through a stack of messages waiting on her desk, organizing them by calls she would return, those for her staff to return, and trash. A text from the Senator asked her to come into her office.

Mac knocked on the Senator's door. She called for her to enter and asked her to close the door behind her. Mac took a seat across from the Senator and waited for her to speak.

"Have you thought any more about what we discussed on Sunday?"

"Yes, Senator. I've been racking my brain, but haven't made progress. I can't remember what was written on that page."

"I see. What about that journal he left for you?"

"We're supposed to get it tomorrow. DHS wants to look at it, of course, but Mark diligently kept his research separate from his thoughts on the process. It contains no research or its results."

"I would like to see that journal."

"I'm sure you could arrange to view it."

The Senator leaned forward. "I would like to see that journal before Homeland does."

Mac squirmed. "With all due respect, Senator, I don't want to get in the middle of a turf war between you and Homeland. I want to put this matter behind me."

"I see." The Senator paused and turned to other matters she wanted her to work on. Mac took notes, and the Senator abruptly dismissed her. Their relationship had clearly soured.

CHAPTER FORTY-THREE

Wednesday, March 25
12:14 p.m.

Relaxing on the same bench, Mac and I basked in the mild sunlight and waited for Doty. Mac vented about her office drama.

"It's weird that the Senator is more obsessed with the research than the Homeland guys are. The relentless tension in the office weighs on me."

"Sounds like it's time to move on."

"Clearly, but finding a new job will take time. Openings for Congressional Chief of Staff positions are rare."

"There's a big world outside Washington."

"Yeah, but I'm really good at what I do, and Washington is the only place that operates by the rules I know."

"They certainly live by their own set of rules. Did you see Banshee's picture on the news?" A photographer had caught Banshee at full extension barking in the face of a startled Don Prost.

"You should frame that. People should know not to mess with you."

"Excuse me," interrupted a man in his forties, dressed in khaki slacks and a tweed jacket with a messenger bag slung over his shoulder.

"Can I help you?" I asked.

He opened his bag and reached inside. Perceiving our tension, Banshee stood between us. The hand emerged with Mark's journal, and Mac and I exhaled deeply. I ordered Banshee to relax, and he laid down at my feet.

"Did Doty give that to you?" Mac asked.

The man smiled. "No, you gave it to me."

Mac and I stared at the man, not believing our eyes. "Doty, is that you?"

He beamed. "I wondered if you could see through my new look. What do you think?" He twirled to show off his new outfit.

"You look great. Have a seat and tell us what happened."

Doty sat between us, handing the journal to Mac. "It's time for me to reenter the world. You made me realize that I have more to offer. Yesterday, I went to the shelter to clean up as best I could and got a haircut and shave. It feels good to be back in clean clothes."

"How did you afford it?"

Doty pulled a bank card from his breast pocket. "I've had money in my account with a very low cost of living the whole time."

"Welcome back. What will you do next?"

He pulled a sheaf of papers from his bag. "I finished my research on the construction of early American government. I have an appointment with the Dean at my old department this afternoon, and I'll submit this for review. Your visit inspired me to get back to living. Thank you."

"Oh, Doty, I'm so happy for you." Mac hugged him and kissed his cheek. He blushed, and a smile warmed his expression in a way I imagined hadn't happened in too long.

"Thank you. I'm back to myself, Danny Simpson. Herodotus lived in the tunnels, but Professor Danny Simpson lives back here, now."

We gave him our contact information and watched the confident professor walk purposefully away.

"I'm glad to see that something good came from this mess. What're you gonna do with that?" I asked.

Mac browsed through the pages. "I'm going to read it one more time. Although Duff promised I could have it, my trust meter is running low."

"Want some company?"

"Sure. The Senator's office can wait. Let's go to my place."

I walked beside her with Banshee staying alert, as usual.

·   ·   ·

Mac lived in another conveniently located townhouse, a rarity in that it had a single car garage as well as a decent view of the Capitol Building.

"I imagine it's hard to forget about work when your office dominates your view," I mused at the historic building.

"It's a constant reminder that despite its many problems, the US government is still one of the best in the world, and Congress is its most powerful branch."

"Some Supreme Court Justices might argue with that assessment."

"Congress makes the laws and controls the purse strings. Decisions of where the money goes control where the country goes."

"I can understand how hard it will be for you to leave the Senator's office, even after what's happened."

"It's time for a fresh start. I'll make some lunch. Feel free to take a look at the journal, if you like."

I sat on the couch with it, while Banshee followed Mac into the kitchen. Mark wrote in very precise block letters with a high quality pen. His entries were meticulously dated and timed, but the content varied widely. Early entries pondered the direction of his research. He initially planned to discover a way to define the changes to DNA over time. I skimmed ahead to where he grasped the possibility that these changes over time could be quantified in a formula. These detailed entries offered a glimpse into how Mark processed problems.

I skimmed further ahead to six months ago, when he made a breakthrough. Although ecstatic with his progress, he gave no details. Soon thereafter, his entries turned dark with Mark's contemplation of how his discovery could be weaponized. He struggled with the dichotomy that his findings could result in astonishing advancement in medicine, but that the potential damage could be even greater. As time progressed, he became convinced that the ramifications were too dangerous to entrust to humanity. His last entries dated a couple weeks before his death expressed his concern that he was being watched. I read his final entry and closed the journal.

"Welcome back, stranger." Mac finished a sandwich at the kitchen table with Banshee under it.

"How long have I been reading?"

"About forty-five minutes. You seemed to be in the zone, so I went ahead and ate without you. Find anything interesting?"

"The whole journal is interesting. I skimmed through most of it, but it's an incredible journey through Mark's mind. He spelled out the evolution of his thought process."

"What do you think about the final entries?"

"Clearly he knew that his research was too dangerous to release indiscriminately. Feelings of guilt over the destruction of knowledge held him back. His conflicting thoughts and emotions are heart wrenching."

"Scientists are wired to share knowledge, not to destroy it."

"Do you trust Duff?"

"As much as I trust anyone in government service, which is to say, not much. He has his own agenda. The journal won't advance his goals, so there's a good chance he'll return it."

Banshee jumped to his feet, growled with hackles raised, and faced the front door. It burst open and masked men surged into the room. Banshee launched at the first man, but the intruder was prepared and tasered him. Barbs embedded into Banshee's chest and electricity surged through his body, as he fell hard to the floor.

I reacted instinctively and rushed at the man who had hurt Banshee. With his attention on my unmoving dog and with my fury focused only on him, I aimed at a point three inches behind his face and punched through my target. He fell to the floor, as barbs from a second man's taser entered the side of my chest wall and sent 50,000 volts coursing through my body. Every muscle tensed in a conflagration of pain. I landed convulsing on the floor next to Banshee. My mind still worked, but couldn't focus on much besides the pain. After what seemed like years, the electricity stopped, and I quivered on the floor.

I watched a third man approach Mac, also with a taser pointed at her, but he did not use it. Instead, he held out his other hand. "Give me the book."

Mac hesitated only a second before realizing the futility of defiance and handed the book to the man. He glanced at it and pocketed it.

"You have one chance to do this the easy way. Write down the formulas he left you, and we will leave."

Mac crossed her arms and stared silently at the man, who turned to nod at his partner, and I received a second dose of electricity. My already tender muscles burned even more hotly, as the current surged through me. Eventually, it stopped, and I once again struggled to breathe and focus on the scene in front of me.

"Last chance. Write the formulas."

Mac cried, looking at Banshee and me on the floor. "I swear. I didn't get to see them long enough to memorize them."

"Okay. I actually prefer the hard way." He deployed his taser, and Mac convulsed on the kitchen floor. He stood over her, removed a syringe from his pocket, and injected her upper arm. Her quivering muscles relaxed, as her eyes rolled back into her head. At that moment, a needle pierced my arm, and darkness consumed me.

CHAPTER FORTY-FOUR

Unknown date and time

Scorching pain stoked consciousness, and I twitched involuntarily. I tried to force relaxation and focused on breathing. Deeper breaths felt uncomfortably tight, but steadied me. Eventually, I gained control of my breathing and assessed the damage.

I wiggled my toes, experiencing only a mild cramp in one leg, a positive sign that I wasn't paralyzed. I curled my fingers and gained confidence in increased muscle control. I slowly opened my eyes, and blinding light seared them. I gasped and closed my eyes tightly. Distantly, speech penetrated my discomfort.

"Doc, you there, Doc? It's me. Wake up."

My foggy mind processed the words slowly, trying to identify the familiar voice. I opened my eyes slowly this time, allowing my vision to transition from black to gray, and finally to light. Squinting, I started to decipher a metal table with hands handcuffed to it in front of me. Slight movement of my wrist confirmed that my own hands were locked in place.

"Good, you're waking up. Doc, look at me."

At a comical pace, I turned my head to the familiar voice at my right to find Mac staring at me. She tearfully flashed a brief, terrified smile. "Glad you're awake. I was getting tired of listening to you snore."

"I don't snore." My garbled words slowly fought their way from my dry throat, as if sandpaper scraped my voice box as I spoke.

"We need to focus on getting out of here."

"Where are we?" My brain fog dissipated slowly.

"No idea. Last thing I remember was that injection, and I woke up here half naked."

I noticed for the first time that she wore only a sports bra and underwear, and her cuffed hands were chained to the table, like mine. "They took your clothes," I observed.

"You're not well dressed yourself."

I looked down to see that I wore only my boxers. None of this made sense. Our chairs were bolted to the floor, as was the metal table in front of us. The four bare walls forming a ten-by-ten foot room held only a camera facing us and a door behind us.

"They must not pay their decorator well. The walls could use some color," I muttered, still not comprehending the ramifications of our situation.

"Not much here except that camera and the accessories on the ceiling." I leaned my head back, causing another wave of blinding pain. The ceiling held a hook with a metal chain hanging from it.

"That's not good. Who the fuck are these guys?" I asked.

"I've been thinking about that. The Russians seemed most likely to me at first, but kidnapping is a big step for them, especially in light of their recent public failures, and those guys at the house didn't sound Russian."

"Could it be Homeland?"

"I don't think so. They can certainly detain terrorists, but I'm not sure about American citizens, and I got no hint from Duff that he even considered doing something like this."

"Mac, this could get crazy bad quickly. Let's just cooperate."

Mac's bright eyes hardened to steely gray. "I can't give them what I don't know. I barely glimpsed the information before the ink disappeared. It was too complex to memorize anyway. Our only chance is to convince them of that fact."

"Agreed. Stick to the truth." My mind had fully awakened, and fear twisted my gut. I tested the chains. I could probably pick the locks, if I had the tools, but I didn't keep a pick set in my boxers. With nothing else to do, we waited, watching the red light on the camera blink every three seconds.

We startled when the door behind us opened. Two men wearing tactical ear pieces, masks, cargo pants, and black muscle shirts that struggled to cover their physiques swaggered into the now claustrophobic room. They each laid a metal cylinder on the table and placed the journal between them.

"I hope now you understand how serious we are. You can still choose the easy way. Write down the formula."

"I told you. I don't remember it," Mac said.

Without hesitation, they lifted the cylinders and jammed them in our chests. Painful electricity coursed through us. We strained against our cuffs as our muscles contracted, and our backs arched. The electricity abruptly ended, and gasping, we flopped forward on the table.

"These industrial cattle prods can be adjusted to five different levels based on the size of the cattle. What you just experienced was level one, the lowest." He clicked a knob at the base of the cylinder. "Next time, I'll try level two. Give us the formula."

"I told you already. I don't know them."

"That's too bad." The door behind us opened, and black hoods were thrown over us, blocking all light. We were doused in freezing water, and the men apparently left, closing the door behind them. A whirring heralded the arrival of frigid air blowing from above. I violently shivered, as some sort of heavy metal music at an impossibly loud level assaulted us. My whole world was reduced to shivering and fighting to think of anything other than the cacophony. Eventually, my mind could no longer process anything and mercifully shut down, as I passed out.

CHAPTER FORTY-FIVE

Unknown date and time

Blaring music invaded my consciousness, but not as loudly, maybe because my ability to hear had been damaged. I still shivered, but warm air blew. My hooded darkness remained. The decrescendo blissfully progressed to soundlessness. My ears rang, and I had never appreciated silence more.

"How are you holding up?" Mac asked.

"That was the worst concert I have ever been to."

"Me, too. One star review."

"What's next?"

"I think round two. I am so sorry I got you into this."

"I'm a big boy and perfectly capable of making my own bad decisions."

"You know they're gonna kill us, right?"

"Most likely. Even if they could get the information they want, we're dead, which proves Mark's concerns."

We lapsed into quiet solitude, mired in our own thoughts. I had never really contemplated my own death, despite confronting it almost daily in the emergency room. I wondered if my nonexistence would matter to anyone. I had friends, but no family, who would miss me, and no one depended on me, except for Banshee. I hoped he was alright and would land in a good home.

The door opened abruptly, and someone ripped the hood off my head. I squinted, as my eyes adjusted. An unmasked guy sat across from me and actually smiled, but with cold, dark blue eyes peering through dirty blonde hair.

"Did you get some rest during the concert?"

"Why don't you stop this shit, and let us go? I don't know the formulas, and no matter how much macho insecurity you need to express in here, I still won't know them," Mac said.

The man looked at his partner standing behind us. "Did you hear this bitch? She wants to talk about everything except what I want to know." He turned his attention back to Mac. "Want to take a guess how long you were listening to that shitty music? You probably thought you were under those hoods for hours. Truth is, that shit lasted only thirty minutes. Next time I put those hoods on, it'll be for a lot longer, and I'm gonna turn the cold water on you the whole time. Write the formulas for me, and this ends."

"With our deaths?"

"Yeah, you smart ones figured us out, but if you tell me what I want to know, I'll give you a merciful bullet to the back of the head. If you hold out, the next few weeks will be rough before you die anyway. Take the easy way. Write the formulas." He pushed the pencil and paper toward Mac.

She picked up the paper and started writing, shielding it with her left hand. She put the pencil down and turned the paper around, so we could all read it.

"FUCK YOU ASSHOLE!" followed by a smiley face screamed from the paper.

The man shook his head. "Tommy, grab that chain."

Behind me, the second man pulled the chain from the ceiling and attached it to my cuffed hands. He released my cuffs from the table, motioned to the camera, and my hands rose with the chain until my arms were stretched over my head so far that my bare feet barely skimmed the floor.

"Last chance."

Mac pointed at the paper and turned to me, already crying, "Sorry, Doc."

I was about to tell her not to worry when the first blow struck the back of my legs, followed almost immediately by the same blunt object striking the front of my legs. I struggled to process overwhelming pain. I looked to see that the man behind me swung a rubber truncheon, leaving my legs in hellish flames. I realized that I was screaming and barely aware of the man yelling at Mac, as the pain spread throughout my legs. He nodded to the man behind me, who delivered three more blows to my chest and back. I struggled to catch my breath, as my chest muscles froze. Agony radiated throughout my body. Weeping, Mac strained at her chains. He grabbed the cattle prod and jammed it into her chest, arching her back over the chair. He turned to send another burst into my chest, constricting my already inflamed muscles. New levels of pain racked through me, overwhelming my senses.

I must have passed out again. I awoke to hear Mac, calling my name. I assessed my predicament. Still chained to the ceiling, my muscles twitched from the electricity, as my chest, back, and legs throbbed with intense pain. Dark bruising spread across my chest and legs. I tried to minimize movement and just breathe.

"Doc, can you hear me?"

I tried to reassure her. "I'm good. Nothing's broken."

"Nothing's broken, yet," the sadist clarified. "For our next round, we will trade the rubber club for a baseball bat, unless Little Miss Maclaw gives it up."

Mac sat up straight. "What did you say?"

"I said you better tell me what I need to know."

"You called me Little Miss Maclaw. Where did you hear that? When was the last time you spoke to Senator Whitestone?"

The man's eyes widened, as he glanced at the camera. "I've never met a Senator."

Mac stared through the camera. "Senator, I know you're watching. Get in here and talk to me face to face."

"There is no Senator, and you're talking to me."

"Shut up. She's calling the shots through your earpieces!" Mac sat serenely, as I watched deep sadness and disappointment rage in her eyes.

Minutes ticked by in silence until the door opened to admit the Senator, who dismissed the thugs and calmly took the seat across from us.

"Hello, Mac."

"Senator."

"I am sorry it has come to this. I wish it could have been avoided."

"You can still do the right thing. You don't have to go through with this."

"Unfortunately, I do not have that option. I need those equations."

"Why, Senator? Why is it worth kidnapping, torture, and murder?"

"It's complicated."

"We seem to have plenty of time, and listening to your explanation is better than having that Babe Ruth wannabe practicing his swing on me," I slurred.

She carefully averted her gaze, as if unable to face what she had done. "I became aware of Mark's research a few months ago. My committee has oversight of DARPA, and we get periodic updates on their projects. His report was purposefully vague and focused on the potential medical benefits, but the military possibilities were obvious. I spoke with a large pharmaceutical company about bringing such products to market to fight cancer, autoimmune disease, and other ailments. Mark's discovery would be worth a fortune to its owner."

"You did this for money? You're already rich."

"I am rich, but not wealthy. Acquiring this information would catapult me beyond billionaire status and would provide an immediate war chest for me to attain the Presidency."

"You greedy bitch. You're willing to do this for money and power for yourself?"

"Not only for myself, but also for my country. We could make our population healthier and eliminate so much pain and suffering, while becoming the most feared country on earth."

"If you want to start eliminating pain and suffering, I can offer a suggestion," I said.

The Senator turned toward me. "I don't enjoy this, but it's necessary. I need that information. Please, just give me the information, and this will be over."

"Even if I had it, I wouldn't give it to you, you evil bitch."

"We will get the information, eventually. I hope for your sakes we get it soon. Goodbye, Mac. I'm sorry."

The Senator stood to leave.

"What did you do with Banshee?"

"Your dog is fine. We sedated him and left him at the house. Goodbye, Doc."

The Senator left, and the hoods were thrown back over our heads. Frigid water flooded over me, and the music blared until I passed out again.

CHAPTER FORTY-SIX

Unknown date and time

The music stopped suddenly, but I feared the beat would echo in my head forever. The door slammed open, and I heard indecipherable arguments in the hallway. I braced myself.

"They're in here. Find the keys, and someone bring me some blankets."

My hood was lifted, and Agent Duff's concerned face studied mine. "Just a minute, Doc, and we'll have you out of these chains."

He moved to Mac, removed her hood, and reassured her of safety. Stunned and aching, I still managed a smile for Mac.

"You look like shit," she said.

"I've never been so happy to see Agent Duff. How did you find us?"

"Let's get you taken care of, and then I'll explain."

Another agent arrived with keys and stood on a chair to remove my cuffs, while Agent Duff held me up.

"Can you stand?" He asked, as the other agent freed Mac.

Mac stood without help, but my first attempt to stand on my own brought a gasp of pain, and I fell onto Duff. My thighs had turned solid black and blue.

"I could use a hand," I said.

With Mac on one side and Agent Duff on the other, they carefully assisted me. I took a few deep breaths and focused on my balance. Standing didn't hurt too much, but walking threatened to be challenging. I shuffled a few tolerable steps, and someone with blankets blocked the doorway. He draped them over Mac and me, and we slowly sidestepped from the horrifying room.

We entered a tiled hallway of a contemporary house with fine artwork lining the walls that led to a well appointed living room. They carefully assisted me to a leather couch. Mac sat beside me, and another agent handed us each a china cup of steaming coffee, which I normally don't drink, but its heat felt magical. Mac reached out to squeeze my hand.

Yet another agent brought our clothes. Mac didn't wait for privacy and slipped her shirt and pants on while sitting on the couch. She sighed, as she pulled on her socks.

"I will forevermore appreciate warm, dry clothes. Want some help?"

I looked down at my chest, as discolored as my legs. "I would love some help."

Mac and an agent gingerly pulled me into my clothes. I leaned back into the couch feeling much better.

Agent Duff sat across from us. "You know I need full statements from you, but right now, can you identify the guys that did this to you? We have some people cuffed in the next room. You up for it?"

"If someone can help me stand, I will be happy to." I trudged to the next room without support. The two torturers sat cuffed on the floor.

"Yeah. That's the guy who asked the questions and shocked us, and this guy clubbed me."

The guy on the floor smiled at us, like we were meeting at a cocktail party. "How're the ribs feeling, Doc?"

Fury surged through me at this callous asshole's joking about his utterly heartless infliction of pain. I moved toward him, and with a primal scream, Mac launched and landed with all of her weight behind her knee, which she drove into the ribs of the man sitting on the tile. I heard the snap of his ribs breaking before his own scream echoed through the house. Agent Duff pulled her up and back.

"Let's get you back on the couch." He nodded to the other agents. "Get these guys moving now, please."

Back on the couch, we sipped our coffee, and a medic offered help. I thanked her and explained that the rubber club smashed soft tissue, but didn't break anything. I accepted a strong dose of ibuprofen and some ice packs.

Agent Duff turned on his recorder. "Please tell me what happened from the beginning."

"Is Banshee okay? Where is he?"

"Your dog is fine. They left him sedated at Ms. Lawton's house. A vet is caring for him now, and we'll get you reunited soon. Now, your story."

Mac began with the break-in, and her voice cracked, as she relived the torture we had received, but became steely again, as she spoke of the Senator's involvement. Agent Duff listened to the entire story without interruption.

"Thank you. I know that was difficult to relive that. You're absolutely sure it was Senator Whitehurst in that room and that she said exactly those things?"

We both acknowledged the accuracy of Mac's statement.

"That complicates things."

"Agent Duff, how did you find us?" I asked.

He turned off the recorder. "Unofficially, we left a couple of bugs in Ms. Lawton's house. We planned to remove them as soon as she gave us the journal, and because you were no longer a high priority, we weren't monitoring them in real time. An agent reviews the tapes every six hours, and he reported the altercation to me. We were able to grab a picture of their SUV and license plate from a neighbor's security camera. We hacked into their GPS to find them here."

"I have never been so grateful for such invasive surveillance. Where exactly is here?" I asked.

"We're in Virginia about an hour outside DC on a beautiful forty-acre estate with a barn and this guest house along with the main house. We're tracking down its ownership, but I'm pretty sure it's gonna belong to Uncle Sam soon."

"I hope the torture room gets remodeled into something more positive. What happens next?" I asked.

"Please stay here, while I make some calls. Check out the kitchen, and find something to eat. The pantry is full."

Mac and I perked up at the suggestion. They left us alone, but watched both doors of the kitchen. I'm not sure why they worried at all about keeping track of us. It would take me about twenty minutes to make it to the driveway in my current condition.

"What sounds good to you, Doc?"

"Grilled cheese."

"Mac heated a pan and gathered ingredients, as I thanked her and sat at the table. After a few minutes, she sat across from me with her own grilled cheese. I bit into the sandwich and realized how hungry I was. Mac devoured her sandwich just as quickly. She grabbed my empty plate. Care for another?"

"I could definitely use another one. Thank you."

Mac returned with more sandwiches and a bowl of sliced apples and bananas. I felt better than I had since our ordeal began.

Tears swelled in Mac's eyes. "Doc, I am so sorry. I couldn't tell…"

I cut her off, pointing around the room and at my ears. Mac understood and continued.

"I'm sorry this happened. You've been nothing but kind trying to help me, and I'm so sorry about what they did to you."

"No one expected this. They hurt you, too, and you lost your brother and were betrayed by the Senator."

Mac's grief transformed to anger. "I can't believe she did that to us."

"Some people can justify all kinds of evil for money and power."

"I swear I won't let her get away with this."

Agent Duff interrupted and sat at the table with us. "The Senator's location is unknown. Until we find her, we need to keep you safe and isolated. You are eyewitnesses to her crimes, and we don't know how many others work for her. We're moving you to another location."

"Where are we going?"

"It's a surprise, but it's secure and comfortable. Your chopper will be here in a few minutes."

"Chopper?" Mac asked.

"It's the most secure and efficient option."

Mac helped me stand, and I walked outside with minimal help from her, as we watched the helicopter land in a meadow. We waited for the rotors to stop, and I needed help to pull myself into it, but soon we were buckled in place.

"Technically, this is the second time we are being kidnapped," Mac commented. She held my hand, as the chopper rose above the idyllic scene of our torment that quickly disappeared from view.

CHAPTER FORTY-SEVEN

Wednesday, March 25
5:10 p.m.

I listened to the thrumming helicopter blades and watched the evergreen forests pass below us to distract myself from the jostling vibration that aggravated my inflamed back and legs. After about twenty minutes, we gently touched down on a landing pad surrounded by trees. The engine shut down, and a friendly marine opened the door. "Welcome to Camp David. I'm Gunnery Sergeant Bower, and I'll show you to your cabins."

The marine helped me out of the helicopter with surprising strength given his size. I gingerly stepped into the back of a golf cart, as the gunnery sergeant took the wheel. "Our first stop will be at medical to get you two checked out."

"That won't be necessary, Sergeant," I said.

"First of all, I was ordered to take you there, so it is necessary. Secondly, Doc, if you don't mind my saying so, you're not moving very well. It won't take long, and the team is waiting for you."

"What did they tell you about us?" Mac asked.

"I was told that you had been roughed up and needed taken care of until some things are straightened out. Our job is to make you comfortable and keep you safe until the bigwigs decide what to do. Here we are."

We walked into a cabin, where military corpsmen greeted us. A woman led Mac into another room, while I entered an exam room like any major hospital room. "Nice setup you have here."

"Thanks. We also have a trauma room and ICU capabilities on site. Do you need help changing into your gown?"

"If you don't mind helping me get this shirt off, I would appreciate it."

The corpsman carefully lifted the shirt off and stared at the continuous patches of deep bruising, that covered my chest and back. My legs looked no better after I stepped out of my pants, as I leaned against the table.

"Why don't you tell me what happened while I get some vitals."

I shared the story of our capture and torture with electricity and the beatings.

"Your vital signs look strong. We're gonna get some blood work to make sure your blood counts are okay with all of this bleeding. We'll get an EKG to make sure the electric shocks didn't affect your heart. We'll get X-rays of the legs and chest to make sure nothing is fractured, and we'll do an ultrasound on the larger bruises in the legs to make sure there isn't a deep hematoma that needs drained. Do you need anything for pain?"

"Not at the moment, but I will definitely take some pain meds for the road when we're done here."

The staff worked efficiently, and within a half hour, the tests were complete. "Good news, Doc. Nothing is broken; the heart looks good; and the labs are normal so far. A few results are pending, but you are cleared to leave. Here is a supply of muscle relaxers and pain meds, if you need them. Ice those areas as much as possible for the next two days, and then you can use heat. You're gonna be sore, but should recover fully in a few weeks. Any questions?"

"No. Thanks for the quick service. I couldn't get treatment this quickly at my own hospital."

"Only the best for our guests at Camp David. Let's get you dressed, and the gunny will get you over to your cabin."

The gunnery sergeant waited with the cart, as I exited the building. "Everything check out okay, Doc?"

"Yeah. Tests looked good, and I got some meds for pain. They warned me not to volunteer to be a piñata again any time soon."

"You can relax and leave the heavy stuff to us. A bunch of marines prowl these grounds. You're staying in the Birch cabin with four suites and a shared common room and kitchen. Ms. Lawton will be in one of the other suites. You are free to walk the grounds, but please stay on the marked trails and follow any orders from staff. There's plenty of food if you want to cook for yourselves, but we have a chef on call, too. Personally, I recommend calling the chef."

"Thanks. How do I make a call from here?"

"That's the one thing you can't do at the moment. Orders are to keep your location a secret, so no contact with the real world. Sorry, sir, but those are the orders."

"Work is going to worry about me."

"Don't worry about that. Secret Service is coordinating your visit. They will contact your work and make up a reason for your absence. They're good at this kind of thing. They should be here with some of your personal belongings soon."

"They broke into our homes?"

"They entered under national security authority. They'll bring fresh clothes and toiletries for you. Here we are."

The wooden cabin looked like it was lifted from a ski resort. The beautiful interior featured high ceilings, dark wood floors and trim, and leather couches and overstuffed chairs. Curled up on one of the couches, Mac rested under a blanket with a book in her hand and a cup of steaming tea on the coffee table in front of her.

"Took you awhile." Concern shone in her eyes.

"I got extra tests for getting my ass kicked. You only got zapped."

"If you need anything at all, just pick up that phone," the gunny said. "It's manned 24/7 and they can answer any questions."

"Thanks, Gunny," we said, as he exited the cabin.

"This is surreal. What do you want to do?" Mac asked.

"I'm gonna lay down on this couch and try to take a badly needed nap." The last thing I remembered was Mac's spreading a blanket over me.

CHAPTER FORTY-EIGHT

Wednesday, March 25
7:16 p.m.

Frantic barking outside the door awakened me. Disoriented from deep sleep, I glimpsed a black shadow racing across the room to land in my arms. My utter joy numbed the initial pain of Banshee's weight, as he smothered me with kisses. Finally, he calmed enough to sit next to me, not on me. I foresaw his clinging to me for the next few days and admitted to myself that I probably needed it.

A man in a dark suit stood nearby, politely waiting for our reunion to end before he spoke. "I'm Agent Hammil with the Secret Service, and that impressive dog amazes me. He was a handful until we got him to calm down. We found him at Ms. Lawton's place, sleepy and still recovering from the sedative he had clearly received. The vet checked him out and said he's fine. Then when his sedative wore off, he became increasingly agitated. Someone finally told him that we were going to find Doc, and he seemed to understand and settle down, although he remained very alert."

Banshee kept randomly kissing me. "Thank you, Agent Hammil. Your bringing him here is the best surprise ever."

"We also brought clean clothes and personal items for you and Ms. Lawton. We'll get them in your rooms and then get out of your way."

Banshee could not contain his excitement over our reunion, although he seemed alarmed by my bruises, as his nose thoroughly examined my chest, back and legs. He seemed upset, and I imagined that the guy who hit me was lucky Banshee hadn't been there to see it.

"What do you say, good boy? How about a walk?"

Banshee barked and twirled in excitement, as I struggled to stand.

"You up for this, Doc?"

"It can be a short walk. I want to see the place. It's unlikely that I will ever be back."

I opened the door, and Banshee bounded outside, free of his leash. He deserved a little freedom after the stress of the last day. Mac and I walked slowly down a trail with Banshee leaping ahead of us and circling back. Mac reached out and grasped my hand as we walked.

"I am so sorry this happened to you. If I had thought even for a moment that it possibly could, I never would have allowed your involvement."

"I doubt anyone could have predicted that the Senator would kidnap and torture us, and that Homeland Security would rescue us."

"When we were in that room with the music blaring, all I could think was that I would rather die than give Mark's research to those people, but I didn't have the right to make that choice for you."

"For what it's worth, I think you made the right choice. Giving powerful technology to evil people would not have ended well for all of humanity. I was sure glad to see Agent Duff, though."

Up ahead, Banshee growled at a bush, as he circled it.

"Do you think there's a bunny in there?" Mac asked.

"He normally wouldn't get worked up over a small animal. Maybe he's just spooked from the drama of the last day."

Banshee's growls turned to full throated barking, as the bush stood up to reveal a soldier wearing a ghillie suit. He smiled at us. "Do you mind calling off the dog?"

"Banshee, here. RELAX."

Banshee sat at my side, but maintained a wary eye on the talking bush.

"Sorry to disturb you folks. I didn't think the dog would be able to smell me. We're testing a new product that's supposed to disguise our scent. Looks like it needs some more work. I'm Sergeant Collier by the way, call sign Squirrel."

"Nice to meet you, Sergeant, and sorry about my dog's scaring you. We didn't know anyone was out here."

"You're not supposed to know we're out here, but we actually appreciate the opportunity to test ourselves. We don't get to work with trained dogs very often. Rumor has it that Scooby here is quite talented."

"Scooby?"

"That's his code name. Everyone out here gets one. He's Scooby; you're Doc; and she's Ribs."

"Ribs?" Mac asked with a raised eyebrow.

"Yes, ma'am. Apparently you busted up some guy's ribs before you came here. You must have impressed somebody, because the story spread to lead to the name."

"I hope the bastard is hurting."

"I heard he needed surgery for some bleeding in his lungs. You folks enjoy your walk, and please stay on the trails. Don't worry about anything. You're safe here."

The sergeant sidestepped into the forest, moved silently into the shrubbery, and quickly disappeared from sight.

"I wonder how many people are watching us out here," Mac said.

"That's probably a national security secret, but I definitely feel safe."

We turned back toward the cabin and finished our walk without incident. After a quick, simple dinner we put together ourselves, Mac engrossed herself in a book, but I was too tired. I took one of the pain pills with plenty of ibuprofen and crawled into bed. Banshee stretched out next to me, and I lost myself in dreamless sleep.

CHAPTER FORTY-NINE

Thursday, March 26
8:27 a.m.

Although still sore in the morning, I pulled myself out of bed much more easily. I found Mac in the living room polishing off the remains of a large breakfast. "Good morning. I felt so ravenous that I ordered breakfast early. I hope I didn't wake you. This chef is as amazing as promised."

Banshee must have agreed, as his nose worked overtime exploring the plates she placed in front of him, disappearing the last piece of bacon. I ordered a waffle and French toast for myself, with some chicken and bacon I planned to share with Banshee. As I finished savoring the best breakfast I had ever tasted, someone knocked on the door. I opened it to find the cheerful gunnery sergeant.

"Good morning, sir, ma'am. I hope you slept well, and I know you've discovered the chef, so I'm sure you ate well. Please remain in your cabin this morning until you are given the all clear."

"Is everything all right?" I asked

"Yes, we follow standard security precautions when VIPs arrive. Enjoy your morning, and call us if you need anything."

The sergeant departed, and another soldier remained outside our cabin. "Why does everyone think we're gonna try to escape?" I asked.

Mac peered at me over her open book from her comfort zone on the couch under a blanket. "I have no idea. I'm happy to stay imprisoned here for a long time."

I strolled along the bookshelves to choose a book of my own and settled on the other side of the couch. About a half hour later, a low rumble grew to a roar as multiple helicopters flew overhead. Mac looked at me. "Sounds like the VIPs have arrived. Do you think it's the President?" Mac asked.

"That's a good guess. This is her place after all. We'll have to wait and see."

We returned to our books until another round of knocking at the door pulled us back to reality. "It's probably the gunny giving us the all clear," I said, as I opened the door to find myself face to face with Megan Taylor, President of the United States.

She smiled warmly and held out her hand. "I am honored to meet you, Dr. Docker. I've heard so much about you. Do you mind if I come in to talk for a few minutes?"

Rarely at a loss for words, I dumbly stepped aside and held the door open for her. She walked over to a wide-eyed Mac who stood frozen in place. The president hugged her briefly and whispered into her ear. Mac visibly relaxed. President Taylor motioned for Mac and me to have a seat on the couch, and she chose one of the chairs across from us. Two secret service agents hovered on the periphery, trying to melt into the background.

"Who's this good boy?"

"That's Banshee."

"I have heard a few things about him. May I pet him?"

"Of course. Banshee, FRIEND. SMILE."

Banshee gave her his best grin and snuggled into the President's hands, as she scratched behind his ears, allowing a moment for Mac and me to collect ourselves.

"One of the worst parts about occupying the office of the presidency is not being able to do simple, normal things like play with a dog. Thank you both for your patience, while we worked to straighten out this situation. I have been fully informed on everything that has happened so far. First of all, how are you feeling? I understand you both were injured. Do you need anything?"

"We're fine, Madam President. Your medical staff is perfect, and the hospitality of the staff has been unmatched. Thank you for the respite and the opportunity to stay here," Mac said.

"You're most welcome. The government does some things very well, and hosting guests out here is certainly one of them. I have to ask for your discretion regarding this conversation. I have no legal right to silence you, but when we're done, I think you'll agree that this topic should not be discussed in public."

"Yes, ma'am," we said in unison.

"Good. I am counting on that. I have been fully briefed on the nature of Mark's research, including it's potential to help mankind or to destroy it. As you know, the Russians are very interested in acquiring this research."

"They murdered my brother."

"The woman who shot your brother is in custody and has been disavowed by the Russians. She will never see the inside of a courtroom, but she will be confined in a military prison for the rest of her life. I can assure you that she has no path to freedom. I hope that is satisfactory."

"Yes, but what about the men who ordered her to kill my brother? Will they ever face justice?"

"Unfortunately, there is not much we can do about that, because he has immunity, but I can tell you that he has been recalled to Moscow. Alina was apparently his star agent, and her very public failure did not reflect well on him. Although Director Petrov will probably not face imprisonment, his career is over. For a man used to a powerful position, irrelevance due to failure is a heavy penalty."

"I guess it will have to be enough. What about the Senator?"

The President leaned back in her chair. "That situation is what we have been working on since her appalling actions came to light. The Senator has been apprehended at her home in California, where it appeared that she was packing for a long trip out of the country. She is currently being held at an undisclosed location."

"What is she being charged with?"

"All sorts of charges were considered, including treason, torture, kidnapping, and attempted murder, but she will not face any of them in court."

"What?" Mac yelled, as she stood up. Both agents stepped forward, ready to intervene, and Banshee stood at alert, sensing the tension. Mac sat down again, dejected, as I calmed Banshee, and the agents faded back. The President continued in a soothing explanation.

"We've reached an agreement with the Senator. She was given a choice. Option one was a public trial for treason, in which she would be humiliated, and we would seek the death penalty. Her reputation would be destroyed, and she would do hard time before she was put to death. Option two was for us to publicize the story that she had suffered a severe stroke that left her so incapacitated that she requires round-the-clock care. Her treatment would be at a military hospital with strict security and no visitors."

"I assume she chose option two. What will actually happen to her?"

"She will be held in much the same situation as the Russian agent. Twenty-three hours a day of isolation, an hour of exercise, and no contact with the outside world. She will die alone."

"She deserves public humiliation."

"While I agree with you, the damage to the country would be substantial. Having a sitting Senator charged with treason would harm our country more than strengthen it."

"What about her estate? The Senator is worth almost a hundred million."

"We hadn't discussed that."

"My silence is gonna cost a hundred million."

The President sat up straighter. "Are you demanding one hundred million dollars?"

"I don't want any of it for myself. I would like it donated to the DARPA research fund in Mark's name. It's the least we can do to memorialize him."

The President considered it only briefly. "I will see that it happens. We would have the right to seize her funds, and a donation to research in the name of a fallen hero is a nice solution. I had heard that you are a problem solver."

"Thanks. Maybe I can use you as a reference on my resume."

"I can offer better than that. My Chief of Staff wants to step down for family reasons. I would like to consider you for the position, if you're interested."

"I would be honored."

"You would start as her Deputy Chief of Staff, working with her for the next several weeks. No guarantees, but if it goes well, the job will be yours."

"Thank you, Madam President."

"Please, call me Megan. We are going to spend a lot of time working together. Now, I'm afraid I need to get going. You are welcome to spend another day here, if you'd like, and whenever you're ready, they will transport you back."

The President stood to leave, but I reached out to her. "Excuse me, but can I ask one last favor?"

"Of course. What do you need?"

"Danny Simpson, a gentleman who helped us escape from the Russian agent at the Smithsonian, was living in the tunnels, but has since decided to rejoin the world. He used to be a full professor at Georgetown before the tragic loss of his wife, and he would like to return. Could you please put in a good word for him at Georgetown?"

"As it happens, I know the Dean personally. I will encourage him to secure a position for Mr. Simpson."

"Thank you, Madam President."

"That reminds me. Agent Duff asked me to give you something." She motioned to one of the agents, who produced Mark's journal from his pocket and handed it to Mac.

"Thank you," Mac breathed.

"You're welcome, Mac. Now, if you'll excuse me." She rose to leave, and Banshee matched her pace beside her. "Do you mind if Banshee spends the afternoon with me? It's not often I get to be around dogs."

"I'm sure he would enjoy that. Banshee, go help the President."

Banshee stayed with her, as they left the cabin.

"Did that really happen?" Mac asked.

"This entire last week has been surreal. I'm glad you got Mark's journal back."

Mac held the journal against her heart, tucked her legs underneath her in the corner of the couch, and opened it to read Mark's thoughts from the beginning.

CHAPTER FIFTY

Thursday, March 26
4:46 p.m.

We accepted the invitation to stay one more night at Camp David. As the sun smoldered low over the tops of the evergreens across the horizon, the gunny brought Banshee back to the cabin and assured us that he had a good day with the President. A secret service agent visited us at dusk.

"I'm Agent Wilson, and I'm here to make sure everyone has their public stories aligned. Ms. Lawton, you were traveling with the Senator, when she exhibited stroke symptoms, and stayed with her by her bedside in Walter Reed Hospital. You didn't speak to anyone except Congressional leaders about the Senator's condition. You have no comment about the situation, other than you wish for the Senator's full recovery."

"Will the story hold up?" Mac asked.

"It should. The staff at Walter Reed is used to ensuring privacy, and we have a limited number of trusted people involved. A full medical record has been created for her, and they show she has already been transferred to a private center for ongoing care. That trail will lead nowhere. Senate leaders are happy to bury her mortifying corruption that can cause reelection problems for members of her entire party. Just stick to your story. The Senator collapsed; you stayed by her side; and you have no further comment."

"Easy enough. I'll just have to remember to look sincere, which will take some practice. It's creepy how easy it is to erase someone from public life."

Agent Wilson declined to comment on that observation and turned his attention to Doc. "We came up with a plausible story to explain your injuries. As you were hiking in a Maryland State Park, you fell down a hill and smashed your chest into a tree. You received treatment at a local hospital, confirmed to have no broken bones, and were discharged with pain medication. A full record of that visit exists in case anyone investigates it. You missed only one shift, and one of our agents called Dr. Pastone to explain that you were finally sleeping in the hospital with the help of some pain meds and couldn't make it in that day. When you show up, joke about the fall and show them a bit of your chest bruising. Remember, fewer details are better."

"That's hardly fair. She gets to be the diligent employee staying at her boss' bedside, and I'm the klutz who fell off the side of a small cliff."

"Sorry. We have to work with the information given. The President also asked me to give a gentle reminder that nothing about any of this can ever be shared with anyone. We all agree that the public mess would benefit no one and may renew security threats against you and the United States."

"I'm happy never to think about that bitch ever again," Mac mused.

Agent Wilson stood and handed us each a card. "If anyone gets too nosy or persistent, please call me, and I will take care of them."

"You don't mean disappear them, do you?" Mac asked.

"No, but we're really good at deception and laying false trails. We can steer them in the wrong direction until they give up. Have a good evening, and best of luck to you both."

The agent departed, and Mac shook her head as she sat next to me. "The government will never cease to amaze me. It apparently supports a whole department for lies and cover ups."

"I must be more cynical. I'm surprised that it's not a full Cabinet position. Secretary of Cover Ups has a nice ring to it. Good night, Mac. I'm gonna get some sleep before we return to the real world."

"Good night, Doc."

.   .   .

The next morning, the gunny helped us load our bags onto the helicopter. "Thanks for visiting Camp David, and safe travels. Make sure to take good care of Scooby. He's such a good boy."

"Scooby takes good care of us. Thanks for everything, Gunny."

We landed at Reagan Airport after only about thirty minutes. Two nondescript government sedans awaited to transport us home. Mac gently hugged me and gave Banshee a vigorous ear scratch before waving goodbye.

Banshee and I rode quietly through the city in the spacious backseat. He rested his head on my lap, as I remained lost in thought. Washington DC would never look the same to me. Hidden tunnels, secret research, and disappeared corrupt politicians revealed an underworld invisible to oblivious tourists walking among monuments. I weighed whether the knowledge of it enriched my mind or uselessly fed my cynicism.

I felt like I had been gone for a month, even though only a couple of days had passed. I put my clothes away, comforted by the mundane routine, and took a long, hot shower, breathing the steam until my skin shriveled. I toweled off and assessed my injuries in the mirror. Although the pain had subsided, the spectacular bruising appeared at it's worst. The solid black and blue contusions beaten into my chest, back, and upper legs would fade with time, as would the nightmarish memories of their cause. Content to be back in the real world, I got dressed in loose, soft sweats and sat down to dispense with my emails.

CHAPTER FIFTY-ONE

Two months later

"We will miss you, Doc. Sure you can't stay for another few months?" Dr. Pastone asked.

"It's time for me to move on, but I'm honored to have had the opportunity to work with all of you. DC is the most intriguing city I've ever lived in, but the heat and humidity is getting unpleasant."

"Hang around for the summer to experience life in a steam cooker," he laughed.

"Not your best sales pitch, my friend. How's the new business?"

"We signed up twelve groups representing two hundred sixty-seven new doctors. We're now the fifth largest ER staffing group in the country."

"Congrats! I bet you land even more contracts."

"Definitely. We have a waiting list to join us, because we're adding only one group every couple of months. We want the growth to be consistent, but steady, so we can seamlessly take care of everyone."

"I'm more hopeful about the future of medicine now that hospitals finally seem to see value in physician-owned groups."

"Hospital administration seems stuck in a quagmire of problems in general, but they do pay attention when they lose a lot of money.

Corporate contracts all over the country are being reevaluated, and it will be more difficult for them to acquire new contracts after the fraud here came to light. If they do get a contract, I expect that their oversight and compliance will be at a much higher level. Watching executives go to jail has a sobering effect on their focus on profits alone."

As expected, the COO of Prime Medical Partners had flipped on his partners. The CEO and general counsel faced a slew of charges that threatened significant time in prison. In addition, the lawyer faced drug charges related to his possession of cocaine and involvement in distribution.

"Couldn't happen to nicer guys. Take care, John. Maybe our paths will cross again."

"I hope so. Safe travels, Doc."

. . .

The morning heat wasn't oppressive yet, so Banshee and I walked to the northwest security gate of the White House, where I presented my ID. I wasn't on the terror watch list, so the guard buzzed me in, directing me to the entrance. I followed the drive, where a Secret Service agent waited for me. We entered the building, and Banshee startled me and everyone else when he barked and surged forward, setting off the metal detector. Agents instinctively reached for guns, but Banshee excitedly circled Mac, who knelt to welcome his kisses. Everyone relaxed and laughed a little, as she looked up at me.

"This dog is a national treasure. I'll vouch for him, but you still need to screen that guy."

I gave up my keys, made it through the metal detectors, and returned Mac's warm embrace. "Good to see you, Doc."

"Good to see you, too, Mac. Nice workplace! I hope you're much happier here."

"I am, thank you." She clipped a visitor's badge to my shirt. "Keep this on, or the agents will make you disappear."

"We know that's in their skill set." We smiled somberly at the private joke.

Mac led me through surprisingly narrow, winding, and sometimes even cramped, hallways to her office in the West Wing. Mac must have read my mind. "Everyone is surprised at the confining layout. This building was built a long time ago and could use a remodel, but there's no space to grow."

Mac entered her office and offered me a chair. "This is nice," I observed.

"It's the second largest office in the White House. The only larger one is oval shaped."

"How's the new job treating you?"

"It's challenging, but I really love it. Everyone wants time with the President, and I'm the gatekeeper, so I'm either appreciated or hated, depending on whether they gain access to her."

"Sounds stressful."

"Not to me. Many requests to see the president stem more from ego than necessity, so I easily dispense with those. The important ones are easy to identify. This job requires multitasking, flexibility, and spontaneity, so I'm constantly challenged and certainly never bored."

"What's it like, working for the President?"

"I genuinely like her, personally as well as professionally. She brings tons of energy and genuine commitment to making the world a better place. She's demanding, but fair. She listens well, considers consequences thoughtfully, and makes quick decisions."

"Sounds like she would make a great ER doctor."

"She would, and that also means you might make a great President."

"I doubt that. I've never been known for my diplomatic skills, and I don't think the country is ready for a guy who lives on French fries, grilled cheese, and pizza to run the place, anyway."

"The White House Chef's job would certainly be easier. How are you recovering?"

"After about six weeks, I felt back to normal, and now all that is just a bad memory. How about you?"

"I try not to think about what happened, but it will take time for the memories to fade. I still have nightmares, but not as frequently. I miss Mark every day. I have an exciting secret to share with you about his research. Please keep it quiet."

"I think I can keep one more secret."

Mac sat behind her desk, pulled Mark's journal from a narrow drawer, and flipped through the pages. "I missed it the first time, his offhand remark about investigating other branches of his research. He didn't have time to pursue it, because he wanted to answer the bigger questions, but it got me thinking. Maybe there's a way to use his research in a more limited way to allow for medical applications, but not military ones."

"Are you working on it yourself?"

"No, but I have oversight of the program at DARPA. A new group is trying to figure out how the information can be used for medical advancement, and thanks to a generous donation from the estate of a certain Senator, they are well funded."

"Did you provide them with any hints to get them started?"

"I may have pointed them in a certain direction. It will take some time and years of trials, but his research may lead to significant medical breakthroughs."

I picked up the piece of amber from her desk and held it up to the light. "Amazing that Tammy here caused so much trouble. Loss of life, destruction of promising political careers, and international incidents happened all because she fell into amber a few million years ago."

"Maybe she will lead us to eradicate cancer someday. Come on, let me show you the Oval Office."

"You're allowed to do that?"

"I make the trip several times a day. It's only ninety-three feet down that hall, forty-two steps at a normal pace and thirty-seven, if I jog."

We opted for a normal pace, and I stared in awe at the room, memorizing details. "It seems a lot bigger on TV."

"Everyone says that. It's actually pretty cozy in here. Come here, check out the desk."

I laid my hand on the Resolute desk, the ultimate symbol of power. Mac moved behind the desk and pulled out the chair. "Have a seat."

"I'm not sure that's a good idea."

"It's okay. Have a seat in the most powerful chair in the world."

I sat down and pulled it up to the desk. The chair felt no different from any other, although it wasn't particularly comfortable, custom made with Kevlar backing for the president's much smaller frame. I placed my hand on the desk, and it felt like any other wooden desk, but I still sensed the history made in this room. The outer door opened, breaking my reverie, and Banshee alerted.

Momentarily startled, the President recognized Banshee and called to him. Banshee responded quickly to receive his ear scratches. I used the distraction to stand up and push the chair back in place. Mac stifled laughter, as she watched me pretend that I hadn't sat in the President's chair.

President Taylor turned her attention to me, obviously sharing Mac's amusement. "Nice to see you again, Doc. How did the chair feel?"

"The chair is too small for me and the seat is way too big."

"That may be the most apt description of it ever, although I think you would be surprised how well you would do in it, actually. What brings you here today?"

"I stopped by to say goodbye to Mac. Banshee and I are moving on."

She hugged Banshee. "I may have to issue a Presidential Edict to make him the First Dog for the country." I must have looked alarmed, because she quickly backtracked. "Don't worry. He's all yours, but he is welcome here any time. Now, if you'll excuse me, I am about to take a call with the President of France. Take care Doc, and thanks for keeping Mac safe."

We scurried from the Oval Office, and Mac walked me to the exit of the White House. "Don't be a stranger. You and Banshee are welcome here any time."

"I appreciate that. If you can get some time off, come visit us in Florida. We'll be there for at least a few months, and the beach is always open."

"Take care, Doc."

After one last hug, we headed across the White House lawn. "C'mon, Banshee, time to make some new friends in Miami."

ACKNOWLEDGEMENTS

The most common question I get from readers is about the accuracy of the conditions and treatments in the emergency room. They are very accurate in terms of content. Anyone who works in an emergency room will recognize the types of cases described. I do condense the stories to avoid an overload of details. In reality, a major trauma could spend hours in the emergency room that would take over fifty pages to detail everything, and nobody wants to read all that. Still, these stories give a realistic portrayal of life in the emergency room.

While DARPA is an actual entity that conducts cutting edge research in a variety of disciplines, the project I described here is totally fictional. The idea of recovering DNA from insects encased in amber was made famous by the brilliant Michael Crichton in Jurassic Park. While his story focused on the implications of reviving old DNA, I chose to use the old DNA as a pathway to quantify evolution. The idea of reducing evolution to a mathematical formula is also fictional but is as terrifying as it is intriguing. Currently, technology allows us to add or remove genes, but we lack the ability to customize or evolve a gene. The ability to do so would have staggering uses in the medical community, but the capability to weaponize such a technology would take warfare to a new level. To my knowledge, no one is working on a way to quantify evolution, but none of the geniuses in the world share their research with me. If someone does figure this out after reading my book, please mention me in your Nobel acceptance speech.

The descriptions of Arlington Cemetery and the Tomb of the Unknown Soldier are accurate but can not do justice to the experience. If you're ever in DC, take a couple hours out of your busy schedule to walk the grounds and observe the ceremony. It will be the best two hours you spend in the city.

Likewise, the descriptions of the Smithsonian and the Library of Congress are accurate but cannot begin to capture the scope of their holdings. One could spend a lifetime studying in either facility and still not have time to review more than 1% of their exhibits. Take some time to visit these places and thank me later.

Camp David descriptions were based on publicly available information. For some reason my requests to check out the place did not get approved.

While I am positive there are secret tunnels in Washington DC, I did not get to play in any of them, maybe because they are indeed secret.

The corporate practice of medicine is a serious problem in modern healthcare that is worsening. Prime Medical Partners is totally fictitious, and the name was used only to get the acronym of PIMPS, to describe their predatory business model that uses medical professionals and patients as commodities to turn a profit. In certain medical fields, large investment groups have bought up a large number of practices, extracted as much cash as possible from the groups while leveraging huge amounts of debt. In a couple of cases, bankruptcy is the only likely outcome, and the investment groups walk away with huge amounts of cash and write off the debt, leaving the system in tatters. Corporate money should be able to be invested into healthcare, but control of operations and decision-making needs to rest with the medical professionals to ensure quality of care.

Many thanks to the team at Black Rose Writing for making this book possible. As a smaller, indie press they have limited resources, and truly accomplish magical things with their small team. The incredible cover is thanks to Dave, while Tony and Minna handle marketing and public relations. Justin is in charge of sales, Mary Ellen helps with edits, and Reagan somehow keeps all of the projects headed in the same direction.

Last but not least, thank you to my wife, Tammy. She has been by my side for over thirty years and deserves so much more than having an ancient termite named after her. In my defense, the termite was a queen and an integral part of the story. Tammy is my editor, and if you found the book easy to read, thank her. I can tell a great story, but she brings it to life.

Thank you to everyone who took time to read the book with special thanks to those who left a kind review or rating. Those are incredibly important for all authors, and if you take a moment to leave a rating or review after reading a book, the author will feel most grateful.

Stay up to date on future projects at www.garygerlacher.com. I am pretty sure Doc and Banshee are headed to Miami in the near future. Be careful out there, and don't try to pick up a golf ball while driving a cart at full speed – that injury is based on a real story.

ABOUT THE AUTHOR

Gary Gerlacher is a pediatric emergency physician who trained and worked in multiple Texas emergency rooms before opening his own pediatric urgent care clinics. His thirty years in medicine have focused on expanding access to high quality care for all children, and his stories give a unique view of the inner workings of the emergency room.

For fun, he's opening a competitive cheer gym with his twin daughters, and he likes to golf and race cars. Gerlacher can be found eating cheese pizza most days of the week. He has three adult children and resides in Dallas with his two rescue dogs and his wife Tamara. Visit Garygerlacher.com to stay up to date on future books.

THE AJ DOCKER & BANSHEE THRILLER SERIES

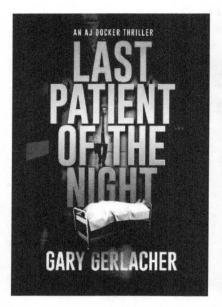

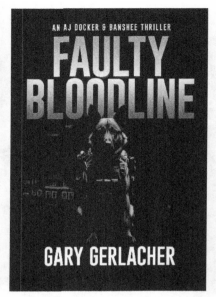

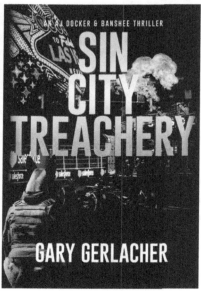

NOTE FROM GARY GERLACHER

Word-of-mouth is crucial for any author to succeed. If you enjoyed *Deadly Equation*, please leave a review online—anywhere you are able. Even if it's just a sentence or two. It would make all the difference and would be very much appreciated.

Thanks!
Gary Gerlacher

We hope you enjoyed reading this title from:

BLACK&ROSE
writing™

www.blackrosewriting.com

Subscribe to our mailing list – *The Rosevine* – and receive **FREE** books, daily deals, and stay current with news about upcoming releases and our hottest authors.
Scan the QR code below to sign up.

Already a subscriber? Please accept a sincere thank you for being a fan of Black Rose Writing authors.

View other Black Rose Writing titles at www.blackrosewriting.com/books and use promo code **PRINT** to receive a **20% discount** when purchasing.

Made in the USA
Las Vegas, NV
26 May 2025

22534007R00156